The Last Witness
The Story of a Man that Never Was

by

Saúl Balagura

The Last Witness
Saúl Balagura

ISBN: 978-0-578-33440-0

Amazon Edition, License Notes

In Memory of

Szmul Zygielbojm, who told the story but no one cared and Sara Zighelboim and Itco Balagule, who told me the story when I was a child, and Meier, Jayah, Sendel, Leibish, Shimen, Abrum, Frieda, Sarah, Erzon, Feihge, Johann, Shmuel, Zeb, Heinrich, Itzic, Max and many others, whom I never met but in my dreams.

PREFACE

When I undertook to write this novel, it necessitated imagining a set of characters that would endure terrible things. It became a heavy weight upon my soul, but what made it even more unbearable was the realization that these imaginary sets of events actually happened if not to my characters, then to others, not imaginary but real people. It makes one infinitely humble to arrive to such an understanding.

A decade after a failed publication of this novel, anti-Semitism has sprung again. Not that it had died, rather, under the colossal shadow of the horrors of the Holocaust, advanced nations and cultures have tamped down their negative attitude towards the Jews. But the kindling was kept, always ready to set alight, always in search of an excuse, an opportunity, a reason. At least half of the world remained anti-Semitic; Jews found refuge wherever they were accepted and in the ancient, newly formed, State of Israel.

I have been keenly aware of a rising tide of anti-Semitism within the civilized nations. The very same freedom that allows cultural diversity also became tolerant of hatred against the Jew, as if the price for freedom were hate. At the same time, the last witnesses that had survived the Holocaust, have been decimated by age. Soon, there will be no more witnesses. Without witnesses, crimes become statistics, and statistics are soon relegated to an obscure corner, or a digitized memory chip. In many schools, teaching about the Holocaust comprises a few paragraphs in history class, if that. Once the victims of a crime are forgotten, it is as if the crime was never committed. At that point, unencumbered, we are ready to suppress it from our minds, and I fear, to endeavor on new crimes once again.

It is because of these current developments that I have reworked this novel, THE LAST WITNESS, including numerous changes. I have failed to attract literary agents and publishing corporations, finally deciding on a combined electronic/softbound issue at Amazon.com.

I wish to thank my wife, Ursula, who tolerated, nurtured and nursed me so that I could be free to climb any ridge I willed to conquer with the knowledge that upon my return I would find a smile upon her face and a stern critic as well. I thank my friend, Irene Zion, for her suggestions and corrections, and Michael Berenbaum for his insight and encouragement so many years ago.

Such a sensitive topic as this novel deals with, surely may offend some, and I sincerely apologize if I cause them pain.

Saúl Balagura
Nov. 23, 2021
Houston, Texas

OH GOD,

through a crack
in the wall
I see light . . .
Through the light
I see darkness
and I see
no end . . .

1

On this one particular morning Jacob Nathan was to have answered, in a most peculiar way, the one question that had relentlessly haunted him during the long span of his tortured life. He was the last survivor, victim or perpetrator, of the Holocaust to remain alive on this Earth. That it was a special day, Jacob had no doubt, but as to how special it would end up being, it was not for him to conjecture.

There exists a twist, a sarcastic shift, an awful rip that has permitted mankind to rot itself within its own magnificent achievements and ride the waves of history blown by human ingenuity, by love, and above all, by an irrational will to live, to survive even when there is no reason to continue living. Jacob, and millions like him, had fallen sick to the contagion that evil can inflict upon children and their parents. But evil bested itself, for many of its victims were left to live filled with guilt for having survived, experiencing the mounting horror of thinking that they, not the perpetrators of those horrible deeds, were the criminals, their lives constantly dangling from memories of having lived one more day because their food rations might have been larger at the expense of another prisoner, or because a guard did not choose one inmate in particular but instead chose someone else for public punishment and death.

Jacob was now one hundred and two

years old and yet, he managed to walk, albeit with short but confident steps. His youthful face betrayed how old he really was, but when he stood naked in front of the mirror, he could see that there was sagging where his muscles had once bulged — a sad wilting of the young image he still had of the time when he was thirty years old. His neck had acquired that turkey like appearance so familiar to those that notice these things, and his buttocks had dried up. He now was thin and wiry whereas before he had been strong and bulky. He had lost an inch in height and his hair was now just a flimsy cover for the prominent skull that he had to guard against the New Mexico sun with his black Resistol hat. His dark brown eyes that once reflected so much intelligence now were encircled by a thin rim of gray that gave them a cold appearance, no matter how warm his heart was, or how tender he felt. Standing in front of the mirror gave him a feeling of going to confessional, except that it was the mirror revealing all the truth. Like it or not, he had to accept that the reflected image was not that of some unknown, old, decrepit human being, but of himself, and could not help wondering how far he had come and how long he had lasted. Was there any purpose?

He was awakened by the summer sun shining on his face as it erupted over the nearby Pacheco Canyon, burning the fog that collected overnight at the bottom of the narrow valleys that sculpted the arid landscape. After his morning ablutions he walked towards the kitchen and, as it had been his habit for a long time, he swallowed a capsule of multivitamins and an aspirin with a glass of orange juice and set another pair aside for Rebecca, his wife of almost eight decades. Jacob opened the door of the cabinet above the sink and automatically took a coffee filter, folded one edge and placed it inside the coffee maker, emptying into it two large scoops of dark ground coffee. Rebecca prepared some slices of bread. Her hands, knotted like the branches of an old tree, still allowed her to perform her kitchen and cooking routines. She took from the refrigerator butter, yogurt and fruit spreads, placing them on the counter next to the sink. One by one, Jacob brought them to the small table by the kitchen window, and then they sat to eat, listening to the morning program on the classical radio station. As he chewed, Jacob was careful not to bite too hard on his right side, he had chipped a little piece of tooth on the corner of a large gold filling and knew that soon he would have to pay a visit to the dentist –not a pleasant prospect at this or any age. The local station took over momentarily to blare the news, often some permutation of a plane crash in Sri-Lanka, two drug related murders, one major highway accident; mild weather in most of the country, or the stock market reaction to the news of possible inflation. As it had been the case for many years, the announcer's personal bias came through loud and clear. Society had accepted this long ago, but it still bothered Jacob like a fishbone stuck in his throat. He looked at Rebecca and simply mumbled:

"There goes my blood pleasure. Damned news!"

Rebecca knew there was nothing to argue about, she had heard these complaints for decades, and she knew most of his arguments. After so many years, they could read each other's thoughts. She smiled. Rebecca and Jacob had lived together longer than most people can ever imagine their own children would live. They were more than just a couple. Yes, at one point, long ago, they had been two distinct persons, but by now, after so many years, they had become one. Sometimes walking at night on a barely visible mountain trail, under a quarter moon, one cannot tell which is the tree and which the shadow it casts; similarly, it happens when two lives coexist within the forest that so frequently human history immolates never learning from the past.

The news was followed by a cycle of Schubert songs that put Nathan in better spirits. Caressed by the music, the two of them sat looking through the window at a chipmunk laboring to stuff its cheek pouches with Piñon nuts. Holding hands, they smiled watching the little clown feeding, as its body jerked from side to side, attentive to predators. A blue jay flew under the tree canopy, making the chipmunk run for cover between two rocks –nothing had changed, it still was a world of survival, being a hunter or a prey. The morning was losing its chill under the bright New Mexico sun.

After breakfast Nathan helped carry the dirty dishes to the sink. On this day Rebecca had an appointment in town and could not accompany him on their usual morning walk. Women's groups, in the height of their self-realization campaigns, had discovered the power that old age can vest upon those few that are not ravaged by mental deterioration. Age had been kind to Rebecca's brain and her experience of survival and love amidst the chaos and devastation of war and her facility to relate to people, made her a perfect candidate for these kinds of educational and self-improving social gatherings and lectures. At eleven that morning, a car would pick her up to take her to town. Nathan proceeded to the small utility room by the back entrance to the house, close to the garage, and sitting slowly on the heavy wooden banco that jutted from the wall, changed his slippers for the stiff walking boots that permitted him to walk with relative comfort on the irregular surface of the high desert paths.

The Nathans' adobe house, perched on one of the many ridges in the foothills of the Sangre de Cristo Mountains, appeared radiant against the impeccable blue of the sky and the deep green of the Piñon trees with colors stolen from a Jean-León Gérôme North African desert painting. The house extended its horseshoe shape over an expanse of hard packed sandy soil, studded with Chamisa and Mountain Mahogany bushes. A magpie was pecking at the tree stump by the back portal. It was indeed a magnificent house. Its U-shape hugged a garden of rocks and Piñon trees with a small Spanish fountain in the middle. Rebecca and Jacob frequently sat on their patio chairs during the shady period of the day, listening to the hypnotic sound of the water cascading in an infinite pattern of melodies, while small birds took their daily baths in the upper basin, feeling perfectly at home with the two humans watching them. The impatience of youth is replaced by the contemplative nature that the sunset of human life conveys to the elder.

Ready for his walk, he grabbed his walking stick on the way out, kissed the small metal container with Hebrew prayers nailed to the door lintel and after walking a few steps, looked back to contemplate the home that God had given him during these, the last years of his life. Two ravens were coquettishly flying in magnificent pirouettes, occasionally fanning their wings close to his head, only a faint hissing sound revealing their presence.

How long had he had that same walking stick? With a smile he remembered the downed old tree lying on a slope on one of the many mountain trails near Snowmass. At the time, perhaps forty years before, he wanted some memento of the Colorado vacation that had turned out so well and Jacob saw in one fallen branch the beauty of a walking stick clamoring to get out. He had broken off all the side branches with his hands and had smoothed the jagged edges against a nearby rock. Weeks later, at home, he would sand off the rough bark, exposing the inner beauty of the wood, scarred by insects and woodworms. After a coat of varnish, he had finished it with a rub of fine steel wool, giving it a soft glow. For a final touch, Jacob had wrapped the handle with leather and hardened the other end so that it would not erode with use. He had excellent manual dexterity, a necessity in his profession, for Jacob was a neurosurgeon. Things had definitely changed from earlier years.

The world has a way of rotating that makes it almost impossible to comprehend the meaning of things. Events are unfathomable until they become history, and even then, they are subject to rewriting. A morning may start cool and cloudless, just to be followed by a stormy afternoon, and a walk in the park amidst the greenness of a forest of urban trees may end up in a robbery, or a murder. The furtive smile of a passing person amidst the congestion of a cityscape may hide a world of happiness, or infinite disdain, and at night, a cloud can hide an entire universe. Why a person is born and why death does not arrive belongs with this mysterious gathering of apparently disconnected finds. But make no mistake, the absence of an apparent connection does not imply that the connection does not exist. For Nathan, life had become impossible to comprehend. Every corner offered a new vista and every blink brought a picture from his past. As to what all this meant, he almost had given up wondering.

2

"*Jakob ist ein schmutziger Jude! —*Jacob is a filthy Jew!"

"Jacob is a dirty Jew!"

The other children were shouting in a singsong. Jacob began crying. Every time he argued with his friends, they called him a "*dreckiger Jude —*dirty Jew". He had not insulted them, he had not offended them. He lived in the same block of row houses and birds flew from rooftop to rooftop without concern that his was a Jewish house and others were not. And if that wasn't enough, he had begun to see posters depicting ugly men with long beards and beaked noses accused of belonging to an inferior race. The entire city was covered with ugly posters ridiculing the Jews. For what he could make out, the Jews —him— were responsible for the downfall of Germany! He had asked his father about it, but the gentle man, would reply without lifting his eyes from the old books he was mending:

"It too shall pass. It too shall pass."

And perhaps he was right. Jews throughout history had endured continued persecution. Since the time of the Roman destruction of the second temple, Jewish history had been characterized by periods of persecution interspersed with brief periods of bloodshed. It had become a pattern that no country had ever abandoned. From the times of the great Roman emperor Constantine and Saint Eusebius, Jews had been allowed to exist as a kind of counterbalance to the developing Christian cultures in Europe, like an example of evil versus good –a philosophical chiaroscuro where occasionally red blood was used to further a point. But Jews had not become overtly reactive to this treatment, rather introspective. They had turned to studying and reading and philosophizing around sacred books. Thus, imposed isolation resulted in strengthening of the Jewish culture, even if physical growth was always curtailed, stunted like a malnourished child. Now, it was the turn of the National Socialists and their leader, Adolf Hitler, to deal with the Jews. Germany had been humiliated by the Allies after their victory during World War I; the economy was depressed and unemployment was high during the decades following the war and Hitler chose to use the Jews as the excuse for Germany's affliction. Little by little he established in the German mind the concept of a Thousand Year Reign and an Aryan super race and at the same time, by any means available to him and his party, the Jews were transformed into the *Untermensch* –subhuman– that needed to be isolated and later on exterminated. This was the environment that began to envelop and sculpt Jacob Nathan's life.

Jacob remembered his father as an old man –how curious that we should remember our parents as old, no matter how long they might have lived or died; perhaps like a defense mechanism that permits one generation to distance itself from the previous one so that their loss will not be so painful. Meier Nathan had a long beard, which he frequently combed with his delicate hands —Jacob had inherited those hands. Meier did not have a long bulbous nose, like those on the posters Jacob had seen all over town, even though he did have one eye set slightly higher than the other. He was about five feet five inches tall and carried his shoulders forward, giving him a small hump on his upper back and he walked with a wobble like atoms do when pulled by their electrons' halos, or like stars wobble under the orbital weight of phantasmagoric planets. His shop smelled of old paper and glue. His fingers often were stained with the various chemicals and powders that were required to achieve a perfect match for an old, dilapidated book cover. Most of the books brought to the shop to be repaired were religious in content, an old Talmud, a disheveled Mishnah, but some were laic literature, both Jewish and non-Jewish — lots of Shalom Aleichem books. Throughout his life, Jacob would be transported back to this room by the faint aroma of an old piece of paper, or the smell of a dusty textbook from the medical library, even by a musty newspaper scent. Seated next to his father, he would watch as the old man stitched the pages like an expert surgeon, converting what initially looked like a pile of papers in disarray, into handsome books. Jacob had been taught to read by him in that very room, surrounded by the indescribable odor of ancient texts that "*Der Buch Artz*" (the book doctor) —as people used to call his father— had tenderly repaired.

His father would say: "There are no old books my son". Then, after a brief pause, while Jacob would tilt his head and look at him inquiringly, rubbing his beard he would add: "The paper may be old, but the words are always fresh; every time you read them they come alive again, as if they had been asleep. Remember Jacob, words never die".

Jacob's memories of his parents were unique in that he could not remember them fighting. Oh, sure, there were occasional discussions, but these were arguments about insignificant things, never about serious matters, never lasting more than a few minutes. Clearly, they loved each other very much. His mother, Chayah, was a kind and intelligent woman who had dedicated her life to maintaining a perfect home. She had given up her job as a librarian at one of the branches of the state library when she married Meier, but her avid appetite for reading good books never flagged. She towered one head above her husband, but this discrepancy did not appear to affect the love between the two. Jacob's memories of his mother always involved her smile, her soothing voice, and the aroma of dishes she prepared every day, but especially the food for Shabbat. On Friday nights, the three of them would sit at the table covered with the white tablecloth reserved only for holy days. He could see her, inclining her head covered with a dark shawl while moving her hands over the lit candles that appeared to grow out from the old silver candelabrum, reciting the blessings and welcoming the holy day –how many times and for how many generations? Then his mother would bring from the kitchen the Gefilte fish embedded in the salty gelatin that he always saved for the end, to eat with a slice of freshly baked Challah bread. And then, in the deep, oval, white porcelain dish, the one with the golden borders, came the sweet and sour beef ribs or a roasted chicken. And at the very end, when it seemed almost impossible to bite into another morsel of food, she would bring the dessert. At times apples and nuts rolled in thin phyllo dough; other times a chocolate-honey torte. All these flavors had become part of Jacob's genetic code, forever carved into his brain. When Chayah died, she took with her all her recipes, only ghosts were left. Sometimes, no matter how old he was, Jacob remembered these comfortable nights of flavors and aromas from his childhood and floating with them the image of his mother and her eyes looking approvingly at his father. A healing balm.

3

The path through the hills and arroyos did not start right away. He walked the stretch of dusty road down the hill to the base of the ridge, where through the years the desert rains had carved the arroyo bed that remained dry for most of the year. Occasionally, thunderstorms coming from the other side of the valley would flood the arroyos amidst awesome thunder and wind, carrying in torrential waters boulders and fallen trees. It was a spectacle to behold: The dark, mushrooming clouds appearing over the distant horizon; the thunder, like the bellow of a gigantic, wounded animal; the gallop of the storm across the valley toward the East, the absolute clarity of the air, the smell of rainwater in the downdraft, and then the waters.

Once in the arroyo, Jacob turned to the East and walked slowly in the direction of the tall mountains, surrounded by twisted piñons, junipers and memories. He walked alone. Max, his dog, the last of a fifty-year dynasty of Rottweilers, had died a year before; his absence leaving a hole next to him. He still had the vivid sensation that Max was just lagging behind and that in a matter of a few seconds would come galloping from behind some trees, searching for his caresses. He missed the touch of his cold nose, the softness of his pelt and the total helplessness of his massive friend. The sandy floor made it more difficult to walk, but Jacob loved to feel his feet sinking into the warm sand.

4

Lifting her glass, Joanna said, "To the best doctor we ever knew!"

"To Doctor Nathan!" they all replied.

The room was filled with people. They had gathered in the main auditorium of the hospital to bid him farewell. The chatter's intensity oscillated like waves against a windblown rocky beach making it even more difficult for Jacob to understand all that was being said. He had finally announced at seventy-two that he was retiring. God knows it had been a difficult decision. He had loved his profession like a wife. Fear had played a significant part in delaying his retirement. How many people he knew had become empty shells after they stopped doing what they had done for so many years? For a doctor to step down meant to give up helping others. The very places where he had been welcomed day after day would be closed to him. His peers would close the gap left by his absence with a replacement. Some would not even address him as doctor but simply as mister: he would become a "Hey you", a "has been". Wait! There was more to him than just being a doctor. He had grown to accept that he had survived the concentration camps so that he could give others a chance to live. But after carrying his bones for so many years, his age was beginning to show. Lately, after each surgery he needed to have a session of physical therapy. Sometimes it was his neck, where pain would concentrate after operating for hours with the surgical microscope, other times his shoulders would feel on fire, as if someone had placed knives into the joints. At times the pain would be in his lower back and his feet always ached. The hospital administrator had directed the physical therapists to take Doctor Nathan at any time and not to charge him. Nathan was very important to the hospital, generating large amounts of money, operating almost every day of the week, sometimes twice in a day. For three years now he was taking anti-inflammatories and pain medications. Even so, he could not find a moment free of pain. He knew it was time to quit even if his hands were still steady and his mind clear and well informed on current neurosurgery issues.

"To the best doctor we ever knew!" resonated in Jacob's mind. It had not always been like this. He remembered when he had first started his neurosurgery practice, after graduating from one of the best programs in the country. After the Birmingham fiasco he had been called by a medical recruiter who convinced him that his place was as a member of the Graham Clinic, in north central Florida.

Initially, Jacob had resisted the idea. He was apprehensive about the South and did not feel comfortable about it. Even in his native Germany he had learned in school about the American civil war and about the black slaves.

Later on –perhaps wrongly– he had associated the South with discrimination. It never failed that if a community discriminated against one social group, it soon would expand its hatred towards others –bigotry is not monogamous. First the blacks, then the Jews and then who knows what.

"This is not the South, this is Florida!" the medical recruiter had replied.

So, Jacob had interviewed with all the key members of the clinic and had been hired on the spot. Rebecca did not object to the idea of going south, rather, she thought, the change to a warmer climate might do them both good.

The Graham Clinic was indeed a pretty sight to behold. It was located in the central part of northern Florida, in a city surrounded by orange groves and small lakes with ducks and geese drifting placidly, pushed along by gentle breezes. Patients came referred not only by local physicians, but from as far away as Georgia, Alabama and even parts of Tennessee. He had been told, this clinic is the "Mayo Clinic of the South", and it did seem like it.

Rebecca and Jacob rented a house at the edge of town next to what appeared as infinite groves of orange trees. It was here that they got their first Rottweiler and called him Max, in memory of an old ghost from the past. Max Grubber, two years younger than Jacob, had been murdered on Kristallnacht not more than twenty yards from where the Nathans lived. Max was a peaceable happy child with a puffy, sad face. For some reason, their new puppy reminded Jacob of his old childhood friend. The memory of his friend would become the love for his new gentle furry companion. It was here, in this bright and welcoming town, that they established the routine of taking daily walks, the three of them. On weekdays, they walked in the evenings, after Jacob's return from his practice when the heat of the day was beginning to dissipate. On weekends, when Nathan was free after his early hospital rounds, they walked early, before the heat would claim the groves all for itself. Invariably they would come across three geese. They had no doubt that the three geese were friends that also chose to stroll at the same time the Nathan's did. The geese would wobble across their path, unhurried, as if sensing that large and gentle Max was no danger to them.

The first few weeks had been wonderful. Life at home just flowed from one glorious day into another, fed by the satisfying challenges at work, the haunting orange grove landscape and the love they gave and received from each other and from Max. Rebecca had no time to be bored having to organize the new household, keeping Max company and reading. Her new country had opened up an infinite treasure of works born amidst freedom, the freedom to write and speak and Rebecca had begun to accumulate a sizable library.

It had been during these first weeks that they had observed Max's peculiar behavior that became known as "love pit-stops". They would be walking along when Max, who had run ahead, would return and block their way, standing between them until he was petted. He would lean his body against their legs, and then after a short while, he would continue with the walk, moving the little black tail stump from side to side in utter happiness and contentment. Rebecca was happy in her new home.

Work in the clinic was also going just fine. The nurses liked Doctor Nathan, the neurologists with whom he was beginning to interact a lot, were a pleasure to deal with, and the other neurosurgeon was kind and helpful. But all this was to change soon as Nathan's fears of the South were dissipating fast. In fact, he had commented to Rebecca that perhaps the South had given up the ugly business of discrimination, after all, the medical recruiter had said: "For Pete's sake, it is the second half of the Twentieth Century!"

The second half of the Twentieth Century! It did have a ring to it. During the first half the world had confronted evil face to face and had fought it successfully. Nazi Germany had been punished. France, always worried of her image, had reclaimed her lost honor. Britain had been scorched by bombings and had survived stronger than ever, and America had become a superpower. But masked by all the glitter were other events that history would show had not been resolved: Minorities were still considered as second-class citizens in every nation, the Soviet empire would continue killing hundreds of thousands of its peoples for decades to come, China would purge itself of many of its citizens, rulers in most African nations had not finished pilfering their peoples of riches and resources, pandemic atrocities protected by the laws of every nation were still to come. Some countries would accumulate thousands of atomic weapons in preparation for their next encounter and as always, the hearts of men, especially as relating to the basic hate centered in race or religion, had not been purified. Jacob Nathan would have ample time to figure all these things during his life.

As Max began to grow larger and heavier, it became clear that he would tear to pieces the back seat of the car unless some preventive measures were taken. So, Nathan designed a kind of wooden platform that would rest over the seat and would be supported with two legs resting on the floor of the car. By this time, he was in pretty good terms with the other neurosurgeon, Bob MacGiness. One afternoon, Max and Rebecca and Jacob went visiting the MacGiness' with the purpose of building the wooden platform. Bob and Jacob worked for about an hour on the platform and installed it in the car. They tested it with Max, who immediately approved of the whole thing. They toasted to the completion of the project with a glass of Beaujolais. Bob asked if they would stay for dinner, just informal, something like hamburgers. But that evening happened to be the first night of Passover, it was the First Seder. So, Jacob declined and said they would do it on another occasion, but not that evening because it was Passover. "Oh, you are Jewish? we didn't realize that." Then, following a few awkward seconds: "Sure, sure. We do it another time".

5

"Come Jacob, it's your turn now"– Jacob could hear his mother's voice. The entire family standing in the middle of the dusty patio at the back of the house with a chicken and a strange little man dressed in black. Jacob never felt at ease to have a chicken floating and flapping over his head. What if the chicken decided to let go and have a bowel movement? But this was the tradition in his home. The day before Rosh Hashanah, the new year, the Shochet, the ritual slaughterer, would come to the house. Chayah would bring a live chicken and then, with his large, white and puffy hands, the Sochet would grab the poor bird by the legs and swing it around and above the head of each member of the family saying:

"May all the bad things that were going to happen to you happen to the chicken instead" –It was the ceremony that transferred all the problems and vicissitudes from human to beast. A mystical transfer of karmas, as if destiny could be so easily changed. Perhaps a leftover from the period of animal sacrifices during the first and second temples in Jerusalem, when man could cleanse himself by a burnt offering to God according to the established commandments of those times.

Nathan still remembered the Shochet, with his black suit and raveled pants. He could still see him –the cracks crisscrossing the dull black leather shoes– extracting from his right coat pocket a long, narrow case and nesting on its blue velvet interior the ritual knife with which he would cut the chicken's throat.   He could hear his rasping voice saying:

"Now you can live to the next year. *Mazel-Tov*!"

"*Mazel-Tov* and *L'Shannah Tovah*" –good luck and a happy new year– he remembered his parents' joyous reply, as they began dancing and singing an old Hebrew prayer written in a minor key, even if it was a happy occasion.

6

In central Florida, many years after his last bad luck had been transferred into a chicken, Nathan's harmony was going to be shattered. Bob MacGiness had not spoken to him for a week, and he did not do so from then on; any neurosurgical discussions came by way of a nurse or a secretary. A few weeks later, Nathan began to notice a certain change in the way some members of the clinic interacted with him. The conversations in the doctors' lounge were cut short and sometimes, some of the surgeons would finish lunch in a hurry shortly after Nathan's arrival to the table. It was like a paranoid's dream coming true. Then, in the doctors' lounge, two groups were established for lunch. At first, the distancing was almost imperceptible, but soon became obvious. There was no doubt; the changes were because of him. And if there were any questions remaining, one day he was called to the office of one of the "core" doctors of the clinic, Robert Besty, an ear-nose-and-throat specialist.

Jacob, with his usual punctuality interrupted his clinic routine and walked the long corridor towards Besty's office. At two-forty-five he knocked at the door and was invited in. He had been wondering what it was all about. Certainly, it could have nothing to do with his performance as a physician; he was respected and appreciated by patients and hospital personnel alike. But it was getting near the time when the Clinic would evaluate his performance so that a recommendation to full partnership could be made.

"Come in, come in".

Nathan entered.

"Sit down".

The room was nicely appointed with the expected furnishings of a doctor's office. One wall dedicated to diplomas and certificates, the remaining ones hidden by bookshelves; a dark burgundy colored carpet covered the floor, in front of the window stood a large desk with patients' charts neatly piled on one corner and family photos on the opposite side.

Without too much of a preamble, Besty began:

"Do you know why I have called you?" Besty had not greeted him, he had not even bothered to look at him with a full-frontal stare. He sat behind his desk. He had a narrow face, ending in a straight nose parting a set of expressionless gray-blue eyes, encased in perfectly wavy brown hair graying at the temples. His physician's white coat was heavily starched, without wrinkle or blemish as if diseases never got close to him.

"No, not really", replied Jacob.

Then, looking absent mindedly to the pictures of his family:

"Do you know what a W.A.S.P. is?"

Jacob knew what it meant, but instead said:

"A flying insect, I believe a Hymenopterous, that can sting?"

Unable to keep disdain from showing in his voice Besty replied: "No, not an insect, a White Anglo-Saxon Protestant". And he continued on the same breath:

"What are you doing here?"

Jacob stood without saying a word. He felt the blood pushing against the skin of his face. He was going to say: "Do you know how cold a winter is when you don't have any shoes?" But realized he would be swimming against an overpowering current. A person like Robert Besty did not waste his time reading history or trying to understand the social and political and often religious conventions that determined who should be hated, or discriminated, or even worst, killed. It was the curse of mankind that history was never to be used as a teaching tool, previous errors did not bring about corrections, and entire centuries of darkness were not necessarily followed by light. He bit his lip and said nothing. He felt lightheaded. His head was swarming with so many thoughts and feelings, all trying to convey horrible memories from the past, all lost in the bottleneck of consciousness. But he knew that just as a great poet could not stop the charge of a hungry lion by reading some of his strophes, he could not argue with Besty's mind. As he left the office, he wondered what he was going to say to Rebecca and how. In his mind the image of Rebecca, with her light olive skin and her green eyes framed by that smooth oval face, kept flashing like a light beacon to a lost sailor in the middle of a storm.

7

On that summer morning, many decades ago, when he had been formally arrested, Jacob was wearing his brown leather shoes. Against his own father's wishes, he had gone and bought this magnificent pair of Italian leather shoes. He had worn them the day he visited the University and met for the first time Professor Gustaf Untergras, the famous anatomist, who had expressed interest in Jacob becoming a physician. And now, for reasons he could not explain, had decided to wear them again as he walked to the gathering place. It had been a strange sort of arrest, in that he had received notification to present himself at a nearby plaza, like a park. When he got there, others were arriving, as if they all were preparing to go on a pleasure trip and were gathering by the side of a large cruise ship. Except that in this case, soldiers were ushering the "passengers" and there was no cruise ship –transport trains awaited them. He could hardly believe the hate and contempt reflected on the faces of the soldiers that escorted his group. On occasion, one of the soldiers would hit with the butt of the rifle one of the prisoners. Every so often the guards would shout "*Verfluchte Juden!*" at them – Cursed Jews! But what had hurt the most had been the way the townspeople looked at them. He never saw an expression of apology or regret in any of their faces. These were not soldiers, these were regular men and women that worked hard to make a living and on Sunday mornings went to church and took along their children, and in the afternoons enjoyed coffee with whipped cream and *Schwartzwälderkirsch Torte* at the neighborhood Konditorei; people that, a few months before had smiled warmly at his parents and at him.

And then came the waiting. They stood on command, under the summer sun for hours. He remembered a single drop of sweat trickling down his face, right over his eyelid and down his cheek until it reached his lip. And he remembered the bitter saltiness of that sweat drop when he licked it from the corner of his mouth – a strange memory to carry for so many years.

Finally, after completing the paperwork on the prisoners, after meticulous checks and counterchecks of interminable lists, crossing every "t" and dotting every "i", the guards gave the order to march to the train station. More ugly stares from the town's people. Then, again they stood still, waiting. Jacob heard the distant screech of rusted metal wheels against the heated rails as a cargo transport train inched its way towards them. When finally, the train stopped, he found himself in front of a cattle car and without further delay, the guards ushered them inside with the encouragement of police dogs and rifle-butts –and then darkness, a suffocating stench and cries.

During the train transport, many people stepped over his Italian shoes and when he had finally, days later, jumped out of the car and for the first time was able to look at his feet, he felt a deep regret that he had worn those shoes. They were now full of scratches and had lost their luster, and he marveled at the pettiness of his observation: All that tragedy and he was fixated on a pair of shoes. Within a few hours of arriving at the camp he had lost his shoes. The guards amid mocking and laughing had allowed the prisoners to run towards a large pile –a small mountain– of shoes and were delighted to see fights break out here and there as the prisoners vented their anguish during this pathetic, warped version of a shoe shopping spree. Jacob finally found a right and a left shoe that were about his right fit and was leaving the shoe pile, when the man next to him said:

"Throw them out, you want to get big shoes, they will be better in the winter".

Jacob, without any hesitation, had let the shoes fall from his hands and, returning to the pile, had rapidly found a couple of shoes that were about two sizes bigger than he needed. He had trusted an unknown's advice. He had begun the process of survival. Later on, in the barracks, he observed that some prisoners were wrapping pieces of cloth around their feet before putting on their shoes. Being summertime, Jacob did not understand the significance of such a custom, but instinct told him to do the same. He found a few pieces of cloth from an old uniform and tore off two strips. He rolled them like a bandage and then applied them to his feet, over his socks. To his amazement, the new extra-large shoes were now a perfect fit.

The summer months passed, leaving in their wake the eroding memories of abandoned homes, of broken families, of shattered dreams. Little by little the rainy season began and with it also cold winds and mud. Jacob's feet were now protected from the cold, or so he thought. Prisoners slept with their shoes on fearing they would be stolen while they slept. The constant humidity inside the shoes macerated the skin between the toes. It was not uncommon for prisoners to lose their toes to horrible purulent infections. Once in a while, they had to remove their shoes, especially when their feet were too swollen or painful, or when after a day of marching in rain and mud, their cloth wrappings became drenched in dirty water and blood. Then, they would sleep with their shoes tied to a leg.

By the time winter came, Jacob had forgotten what it was to have warm feet. He experienced a constant ache, a constant feeling that he had cold metal driven through the bones of his feet and legs. He could not keep his feet in one place, he had to move them constantly, there was no comfortable place for them. Often, when the night was not too cold, a horrible itching sensation would replace the driving chill in his feet. He had to restrain himself from scratching to relieve the unremitting itch between his toes. Scratching could irritate or even tear the skin and this would surely bring an infection. Sometimes, after unwrapping his feet, he could not stand the stench of the bloody pus that bathed his toes.

Then, the itch would be replaced by the cold, and the feeling of strips of metal penetrating his legs would overcome him once more. How had he arrived at this? What had he done to deserve this? Jacob was learning one of the essential tenets of persecution, making the victim search for reasons of why he or she is being persecuted and by definition making them feel guilty –a question that would be repeated over and over during his entire life. How he hated that awful smell of blood and pus! By the following day, the guards would make them stand in the freezing cold and march them, again and again, through muddy fields and Jacob's feet would again become the center of his world. We think we are advanced thinkers, because of what we can accomplish when left to our own. But when we are afflicted with some illness, or have a cut, or condition that causes pain, then, we revert to the primal state: all that concerns us is to avoid further pain. Studying is important, but wet, infected, painful feet are even more important. This was the truth, this was the very extract of all human wisdom, and Jacob was given free lessons day after day.

8

That was all that the meeting had been about. Jacob had left Besty's office and walked slowly to his own; like the two sides of a coin, one showing a normal face and the other a distraught one. He had called the two neurologists on the phone and they were on their way to his office. While he waited, he remained seated, somewhat numb. Cistros and Nallan walked in, their faces reflecting concern. Nathan told them of his meeting with Besty. It was clear they already knew that something bad was going on. It was clear they did not share the same anti-Semitic opinions of other members of the clinic. They had found in Jacob the "best neurosurgeon they had ever seen". They did not want to lose him.

Abel Cistros had immigrated to America in a quite circuitous way. He had completed high school in Ecuador and then, with his parents' blessings, had migrated to Spain. He completed his medical studies in Madrid just to find out upon graduation that there were so many doctors that a substantial number of them were driving taxis to subsist –Franco's Spain had more jails than hospitals. That's when Abel immigrated to America and did his Neurology training at Vanderbilt. From there he had come directly to the Graham Clinic. He was the token "Latino" at the clinic; of course in his favor was the fact that he was not a Jew, but a fellow Christian, it didn't matter that his skin was a shade darker and his hair black and thick like a corn field on a moonless night.

John Nallan was a native of Florida. He was tall and thin and elegant having compensated for his balding head with a short, full beard. His family had arrived from Spain to Cuba in the seventeen-hundreds and had settled in Tampa after the American-Spanish War, first rolling tobacco leaves, then advancing to lawyers and even dentists. John graduated from Gainesville and then did his Neurology training at The Mayo Clinic. He returned to Florida and after one year of solo practice in a dingy office in Ybor City, joined the Graham Clinic. Unlike many of his clinic colleagues, he was not a bigot; perhaps growing up in a culturally diverse environment had broken that insidious and infectious prejudice, or maybe his immigrant roots were responsible for his open mind.

Cistros said, almost avoiding Nathan's eyes: "Look Jacob, this is just the work of a few".

"Yes", Nallan intervened, "This whole thing will pass. Just lay low for a while. Listen to me, just lay low and it's going to pass", he said in his characteristic muffled voiced.

So, Jacob went into waiting mode, just like the Jews of Spain had done centuries before: Lay low and it will pass the rabbis had said. Lay low and we will ride the wave; the king and queen will see their error and will allow us to be again part of the community. Don't distress because our synagogue has been turned into stalls for the

Count's horses, it will soon be ours again. But the Spanish Jewish sages had been wrong. Seldom had persecution been so effective. It would take four-and one-half centuries to reincarnate itself in the form of the Third Reich. Pope Gregory IX established the inquisition in the Kingdom of Aragon in 1232 to be later revived by Ferdinand II of Aragon and Isabella I of Castile together with Pope Sixtus IV and it did not matter that Jews had become virtually invisible, many converting to Catholicism on their own to avoid being murdered by local zealots. But it did not matter, soon they were ordered to convert or to stay clear from the kingdom's territories, and even worse, even those that had converted were punished, for the Church doubted the sincerity of their conversion. The Inquisition was now fully developed. Later, Hitler would also doubt the loyalty of the Jews towards Germany. Their assimilation would prove to be no shield against the hate instilled by daily sermons.

For Jacob, lying low for a while did not seem to ease the situation either. A few weeks later, he was called to the office of the clinic's senior partner and co-founder, Doctor Robert E. Smith III. The oil painting of Smith hanging on a wall in the doctors' lounge did not reveal the greenish tint or the dried out wrinkled skin that so characterized the chain-smoking physician. In no uncertain terms, and with assurance derived from being one of the founders of the clinic, he had stated in his raspy, whispering voice:

"I do not see Nigger patients and I do not refer patients to Jew doctors".

Again, Jacob had called his two neurology friends and they had convinced him to go and see the Chairman of the Board, a thoracic surgeon by training; for sure he would help –a man capable of making life or death decisions to save patient's lives.

"Just, don't be too controversial, just ask him if it is OK for you to stay in the clinic". They convinced him to plead, they had seen the writing on the wall and were about to lose their neurosurgeon. And Jacob Nathan, the survivor, had dutifully gone to the Chairman's office, dutifully following his friends' advice.

It is difficult to explain why Jacob did not pack his bags and leave the clinic. God knows he had received plenty of signs that he was not welcome there. Perhaps it was the plea from his two friends, or perhaps some powerful mechanism was forcing him to remain at the clinic. Nathan had a deep knowledge of biological mechanisms. He knew that often animals would rather starve than venture out of a known territory, or that captive animals may be reluctant to leave their cage, even though it is confining. The comfort of the known is often preferred to the promises of the unknown. Now, Jacob was following these same powerful biological lines of behavior that, in the long run, had protected many, even if by any logic, it would have been better to flee.

While the Clinic pursued the protracted process to expel Jacob, he was expected to continue with his clinical duties, including the coverage of the emergency room. By then, not too many people were looking at him with a positive attitude. It was under these circumstances that he received that emergency phone call.

"What is it?" he had inquired looking at the clock on the night table. The clock indicated it was two thirty in the morning. He had been asleep for just two hours and felt depressed and tired.

"Some John Doe got hit by a car," replied the nurse on the other end of the line.

Jacob left the house in a hurry and had driven faster than recommended, as he usually did when called to the emergency room. As he arrived, he asked the whereabouts of the patient. A disinterested, sleepy nurse indicated with a minimal gesture of her hand:

"He's on a stretcher in the back".

Jacob walked hurriedly towards the back of the emergency room and could not see any patient on a stretcher, and then he noticed that there was a stretcher in the corridor that led to the janitor's closet. He hurried towards it. Years before, Doctor Kalrsman, his mentor and professor of neurosurgery, had said to him in that soft voice that Jacob still could hear:

"Jacob, if when dealing with emergencies, people don't think you are a son of a bitch, you are not doing your job well".

Jacob would never forget that advice. Throughout the years it saved many lives.

On the stretcher Jacob found a man, perhaps 20 years old, naked, covered in mud. He had no intravenous lines in him –the nurses had not bothered with it. He was unconscious. It took him a few seconds to realize that he was comatose, paralyzed on the right side, and that his left pupil was large and unreactive to the light from his powerful flashlight. Nathan knew that the patient was dying. He called for a nurse. No one came. He then shouted with the full power of his lungs:

"I want a god-damned nurse here with this patient. He needs an i.v."

A nurse came reluctantly as if she were walking on a freshly tarred road. Jacob asked the emergency room clerk to call radiology for a CAT scan and to call the operating room to have a room ready for a craniotomy.

"X-rays says they have the machine warmed up, but the radiologist does not want to come", the clerk informed him −no Jew doctor was going to get him out of bed at three in the morning.

"I do not give a shit about a radiologist, I need this patient in x-rays now" Nathan shouted, knowing very well that he could read a CAT scan as well as the radiologist.

"There is no messenger to push the stretcher".

"I don't give a shit; I'll push it myself" and he had begun pushing it under the protestations of the nurse who had just finished establishing an intravenous line and was now filling out papers by the foot of the stretcher under the flickering light of a distant fluorescent ceiling bulb.

A few minutes later, the patient was inside the CT scanner long narrow tunnel and the first images were appearing on the monitoring console. A large Epidural Hematoma. Jacob could see the large collection of blood occupying the space between the skull and the thick membrane that covered the left hemisphere of his patient's brain, Mr. John Doe. He did not finish completing the study. He asked the technician to help him put the muddied patient on the stretcher again. He asked the nurse to call the operating room and inform them he was coming up with the patient.

"We do not have an anesthesiologist; we cannot give you an operating room without one!" barked the operating room nurse. It was clear that the clinic's attitudes were spreading to many of the employees in the hospital. He took the telephone from the nurse and in a commanding voice said:

"Hello, this is Nathan, I am taking the patient to the operating room NOW, you can call the anesthesiologist or you can call the police to stop me. Have a craniotomy tray ready". He listened to the nurse's reply. Then he said: "If we wait for an anesthesiologist, we will not need one. Patient will be dead. Understood?" Jacob hung up the phone and began pushing the stretcher. His heart was pounding against his rib cage and he felt hate against a system that took revenge on an innocent patient because he happened to have a Jewish neurosurgeon as his physician on this faithful night.

He got to the double doors of the surgical suite corridor and told the nurses to place the patient on the surgical table while he changed into the operating room attire. When he entered the room the nurses' eyes sparkled with rage; he paid no attention to it. Jacob began shaving the patient's head with the straight razor blade. He positioned the head over the horse-shoe shape rest holder and ordered the nurse to give the patient's head a good Betadyne prep scrub while he proceeded to wash his hands with sterile technique while his mind rushed over all the possible surgical scenarios that could face him in just a few moments: Was the patient going to die on the table? Was he going to encounter uncontrollable bleeding? He returned to the room and got dressed by the circulating nurse with the typical sterile gown and gloves. He then began placing drapes on the patient to isolate the operating site. Still, the anesthesiologist had not shown up.

"Scalpel". None was given.

"SCALPEL" he shouted. He began to make an incision on the patient's scalp. This time he did not take the time to stop the bleeding from the scalp vessels, as was his custom.

"DRILL". He noticed the contempt bursting from the partially covered face of the nurse. But this time she did not delay her response to his order. He placed the metal tip of the air-powered drill on the skull and activated the switch. He applied pressure and the drill began to bite the bone and then stopped automatically when the tip went through it. The dark black-red gelatinous blood clot began oozing from the hole. Jacob asked for a suction and began suctioning as much as he could of the tenacious bloody mass. At this point, the anesthesiologist entered the room. He was spewing insults that he probably had begun uttering in the dressing room.

"Who the fucking hell do you think you are", he shouted at Jacob.

But Jacob was too busy doing his surgery to entangle himself in a verbal tournament.

"Just do your part of the job", Jacob replied. The patient was beginning to move as the thankful brain began responding to the decompression.

Baker, the senior anesthesiologist at the hospital, was fuming. Here was a (Jewish) doctor performing surgery on a patient that was not under anesthesia! He had not waited for his arrival! Who had heard of starting a case without anesthesia! Of course, the fact that he had delayed his arrival as much as it was possible escaped his mind. Still mumbling insults, he got under the surgical drapes to get access to the patient's airways. Then, the noise stopped. He intubated the patient, introducing the curved, clear plastic tube into the trachea and connected it to the machine that provided the gas mixture, respecting as much as possible the sterile surgical field. When he emerged from under the drapes Baker's face was that of a different man.

"Doctor Nathan, all is now under control" he said, in a soft, almost tender voice, his rage now forgotten.

"Craniotome". With the bone cutting instrument, Nathan proceeded to open an oval shaped window in the skull, beginning and ending by the small burr-hole he had initially made. The larger aperture allowed Jacob to remove all the blood clot and to observe the brain returning to its usual space.   He then began applying tenting sutures to the thick dura membrane to prevent blood from re-accumulating.

"Do you know who this patient is?" Baker said to no one in particular. He answered the query himself:

"This is Mickey Bennett's son. This is Joe Bennett. Mickey...my best friend..."

As it turned out Joe Bennett was not only the son of Mickey Bennett, the latter happened to be also the richest man in town.   The newly baptized Joe Bennett, never to be known again by his recent alias John Doe, was transported to the recovery room, where a team of nurses from the intensive care unit had been called by Doctor Baker to supplement the recovery room nurse on call. Joe Bennett deserved the best medical care the hospital could provide. In the recovery room, Joe opened his eyes and began moving his right side. The left pupil was coming back to a normal size and was reacting to light.   Joe could not speak.

On the following day, Joe began speaking. He complained of back pain. An x-ray ordered by Doctor Nathan demonstrated a fracture of the sixth thoracic vertebral body. An orthopedist was consulted and it was decided to place the patient in a thoracic brace. Eventually, Joe recovered completely. He had been the victim of a hit and run accident, complicated by the fact that the driver of the car had stopped to rob him of his wallet and all his identifying documents.   But Joe

Bennett had almost become the victim of a second hit and run accident, when as a John Doe, he had been abandoned by the very hospital system that was supposed to help the sick and the wounded. Abandoned by all, that is, except Doctor Jacob Nathan.

9

Within weeks of the emergency room incident, Jacob had become the hero of the Bennett family and the villain of the Clinic. His success with the younger Bennett only made the resentment towards him grow. Jacob continued his clinical routine, seeing the patients that Nallan and Cistros referred to him and operating on those that required it.

Jacob was an expert in micro-neurosurgical techniques. Operating under magnification permitted a much greater degree of delicacy and control. One Sunday afternoon, while a reporter from the local newspaper was interviewing Jacob at his house about the expertise that he had brought to the Clinic in the neurosurgery field, the telephone rang. Rebecca had come into the study, interrupting the interview:

"It's the Chairman of the Board of the Clinic" she had said.

Nathan apologized for the interruption, but on purpose, took the phone call right in front of the reporter. The Chairman informed Jacob that the Clinic had cancelled the surgical procedure he had booked for the coming Monday –He was out. The reporter overheard the conversation and decided to give the story a new twist.

The following Sunday the paper carried in a full front-page article the story of the dedicated neurosurgeon that had brought a new level of surgical care to the area and the Clinic that was undermining this effort. The article polarized the community. Jacob received many calls from thankful patients and their families. One of them even offered to kill any member(s) of the Clinic. Jacob thanked him and declined. For several months the newspaper continued to publish letters to the editor, but eventually, as is often the case, all died down. This too he had learned: that time has its way to smooth out rough edges, to mitigate indignation, to quench the irate righteousness. He had seen it happen in Germany, he had seen it happen with his own patients, when the storm had passed and their loved ones had been taken by the ravishes of nature and now, the town that had welcomed his neurosurgical expertise would also rest in silence after the prescribed time had passed.

Jacob and Rebecca moved on, but during the remaining years of their lives never forgave themselves for having allowed the Clinic to go unpunished, for not having submitted the Graham Clinic to a discrimination lawsuit, for having bent their necks once more to the face of persecution. There would be no sunset contemplation without some painful memories of this period in their lives. How could there be a statute of limitations for a crime that alters a life forever?

How had he permitted this to happen? Jacob Nathan had lost all he had ever loved when a whole people, he amongst them, marched in tortured silence to certain slaughter. And after his camp was liberated, with his first recovered strength, when he still had not been capable of walking, when he had just begun to gather some coherent thoughts, Jacob had promised to never be passive again. And now, years after those gates had opened on that faithful winter morning, he had remained silent again! How had this happened? How was it possible that history had rolled over him for a second time? His entire life was never at ease again. He had betrayed Leibish and Shimen and Abrum and Frieda and Sarah and Erzon and Anna and Max and all the others. Now and forever they would haunt him. He had failed them all!

10

There had been no farewell party on the day the camp was left unattended with its gates wide opened. The morning sunlight, filtered by the ever-present low-lying smog saturated with the odor of rotten bodies, of burnt flesh, of ashes, of putrid still living human beings, had bathed the camp without yet casting upon the ground the shadows of the guard towers and the barbwire with its curving poles. It had been like any other day on that cold winter, except that there had been no call to stand at attention on the campground in front of the officers and soldiers in charge of slaughtering them. That morning, the activity inside the barracks increased little by little, gently, like newborn puppies excited by the presence of a different smell. Winter had not been kind to many of the prisoners. The frigid nights of January, combined with malnutrition and disease took their toll. Every morning there were many that never moved again. Nathan used to think that they simply continued dreaming for eternity, dreams of harmony and peace, he hoped. Dreams not too different from what he dreamed on occasion: A lovely winding path amidst rolling hills with birds jumping from tree to tree, chirping happily.

The rumor started by the new inmates, that the allied forces were getting closer, had coincided with a decrease in the amount of food that was distributed by the guards at mealtime.

The single piece of bread was now half of what it used to be and the soup was even more watery. In the mornings the surviving inmates were forced to clear the bunk beds of human remains. A death offered the opportunity of acquiring an extra blanket, or another jacket, or a pair of pants, so that in a way, the survivors would find themselves better equipped against the pervasive cold and clammy nights, and at the same time would feel the horror of welcoming another death. It was a dirty trick, one that would hunt the survivors for many years to come: to wish death upon another human being so that one could have his socks or his jacket. There were moments when Nathan would become painfully aware of the changes that had taken place in him. He had started by wanting to become a medical doctor so he would help others in need and now, especially during those cold winter nights, he couldn't help wishing that someone would die in his barrack so he could get a blanket or a pair of pants. Yes, they all had been inoculated with the guilt virus. For those destined to live, life would never bring happiness without a healthy serving of guilt. Why, they would ask themselves in the solitude of dark nights, was I spared? What kind of person am I to have wished death upon others? How could I have rejoiced by Smulik's death? Why me? Why me? These thoughts would bump inside the survivors' heads like bouncing balls against their skulls keeping them company during insomniac nights, bringing misery even to the happiest moments of their existence.

On this particular morning, Jacob elbowed his dear friend, lying by his side.

"Leib, Leibish, wake up, wake up, Leib! There is something wrong!"

Leibish had opened his dried and crusted eyelids and immediately became alarmed by the silence.

"We are dead", he said.

"No, no, I think we are alone".

Leibish looked into Jacob's deep dark eyes and became more aware of his surroundings. They helped each other crawl out of their bunk beds and slowly inched their way towards the entrance door of the barrack. Too tired and weak to continue, they sat on the cold, harsh floor against the open door.

For the last two weeks, the newly arrived prisoners spoke of evacuations of the camps, of forced marches, of train rides. One morning, during one of the last incoming trainloads, Jacob was delegated to clean the barracks. His companion for the task was Abrum. He had come on a transport just one week before. Abrum appeared somewhat stronger than Jacob. These last weeks of diluted food portions were taking their toll on all the inmates. Jacob needed to stop frequently to rest as they moved from one bunk bed to the next, removing the dry excrement encrusted into the cross boards of the beds. To fill the time, they spoke; Abrum more than him.

"Jacob, I was in a camp in Eastern Poland." Abrum said without any prompting. He spoke in Yiddish. Although initially Jacob only spoke German, he had learned Yiddish, which appeared to be the universal language in the camp.

"Me and my cousin Laedl. We could hear the sound of bombs in the distance. Every day getting closer and stronger".

"Come, help me scrape this bed or they will kill us both", interrupted Nathan. The two of them rubbed their fingernails against the dried feces until the grain of the wood came through. Jacob, exhausted, sat down. Abrum continued:

"One morning, during roll call, we were ordered to form lines of five and they kept us standing for hours. Finally, late in the afternoon, SS troopers surrounded us and gave the order to march."

With tears in his eyes Abrum continued:

"Jacob, we marched through the gates of the camp!"

"Oh, how for a moment, if only a moment, I thought we were free! But the SS sergeant began trotting and we were forced to follow. As the sun set, the cold of the night began intensifying. Running helped keep us warm, at least in the beginning. But then, with no stamina or energy reserves, some of us began lagging behind. At first, no one thought much of it, not until we heard the first shots. Then we saw that SS guards were shooting anyone who had fallen or could not march at the pace of the group."

Jacob's eyes were fixed in Abrum's. He held his hand over his mouth as if silencing a shout, a cry that would never emerge. The smell of feces on his hands did not matter any longer.

Saúl Balagura

11

It was a glorious New Mexico day. The heat of the Sun was not yet suffocating. The air was so clear and infused with the aroma of the evergreen forest that created the impression that one was taking in with every breath the very essence of God. The soil was dry and smooth swept by winds the night before. Jacob's feet were stepping on virgin ground. Here and there bushes of mountain mahogany sprouted from the dry sandy landscape extending their branches like hands clamoring for water. The ground began sloping gently. On the virgin sand he saw the delicate footprints of a coyote. He wondered if it had had good luck with its hunt. He wondered if it had been alone or in a pack. Coyotes often crossed the dried arroyo behind his house on their way to their daily hunt and back. They had a scraggly look and a sad howl. Even the palaver echoed from hill to hill in their high-pitched barks and lonely howls seemed to be written in a minor key. Only rarely he had seen them, walking cautiously at a constant pace with their noses to the ground, following an invisible rabbit trail, always alert to the bark of the neighborhood dogs.

It did not escape Jacob the cruel destiny that nature had imposed on these two cousins, the dog and the coyote. The dog had given up his freedom genes in exchange for food, shelter and eventually love from its master. The coyote had become even more cautious, more elusive and reclusive to guard its freedom. When Max was still alive, Jacob remembered how on occasion, on hearing the distant coyote palaver, Max would bark and even howl from the safety of home while the coyotes would become even more cautious as they pursued their prey worrying that dogs would perhaps block their run. Was there a parallel to be drawn? Had Jews not kept a similar attitude during the past twenty centuries? Like coyotes, Jews had survived and like coyotes, they were taken as dangerous parasites, upon which periodic cleansings and open hunting were instituted. Yet, like coyotes, Jews had an intrinsic pride, a certain self-assurance that gave them, no matter how arid their environment, a certain dignity in their survival.

On very few occasions, Jacob had seen coyotes cross his path: Lanky, thirsty, solitary, almost Quixotic in their appearance, yet never running away from him; just walking with certain noblesse, looking him in the eye while they trotted silently into the underbrush. He had walked like that, many years before, trying to convince himself, if not others, that he was still an individual, with rights and duties no different from the people that watched him with contempt. Nothing could make him forget. Everything reminded him of those terrible days.

12

Abrum, collecting a little saliva, forced himself to continue with his story. His voice almost a murmur, his throat sore from ulcers, his eyes fixed on Jacob's. Outside, ashes were falling on the prisoners that remained in the camp. Later on, the wind would blow the sediment, rising as twisted fingers in a final gesture, bringing people to rest on top of rooftops and trees and the almost infinite fields that surrounded the nearby woods.

"The only way to survive was to keep up with the pack. As I felt the pain in my legs, I begged for the whole group to slow down; I thought if we all did, they would not dare shoot us all. My entire body was concentrated on just two things: running like all the others and praying that we all would slow down. And as the pain increased in my legs, and my breathing became shorter and shorter, I saw death coming. It could not have been too far from me. From my legs the pain began creeping into my back. I realized that I had to stop. I could no longer move my limbs. I began floating, gliding in the air just with enough speed to keep up with the masses. Someone next to me fell down. Others trampled over him and then I heard the shot. The cold began to penetrate into every crevice of my body. I felt a sensation of tingling advancing from my feet upwards. My arms were dangling by my side as if they belonged to some cadaver standing next to me."

Abrum's face was almost rigid. Some tears collecting on the wrinkles around the sockets of his eyes. "The road, that before had been muddy began to freeze, leaving some stretches with jagged edges and others slippery like a frozen lake. More people fell and more shots were fired. I saw my cousin Laedl fall, and two of my bunk bed neighbors. I kept floating. Then, my lips became parched like desiccated mud, my tongue was dry and stuck to the bottom of my mouth. Each breath brought intense pain to my chest. I knew this was the end."

Jacob moved slowly to another bed. They found a blanket and with great difficulty were able to rip it in half and each wore it like a shawl. Abrum continued:

"Suddenly, we all stopped. We had arrived at the destination for that day. I could see the SS troopers eating and drinking, but they never gave us any food. We drank the snowy mud from the side of the road. We huddled against each other so that we would not freeze. We slept like the dead until we were awakened by the shouts of the living guards."

Abrum's chest heaving in short bursts indicated he was crying, even though no tears sprung from his eyes. "And we began running again. Just this time, we knew what was going to happen. Each one of us knew exactly how the pain and agony would begin creeping and each one knew how we would die. After many days we arrived at this camp. I don't know how many of us died, but when we started, I could not see the end of the line, and when it ended, we were not more than four hundred men."

"Jacob, Jacob!   Listen to me" he said almost in a whisper, "if you want to live, don't go on one of those marches".   Abrum stood in silence for a moment, and then began walking slowly towards the barrack's door, his image turning into a dark shadow as the outside light tumbled into the room.

Jacob never saw him again. Had he been an angel sent to save his life? Abrum's skeletal body and oversized head had not appeared different from all the other prisoners, but there had been something in the way those dried eyes shone that kept Nathan wondering for the rest of his life. Perhaps not all angels have to have wings; perhaps some of them, instead of wings have dried up eye sockets. Who can tell?

13

It would never cease to amaze him how the piñons curled and gnarled and wrinkled as the years went by so that Jacob could almost see in them what he, himself, was becoming –had become.   And in the middle of this desert mountain there were beautiful gray and green and even some red feathered birds that kept chirping all along his daily walks. To the left, not ten feet from him, he saw a small sparrow pecking at the bark of a Juniper. On this riverbed, Jacob had to walk carefully, for the sandy soil hid occasionally the old roots of long-gone trees that would wait for his feet like the hands of long-gone dead people eager to snare him and cause him to fall.   He knew each of these paths like the inside of his home. A few steps more and the trail would make a left turn and open into a narrow sandy passage shadowed by 200-year-old piñons. And fifty yards ahead, he would encounter the ground studded with rocks covered with soft, green moss, a sight that never ceased to amaze him, and not too far ahead he would find two granite boulders jutting out from their sandy prison like giant bones.   The muscles in his thighs began to ache and Nathan decided to stop for a moment, shifting some of his weight onto his fateful cane. This would be a perfect time to caress Max, but his faithful dog was dead, leaving moments like this saturated with emptiness. High above his head he could see the sun reflected on a passing jetliner, like a bright star in the middle of the day, its contrail bowing to the winds, giving it the appearance of a comet –the sound of the powerful engines had not reached him yet. After a while, his heart rate had normalized and his legs stopped aching. The air was clean and he continued his walk watching in amazement the occasional row of ants marching in a single file across his path, on a path of their own. He had walked about three-quarters of a mile into the hills when he saw an old stretch of rusted barbed wire –unearthed by recent rains— and he froze.

14

The train had stopped with a horrible screeching noise that almost woke the inmates that were already dead. Nathan had been standing inside that wagon for five days and four nights. It had been impossible to lay or sit. Just standing, kept in that position by all the other people that had been crammed into the transport wagon, men, women, children, old, young, sick, mothers breast feeding, stroke victims, strong men, beautiful women, doctors, musicians, all standing, pressed against each other, barely able to take a deep breath. He had felt like an animal or less. That feeling that a person has that is never felt until it is taken away, he felt for the first time in all its might and meaning when the SS guards shoved the last fifty people into the wagon, and the old man next to him wet his pants. As Jacob felt the wetness advancing and covering his own right leg, he turned and looked in disbelief –as if to say "what the hell!"– just to find those sad, terrified gray eyes of the old man that just moments before had been desperately calling for his Frieda: "*Friedale, wo bist Du Friedale*". But Frieda had not responded. And now Jacob knew for the first time that this was the end of humanity and he had cried.

Years later, some would criticize him: "Everything reminds you of something in the past". That is what they would say. But how could he not be reminded of being a part of this trainload of people when he would find himself in a crowd packed room, even if it was just in the lobby of a theater, even if instead of going to a concentration camp, he was just going to listen to the great Isaac Stern play at Carnegie Hall, even if there was ample space to move around, to turn, to hold a glass with champagne? Yes, everything reminded him of those times, because, after all, he was the past that had not died and now was living in the present, a future that he could never have imagined in those dark oppressive days.

It had been four-thirty in the afternoon the day that the SS guards had transferred him from the detention cell to the train station. Until that point, he still had been hopeful that after the war, when the nightmare had passed, he would walk again the streets of his beloved Berlin and finish his studies of Medicine so that he could, in turn, teach young men and women at the university. It was a very long line of people: Women, children, men, all carrying some belongings packed either, in formal luggage or hastily held together by a knotted bedsheet. Everyone was wearing a winter coat even though it was a hot summer day —deep down they all had known. For a moment it had occurred to him that they were waiting to board one of those luxurious cruise ship on its way to an exotic vacation, but the somber faces reminded him that it was not going to be pleasant to climb into a cattle car. At three in the morning, he could not hold his urine any longer. It had been eleven hours, and like the old man next to him, he let go and he felt the warm fluid bathe his legs and for a moment enjoyed the relief, and then he realized that the only thing that differentiated him from Frieda's husband, was ten hours and he cried again.

They all stood packed in the cattle wagon for the longest time. Immediately next to him was Anna. Sarah with her long red hair stood dressed in a dark blue suit, and there was Erzon with his broken wax mustache and flannel shirt, and Feige, fat and sweaty, and Johann tall and strong like a bull, and Shmuel with his long hair hidden by a black hat, and of course Max, Frieda's husband, and all the others, with their faces erased by the dusty, pervasive twilight contained within the walls. Night came and the train did not stop and no one got fed.

"*Am Morgen*. The train will stop in the morning and they will let us walk and sit and we will have something to eat. *Am Morgen*", Sarah had said.

The rail tracks rocked the train from one side to the other and they all danced along, their bodies compelled by the pull of gravity –like a sad group of dancers, following the hypnotic howling music of the wheels hurling along the metal railroad tracks. Sometime that first night, Jacob started a conversation with Erzon, his mustache now in total disarray.

"After all this is over, I am going to study Medicine", Jacob had said at one point.

"And I will become a famous painter", Erzon had replied, half of his moustache flipping as his lips moved, giving his face a tragic and comic expression. It would be a long and intense friendship, the one they had inadvertently started in the hot and crowded train on their way to a place none would have imagined could exist.

The morning came and the train did not stop and as the day advanced, the mid- day heat began to take its toll. With nothing to drink, Jacob felt the urge to urinate only once on that second day. On the morning of the third day, all were very tired and exhausted. Jacob's head was moving at the rhythm of the railroad tracks, following the bobbing of the moving train back and forth, side to side. It was then when he noticed that Max's head was tilted, and then, on closer inspection, he realized that his eyes were open and were not blinking, and he had stopped calling his Frieda and he was dead. And horrified, he had thought how strange it was to be standing next to a standing corpse. He prayed that all this was nothing but a bad dream, but he knew he was fully awake. Jacob Nathan realized that he had arrived at the edge of hell. The air that he was breathing was now heavy with the urine and feces and sweat that each one of them emanated unwillingly and in shame. And then, one early afternoon, the train had stopped and they heard dogs barking and guards shouting and the screech of doors sliding open. Their turn came soon enough, and as the doors opened and the brightness blinded them, they were ordered out. A plank of wood had been placed by the wide door, and people were erupting out of the boxcar like pus out of a bursting boil, and the wagon emptied, except for the dead. Nathan noticed that the standing dead had now fallen and he counted ten; "a minyan" he thought and then it was his turn to jump. Jacob jumped from the threshold of the wagon into a dry and dusty soil, and it was then that he saw the coils of barbed wire progressively narrowing, funneling into the entrance gate.

15

The constant churning of the train wheels against the metal rails was lulling Jacob into a deep sleep. Jacob's thoughts were lost in the immensity of the landscape that glided rapidly through the window of the train. The fields were green, scarred in orderly lines by the plow that constantly defiled the fertile ground to demand from it one more time potatoes and beets. The orderly fields were interrupted by narrow strips of woodlands left in place to break the winds and preserve the fertile topsoil. Here and there he could see the steeple of a church. This was the first time he traveled alone. He was thirteen years old. He felt like a grown man. He had the feeling he was a person, a real person, needed by others to complete a tradition that had started centuries before he or his family or for that matter even Germany had been born.

The Nathans had cousins in the town of Eberswalde about 40 km to the northeast of Berlin. The Jewish population in town was too small to complete a minyan. They were always in desperate need for a tenth Jew. So when Jacob had his bar-mitzvah, it not only brought great happiness to his parents, but it gave new hopes to the small Jewish community for Jacob was seen as the manna that the Jews of Eberswalde had been praying for all these years. For the first time in recent memory, they would not have to disband during high holidays. Now Jacob would be their tenth man.

The train ticket had been paid by the Eberswalde Jewish community. Jacob was seated in a compartment by himself. His legs barely touched the floor as he sat on the soft and velvety bench. A small table, jutting from the wall just under the window, was adorned with a tiny porcelain flowerpot and a single hyacinth. Overhead, too high for him to reach, there was plenty of space for luggage and even a sleeping berth.

Jacob could not remember a time in his childhood void of his cousin Heinrich. The family from Eberswalde visited the Nathan's household often. Heinrich was a year younger than he, had blue eyes, blond hair and a soft, gentle way about him. The two of them often played hide and seek in the house and around the neighborhood. The two of them would whisper children's thoughts in the middle of the great synagogue to break the boredom inflicted upon them by endless hours of praying. He had not seen Heinrich since his bar-mitzvah and was looking forward to the meeting, although now he had to behave with some dignity, the two could not chat during services, the other adults were counting on him praying.

The train began slowing down and the change of rhythm woke Jacob up. He was wearing the same brown striped suit his parents had bought for him on the occasion of his bar mitzvah, a few months earlier. He felt comfortable and warm. He was the tenth man for the minyan. He thought he liked riding on trains.

16

Jacob felt the New Mexico sun stinging his hands and realized that he was sweating and that he must have been standing in that same spot for some time. He shook his head and continued his walk and automatically whistled to call Max but cut himself short: Max had died a few years before. At his age time was beginning to lose its temporal sequencing. Time was ceasing to be time. Years could collapse into just brief moments, yesterdays seemed far away, and events that had happened long ago, could jump to the foreground evoked by a common thread, sometimes too small to perceive. Age had given him the power of teleportation across time and space. And as he aged, he realized that what to others might have appeared as senility was in fact the product of an active mind, sharpened by the passing years, as other less meaningful events began to peel away exposing a core of experiences that could never be forgotten. Daily living was not as important as having lived. The rusted barbed wire followed Jacob's path for a few yards and then dipped into the sandy ground – there was nothing to enclose.

Rebecca and Jacob had flown a thousand miles to get him, Max. They had decided after the death of their last Rottweiler that there would be no more Maxes.

"A dog would tie us up", she said.

"We can hardly take vacations and go on trips", Jacob affirmed.

But the hurt of losing Max began to subside after one year had passed, and the memories of pain began to be replaced by memories of warmth and feelings of emptiness. They remembered Max's love pit stops, when the old dog used to stand in front of them in the middle of a walk, begging for caresses. They remembered the puppy smell he retained even as an old dog. They remembered, with tenderness and lessened pain, how he would sometimes sit and just look at a beautiful sunset as if he were just another member of the family enjoying the quiet end of a day. And those soft, brown eyes that reflected their own souls, they remembered that too.

The decision to get another Max was not forced upon them by grief but by love. This time they had decided to get a "reject". Up to then, each Rottie they owned had been a pure breed, with a lustrous pedigree. But recently, a friend had introduced them to a Web site for rescued Rottweilers. They had been made aware that thousands of Rotties were abused and rejected each year, and that some recue groups dedicated themselves to the salvage of these unfortunate animals. So, Rebecca and Jacob had made contact with one of those rescue center in Ann Arbor, Michigan, close to the university, and had made an appointment to visit.

The whole endeavor required a lot of planning. Airlines did not want to transport a massive, adult Rottweiler. They did not want that liability, especially during summer months, when a cage left on the tarmac could reach temperatures well above 100 degrees. This meant they would have to drive with their new dog all the way back from Michigan, some seventeen-hundred miles. It also meant they had to get there by plane and pointed to the obvious need to rent a car one way. All this had to be coordinated with motels along the road that would accept overnight pets of the size of a grown leopard. And of course, they were worried sick that they would not find a dog with at least some of Max's characteristics. Over and over, they had said to each other, "This is not a replacement for Max. It's just another dog". They were afraid of betraying their old, dead friend. It is human nature to fear that meeting someone new somehow puts a limitation on how one feels about someone old, as if our hearts are not big enough to extend our love. It is the guilt that inhibits friends from expanding their circle, it is the fear of a widow to remarry for fear of betraying her dead husband. But the human heart can cover many with its warmth and no disrespect is given to old loves when new ones are found. Love is infinite when there is a need to give it and almost as large when one needs to receive it.

As they approached the wire-fenced facility, about thirty dogs became active and began pacing the grounds, some barking. Mary, the lady in charge of the rescue mission, was about five feet six inches tall, with sun wrinkled skin and laborer's working hands and a sweet smile that surfaced when she looked at her dogs. As the Nathans got closer to the fence, Mary motioned to them to stay behind. She would bring the dogs one at a time. Rebecca and Jacob knew that whichever dog was chosen would find heaven on earth. Rescuing one meant not rescuing the others; it was so painful to reject any of them. And then Mary let him out. It was a magnificent dog, gigantic. He ran in their direction and jumped on Jacob, placing his massive paws on his shoulders, standing face to face. He had a sad expression even though the little stump of his tail was wagging wildly from side to side. He had a little white spot on his left ear and one on his nose. Rebecca recognized then that the dog had been abandoned because he was not a perfect specimen –white is not tolerated in any pure breed Rottweiler.

The rescue ladies had found the dog roaming in the municipal garbage dump. His skin had entire patches without hair. He weighed eighty pounds and looked like a sack of bones. Under the care of the rescue mission, the dog had regained his normal weight of one hundred and fifty pounds. Six months had passed and no one had adopted him. The Nathans had fallen in love again. Rebecca indicated to Mary that this was the one, but that they did not like a jumping dog; as big as he was, he could throw someone to the ground. Mary had said, "No problem" and proceeded in just two trials to teach the dog not to jump on people. It was as if the dog had sensed that not jumping was his ticket to a new home.

The Nathans rented a car and even placed sunscreens on the windows to protect the dog's discolored nose from the summer sun. They called him "Max" and from the very start he had positioned himself on the back with his massive head between the two front seats over the middle armrest. He traveled the seventeen hundred miles return trip in silence and tranquility. He knew this was his new family. There had been no need for acclimation between the Nathans and Max. After the first night at home, they had all gone for their morning walk as if they had done it always, almost as if the old Max had entered into the new one, and a long love affair had continued, interrupted briefly by death.

17

The dried arroyo was narrowing and its banks were becoming steep so that Jacob made it a point to keep an eye open for the next spot where he could climb out of the canyon which was getting ever deeper. The walls of the arroyo, carved by gentle but relentless erosion, exposed the roots of any tree that dared grow along its banks. Roots as thick as the tree trunks they sprouted from, twisted into the ground, branching into hundreds of dried wrinkled arms desperately holding on to rocks and sand and dirt. As Jacob walked the arroyo bed, stones became more prominent and signs of recent erosion showed a large Juniper, perhaps a hundred years old, fallen into the canyon opening a natural path for him to climb out. Once on higher ground, the soil was again gentle, offering a carpet of sand, dried twigs and small pebbles, and now Jacob only had to worry about finding a clear path among the ancient stocky trees that partially shadowed the landscape.

Jacob's eyes were always searching the sandy ground for any relics or archeological objects. Their friends kept telling them about all the arrowheads and bullets that they had found during their walks in the woods. Jacob knew that these Tesuque hills had provided the backdrop for many a battle between Indians and Spaniards centuries before. In fact, one of the neighbors, Martha and Paul Gallaway, had told them of a peculiar event they had experienced.   After moving into their house atop of one of the ridges, Martha began experiencing a general sense of malaise. At first, she assumed it was due to the stress of the move from California, but it did not resolve with time.   In fact, she began having headaches, bad headaches. The Gallaways had consulted a physician, but after all the tests came out negative, he gave Martha a prescription to take care of her headaches as need be. Neither Martha nor Paul were satisfied. Then, about six months after they had moved to their new house, she began having nightmares.   At first the nightmares were infrequent, but as they became more and more pervasive began to take a toll on Martha and for that matter on Paul as well. They were very discontented, even though they were living in a million-dollar house on top of one of the most beautiful landscapes that nature can offer. Finally, Martha read in the local paper about an old Indian woman that had magical powers. Since they had exhausted the western medical sciences, they decided to consult the old Indian.

She said her name was "Mategooh". Her lips, smiling almost all the time, showed a mouth void of most teeth. She wore a white cotton shirt over a black wool skirt and dark brown leather sandals.   Around her neck she wore a silver necklace with blue and green stones. Her skin was a wrinkled landscape ravaged by the heavy sun and rarefied, thin air. The Gallaways picked her up, for she had no means of transportation. She lived about ten miles, as the crow flies, from the Gallaways, in a small adobe hut next to the

Rio Grande, under a large cotton tree. When she stepped out of the car, she made a hissing sound and then, shaking her head from side to side she said:

"No good. Land no good."

"What is it?" inquired Martha, conditioned to believe almost everything if it could stop her painful nightmares and already expecting the worst.

"It is the spirits. Too many spirits".

"What do you mean, spirits?" Paul interjected.

"Many years ago, when the People were living in the valley of the big river, white men came on top of horses. They had fire-tubes that killed many women and children." The old Indian woman stopped talking for a moment and pulled from a pocket of her skirt a small leather pouch with a brownish powder, perhaps some pollen. She pinched with the index finger and thumb of her left hand a small amount and said:

"Follow me".

The three of them walked around the house at an even, deliberate pace, as Mategooh released into the air small amounts of the powder. Then she said:

"The young warriors took to the hills and hid from the white man. But the white man looked for the braves. It was on this ridge that they were finally found." She listened with intent, tilting her head: "Can you hear them? "

She took from the other pocket a black pouch and this time grabbed a pinch of an ash-like substance between her thumb and middle finger and they all went around the house in the opposite direction and as she dispersed it into the air, she began making peculiar guttural sounds in rhythm with her step. When they were back to where they had started, she spoke again:

"The sun was high in the sky when the fight began. When the sun began to kiss the mountains for the night, the war had ended. All the warriors had died".

The old Indian seemed tired and became quiet for a while. Paul interrupted the silence:

"But what do we have to do with all that?" –inflection on the we.

The Indian seemed to have been awoken from a light sleep:

"The young warriors were never given proper burial. Their spirits move all the time around this hill and your house. They have not found peace."

Martha was crying. Paul held her hand as he asked:

"What can be done?"

The old Indian woman replied:

"Give me hundred dollars". Paul got his wallet out of the back pocket of his trousers and gave the woman two fifty-dollar bills –he was prepared. She rolled the bills and placed them in a satchel inside her blouse. Then she said to Martha:

"Bring dress that you love the more to me".

Martha ran inside the house and moments later she came out holding in her arms her daughter's wedding dress. The old woman asked Paul to dig a hole two feet long and two feet wide and three feet deep in the middle of the patio around which the house wrapped its square corridors. It was not an easy task. The ground was packed solid. Thirty minutes later, Paul, all sweaty, had completed the task. The old woman began chanting in a manner that reminded Martha of the sound of sea waves as they brake against a rocky beach. She folded the dress and placed it in the hole and emptied the contents of the two leather pouches over it before Paul filled it back with the sandy, rocky soil.

They drove the old Indian back to her home. That night was the first night in many months that Martha had a restful sleep. She never had headaches again. Had it been old Indian magic, or had burying the dress permitted her to bury her guilt? These were incredibly beautiful foothills and many years before had been inhabited by native Americans. Some people felt that even though they had paid for the land, it was not theirs –the old guilt contaminating the beauty of the land. And no matter how hard Jacob looked for old arrowheads, he never found one, not one in many, many years.

The flutter of a bird's wings made him turn his head and he noticed the peculiar rock, protruding from the sandy soil. It reminded Jacob of an exposed brain.

18

"Look", Nathan had said, "this is the time to tell all the jokes you want, as long as they are good and you promise to be quiet when we get to the exposed brain".

The room was full of gadgets and instruments. Smooth white mosaic covered the walls and gave the operating suite the aspect of immaculate cleanliness, which in fact it was. Bob Holgers, the anesthesiologist, was seated in his little cubicle hidden by a tent of sterile drapes. Jacob loved to operate with him. Holgers was the best anesthesia man he had known. He was a typical small-town Texan, complete with accent and mannerisms and wrinkled leather boots, but he was also board certified in Internal Medicine as well as in Anesthesiology. His sense of humor and timing were a joy, and his knowledge of Texas history was encyclopedic.

"Y'all know what day's today?" he said whistling slightly the 's' sound and exaggerating his accent to make it appear as a hillbilly.

"Let me see, I believe it's Tuesday", Nathan replied knowing very well that Bob would come out with some incredible story.

"No sir. Today is the anniversary of the day when General Santa Anna began his northern campaign towards San'Antone".

Almost without taking a breath he added, "That sucker came with enough troops to wipe out the entire country of Texas. Yess-sirr-reee".

"No sir today is the anniversary of my first day in the neurosurgical program at John Fox Municipal Hospital", Nathan countered, with a painful smile under his surgical mask –another battle he had survived.

19

Things had definitely changed for the better since that first time. He recalled that day in July when, still dark, he had kissed Rebecca good-bye, not knowing what the rest of the day would bring. In fact, he had no idea as to how the rest of these, tough, training years would turn out. He took the elevator to the basement and walked briskly towards his car. They had bought a Peugeot after they had decided that it would be better to live in Manhattan and commute to work in the Bronx. The Upper East Side was a wonderful place to live. Within walking distance of their apartment there were at least some twenty restaurants: three or four Chinese, two Hungarian, one Czech, four Italian, one Irish, one Spanish, two Mexican and a Deli and then some. Every imaginable service was within three blocks of their building: two banks, two supermarkets, one drugstore, several laundries, one auction house and even a bagel factory.

Rebecca was able to walk to work. She had gotten a job as secretary to Sal Rosenberg, a neurologist at Memorial Hospital. Her working hours were from 8 in the morning to 4 in the afternoon, with one-hour break for lunch. Rosenberg was a kind and dedicated man. By the time he arrived at his office, at 8:30 in the morning, Rebecca would have all the charts in order, the appointments at the tip of his fingers, and a cup of fresh coffee as well. Rebecca was an organized and efficient person, the perfect employee to have in a medical office. Her smile and clear understanding of human suffering gave her a "natural" way to relate to the patients; in return, the patients trusted and respected her.

Yes, she understood human suffering. She had studied under the best teachers Germany could offer. She had grown up under the shadow of European *hoch Kultur*, she had seen the Sun lose its shine during the war years, and then, she had found Jacob and had nursed him like only love can nurse. And throughout all those years, she had learned her gentle way.

Jacob turned the ignition key and the Peugeot responded immediately with its characteristic purr. He drove out of the garage and joined the traffic going north towards the 3rd Avenue Bridge. During the six years that it took him to finish his training, he often wondered how long it would take him to die if his faithful Peugeot were to break down in the middle of the South Bronx. All the deadly head bashings he was to see and treat at the emergency room during his training would come from this fertile ground. He got on the expressway and drove at a brisk pace against the traffic that was pouring into Manhattan. Jacob found the esplanade where the hospital buildings stood and parked his car in the designated space for the residents. He proceeded to enter through the emergency room entrance and walked briskly through the corridor that took him to the main elevators but chose the stairs next to them and climbed to the third floor. The neurosurgery ward occupied the West wing of the third floor.   Nathan crossed the threshold marked by the double doors and walked in the direction of the voices. A group of doctors and nurses were gathering in the first room to the left of the ample corridor. It was the "Doctors Office", with its government issued metal desk, three wooden chairs and one decrepit sofa. Behind the desk, that was facing the room, there was a wooden reclining chair and behind it, a window with the shades drawn. The walls were painted in light gray and save for a photograph of the front of the building –perhaps taken on opening day— they were void of any warmth. At 7 a.m. on the dot, the group moved to the corridor marking the beginning of the formal rounds.   The chief resident, Ted Goldberg entered the first patients' room and behind him walked, by seniority, the rest of the doctors and nurses. Since this was his first day in the service and he was the junior resident, Nathan was last to enter.

The room contained six beds, three on each side; next to each one there was a night table and a respirator. On the wall facing the door a set of windows with closed blinds partially blocking the view of parked cars that covered every available inch of the parking lot surface down below and the distant grass and verdant trees that were invisible to the comatose patients occupying the six beds in the neuro-intensive care unit. The bed covers were immaculate laundry-white, with a sharp crease along the very middle of the bed, as if slicing the patients in half. Each head was resting, dead center, on an equally immaculate clean pillow. The morning crew had prepared for the show —as if paraphrasing the old adage, a sound mind in a sound body—with an exhibition of clean laundry over soiled patients.

Ken Siegel, the senior resident, looked briefly at one of the patients' charts and then questioned the doctor standing just in front of Jacob. Nathan observed the change in color of Nalan Patel's neck. Then, almost inaudibly, Patel began to answer:

"This is Teddy Gonzales, who was admitted…"

"What's the sex and age of the patient", interrupted Goldberg.

"I'm sorry. The patient is a 23-year-old, black male who was admitted last night with a baseball bat injury to the head. A skull x-ray done in the emergency room showed eggshell fracture of the skull…"

This time Siegel interrupted: "Jacob, what's an eggshell fracture".

Nathan suddenly realized that he was experiencing the same skin color change he had observed on Nalan Patel's neck just moments before. He shifted his feet, taking the time to think about an answer.

"It is a multiple fracture of the skull that resembles the appearance of the shell of a hard-boiled egg when it is hit several times before peeling it."

"Go ahead" Goldberg indicated to Patel.

"At about eight last night, the patient, Mr. Gonzales, was talking with his girlfriend, when a drunken ex-boyfriend showed up at the stoop of the brownstone rental where they were sitting.

The two of them got into a fight and the ex began hitting Gonzales with a baseball bat until some neighbors stopped him. The patient ended up on the ground, unresponsive, spouting blood through the mouth, the nose and his left ear. Someone called the emergency service and the ambulance brought him to the hospital within 40 minutes of the incident."

"Did he regain consciousness at any time? Goldberg asked.

"No. The ambulance attendant reported the patient was breathing with difficulty and that he was unable to arouse him".

"What was done?" again asked Goldberg.

Patel proceeded to recount the events that had robbed him of his sleep the night before. "I was called when Gonzales arrived at the Emergency Room. On examination, it was clear that the patient had sustained severe head trauma" –he spoke in the typical Indian singsong. "There appeared to be no other injuries. The patient was not responsive to verbal or painful stimulation. It was clear that the airway was compromised by blood and I proceeded to intubate the patient."

Siegel looked at Nathan: "Got a question for you: What's the advantage of intubating the patient?"

Nathan's mind had to shift from the thousands of textbook pages he had almost memorized, into a practical explanation for this particular application in the real world. He began answering almost simultaneously:

"There are several advantages to

intubating a comatose patient. First, one minimizes the possibility of aspirating vomit or blood which could severely impede breathing and cause pneumonia; second, after head trauma there is going to be some degree of brain swelling and one way to partially control it is by keeping the PCO_2 below 35, by hyperventilating the patient."

"Good" said Siegel.

Goldberg asked what had been done for the patient in addition to ventilating him. Patel continued:

"Patient was taken to x-ray and a cerebral angiogram was performed. It did not show a shift and we assumed that there was no blood clot but just generalized swelling. He was placed on Mannitol i.v."

The group moved to the next bed and then the next. The scut work list of to-do-things in Nathan's possession became longer and longer. Just as the procession was leaving the neuro-intensive room, Nathan noticed that the patient next to Gonzales, a man with a tracheotomy, was having difficulty breathing because a plug of mucus was partially blocking the opening of the plastic breathing tube. The patient was drowning in his own mucus! As the group exited the room, Nathan said to the head nurse, Ms. Harmon:

"I think the patient needs suctioning". To which Ms. Harmon replied in a tone of voice that denoted annoyance:

"You should be glad I came to work today; I could have stayed home". And she walked out of the room, indicating with her demeanor that her mere presence in the ward had been enough work for one day. Jacob turned on the suctioning machine and applied the suction catheter to the thick mucus; the swishing sound of the yellowed infected spit was followed by the clean sound of air entering the lungs unimpeded. This would not be the only time when Jacob woke to the reality of health care professionalism. Mediocrity, as he had always known, was not the privilege of the few but of the many and it extended across all professions; doctors or nurses were no exception, even patients could be mediocre!

20

Yes sir. Today is the anniversary of my first day at the Bronx, Jacob thought, as he remembered with profound disgust the fleshy, rounded face of Ms. Harmon, the nurse in charge of his patients when he had started his training; the angel of the neurosurgery ward, the dedicated union card carrying public servant. *Not much of a change from Brooklyn,* he thought.

"O.K., the day General Santa Anna invaded the Bronx", laughed Holgers. And they all laughed.

The patient's head was clamped securely to the operating table in such a way that she was half seated with her neck bent down, facing Holgers. The endotracheal tube sprouting from her mouth connected to the anesthesia gas machine. On the other side of the sterile drapes, all that could be seen of May McCoy was a strip of shaven scalp. Nathan stood right in front of it and asked for a syringe with local anesthetic.

"Lido with Epi" he demanded.

Mary, his red-hair nurse assistant, handed him the plastic syringe and, with a series of rapid pricks, he began to infiltrate the entire patch of exposed skin. How many times Jacob had thanked those heavy sterile drapes for covering the patient; seeing only a small patch of skin made it possible to be daring, to cut into flesh without thinking that he was cutting into a human being.

"Scalpel"

Jacob, himself, was hardly recognizable. He was completely covered in a sterile surgical suit, and his head, neck and face were covered as well. A plastic ring around his head held in place a fiber-optic system that projected an intense beam of light right onto the operating field. A pair of magnifying lenses, that made him look like a cartoon character popping its eyes, covered his. His hand pushed the cutting blade softly from the top to the bottom of the exposed skin, and a trickle of blood began to flow.

All along, Chung, the circulating nurse, was busy making sure that everything was in working condition and that all the sterile seals were intact. She constantly watched to make sure all the control pedals were within easy reach of Nathan's feet. She checked that all medications and chemicals were labeled appropriately. Chung was there to assure that all went well. She always looked after Nathan and he was fully aware of it. Chung was the antithesis of Harmon, she was the perfect nurse, the angel that every patient should have when his or her life depended on detail. A hospital needed a handful of them to be able to survive, to keep afloat over the miasma of mediocre personnel and yet, people like her were never recognized and compensated enough, they did their job because it was whom they were and nothing more. Of course, these were thoughts that passed in a matter of microseconds, as his hands worked in Mrs. McCoy's head.

21

The meeting of the surgical department had begun as usual. The minutes from the previous meeting were read and approved. Next, they discussed a series of two post-operative infections. It was determined that no rule of sterility had been broken in the operative area, the infections had occurred as a spurious phenomenon. Next on the agenda was the relative decrease in hospital revenues and the need to slim down the budget. The discussion shifted to getting rid of some of the nursing staff. At this point, Jackson spoke:

"I think that before we begin firing indiscriminately, we should get rid of the people that cannot speak English. Hell, I can hardly understand some of them nurses", he said in a smooth, southern drawl.

Jackson was a Urologist that had joined the department about fifteen years before Nathan's time. He had trained in New Orleans. Everybody knew he was a racist. Nathan waited for anyone to respond, but no one did, and it was almost time to vote. Nathan realized he was a relative newcomer to the department, and that to take a position against Jackson was not going to help him. But Jacob was astounded that no one had spoken to defend Chung, the obvious target of Jackson's invective. Bigots always counted with the passive silence of the people. It was how they could steer an objectionable act, even in the face of being a minority. Passiveness is the most destructive force in the human arsenal of persecution wars. Racists, bigots, tyrants, they all could count with the purulent laziness of society, at least at the beginning, before they could establish their internal police, that in turn could silence the occasional protesters. Throughout history, more people have suffered under the banners of silence that under martial songs.

Chung was a fifty-year-old Korean woman. She had never been late to work, nor had she ever taken advantage of sick-day leave. She was one of the most dedicated nurses Nathan knew. She even had built small containers for Nathan's delicate surgical micro-instruments so that they would not be damaged during the regular handling and sterilization that took place after each case, saving the hospital tens of thousands of dollars in repairs and replacements. Now she was about to be dismissed because she had a heavy Korean accent. Jacob could not believe that no one contradicted the clearly bigoted statement. He felt outraged. He wanted to punch Jackson, instead he said:

"I want to state in the strongest terms that Ms. Chung is the best nurse we have. I do not want to see her fired just because some of us hide under white sheets at night, burning crosses. If she goes, I'll go".

Jackson looked at the Jew who had exposed him. Jacob remembered that stare, it was the same one his guards at the camp displayed when they had pointed at the large stack of shoes and mockingly told him to go for them. After a prolonged and heated discussion, it was agreed that the lull in surgical procedures and decrease in revenue was probably a transitory event, and that it was best to keep all existing personnel.

22

"Cautery, suction!"

Nathan continued working on the wound that now was quite deep.

"Retractors!" The paraspinal muscles separated at the bottom of the exposure and the clear creamy color of the base of the skull became visible at the top.

"Mary, get me the air drill, please".

Mary positioned the drill handle in his left hand and held the extension tube in the air to stabilize the instrument so that it would not pull at all by the tip. Jacob pressed the pedal with his foot and the drill bit began spinning at 80,000 revolutions per minute permitting him to cut the bone as if it were butter. He was glad the hospital had agreed to spend such a large amount of money; the drill was worth every penny. His left hand moved slowly and meticulously making the drill bit tip caress the bone surface while his right hand held a suction tip and Mary irrigated with a saline solution the dry bone dust towards the suction tip. Even so, Jacob could not avoid breathing the acrid odor of bone dust. Little by little the bone covering the most lateral and inferior edge of May McCoy's right cerebellum was thinned out until it became transparent. Nathan requested a bone rongeur and delicately began biting the last remnants of bone, exposing the thin membrane that covered the delicate tissue of the cerebellum with its countless narrow, horizontal lines and its propensity for bleeding at the worst times.

"Vascular scissors and small forceps".

Mary had anticipated his demand. Now delicately, Jacob cut a U-shape opening in the Dura Matter exposing the tender neural tissue. A small nick on the Arachnoid membrane made it possible for the cerebrospinal fluid to begin dripping out, providing some decompression to the soft lobule.

May McCoy had been referred to Dr. Nathan by a local neurologist. She suffered from Trigeminal Neuralgia, a condition that gave her the equivalent of an electrical current being applied directly to the teeth in the right side of her jaw: The pain was excruciating. Initially the pain had been kept under control with anti-epileptic medication, but during the past months, the illness had escaped the drug's beneficial control. She was the perfect candidate for the procedure that Jacob was now performing on her. The cause was a small blood vessel pressing on the Trigeminal nerve, producing a kind of local electrical seizure that translated into horrible, agonizing pain in her jaw. The treatment was straightforward: it was necessary to separate the blood vessel from the nerve without damaging either and without killing the patient.

"Greenberg self-retainer", Nathan demanded, and quickly applied it to the open wound. He proceeded to attach a cerebellar retractor to the muscle edges.

"Let's get the microscope in! Get the loops off of me!"

Chung, the circulating nurse, took the magnifying glasses from Nathan's face and then proceeded to free him from the fiber-optic headlight. She carefully placed them on a steel table and proceeded to push the heavy operating microscope into position. The microscope, draped with a sterile transparent plastic sheath, with its complex electromechanical design permitting Jacob to move it with two fingers even though it weighed about four hundred pounds. He turned the oculars and adjusted the focusing system until he could see the operating field clearly and in perfect focus. The optical system of the microscope was connected to a large television screen and a video recorder. All in the operating suite could watch the operation.

"Get me the arm support, please".

A modified tray-stand with two foam pillows wrapped around its horizontal surface and draped sterile was placed between Jacob and the patient.

Jacob rested his arms on the padded armrest and began to guide the smooth retractor along the very edge of the cerebellum, excerpting a mild retraction to separate it from the inner surface of the skull. Small veins linking the two were cauterized and cut. Little by little, the surgical focus advanced deeper and deeper until finally the eighth nerve complex was exposed. A bit more dissection advancing the surgical field still deeper finally exposed the Trigeminal nerve.

Jacob saw immediately that the nerve was severely compressed by the anterior inferior cerebellar artery. He knew that the delicate part of the surgery was beginning.

23

It was still dark. Incredible as it might seem, they had survived one more day in the hospital. Nights came as a balm for the patients, the medical personnel did not practice at night. There were no private rooms, just several cells, more like cages and a relatively large wardroom. The floors and walls were gray and filthy, ventilation was poor. The beds were narrow with metal frames that held either shallow lumpy mattresses or boards. All the patients were motionless in their beds for fear that any movement would attract one of the nurse-guards. Bothersome patients ended up dead. During these days, medicine was not too advanced, and whatever effective treatments existed were mostly reserved for the soldiers. In general prisoners were given a better diet than at the barracks and depending on the type of experiment in which they were guinea pigs, even an almost normal diet. Pet prisoners were treated better than the others, but the extra care came with certain demands. If one was unlucky to be taken to the infirmary, it was well known that the best way to come out alive was to not attract attention. They also knew to stay on the good side of Hermann. Hermann did not have a kind face. Before the war, he had been a potato farmer. His hands were as big as any Jacob had ever seen, and he used them to hold the patients down while the camp doctors practiced different sutures and knots on them.

No one wanted to become a hospital guest, but after several days of diarrhea and vomiting, dehydration would set in making it difficult to fake a sense of well-being. Then, too weak to resist, there was nothing anyone could say or do while being dragged to the hospital barracks.

The sun brought with it light and life to the ward. The putrid stench collected during the night was ventilated as windows and doors were opened. That morning, Jacob knew that his chances of being selected were low since the day before they had used his back for surgical practice. They had practiced only a flesh wound, still, doctors preferred a fresh patient. He felt lucky they had not messed with the bones –his mind had registered the horrible howling of the patients that were used for the bone fracture and infection experiments. His dehydration was improving now that the vomiting had ceased and he was able to retain the daily watery soup. The pain on his back was subsiding. The hospital was kept comfortably warm for the comfort of the nurses and doctors. Perhaps in one or two days he would be able to return to his barrack and resume his normal living. After six days, the cuts on his back were not bothering him as much as he thought they would. He never thought possible to feel homesick for the hellhole that served as his living quarters in the camp of infinite suffering and hopelessness and hope.

24

The ooperating room bright overhead lights had been dimmed and now the room appeared ghostly, lighted by the concentrated beam of the microscope pointing down into the surgical wound and the light of the television monitor showing in vivid colors a landscape of shiny tissues and blood vessels, constantly bathed by the cerebrospinal fluid. Behind the drapes, the anesthesia machine and its monitoring screens added a greenish tint to the ambience. The voices had quieted down and the room was filled with the constant hiss of the suction and the intermittent blow of the breathing machine with its live giving singsong of inhalation and exhalation.

"Give me the micro-scissors and the micro-number four".

With the two small instruments Nathan began to dissect out the small arachnoid adhesions that entrapped the artery and nerve in Mrs. McCoy's head. Jacob knew that this was the part of the procedure when a false move could cost his patient dearly. His instruments followed up and down and in and out the movements of the nerve-artery complex induced by May's heartbeat and breathing. Having finished this maneuver, he asked for a blunt nerve hook, and sliding it under the artery proceeded to pull it away from the nerve. Now it was a matter of placing a small sponge in between the two and this part of the surgery would be complete.

Jacob looked at the nerve-sponge-artery complex to assert that there were no kinks in the artery and no displacement of the sponge, and then began to withdraw the retractor from the cerebellar surface. Small points of bleeding began to develop. He had learned long ago that this was a part of the operation where patience was king. Slowly and methodically, he cauterized the bleeding capillaries until there was absolute hemostasis. Satisfied, Jacob asked for dura stitches and proceeded to close the membrane in a watertight fashion. A small patty of bone dust covered by foam was placed over the window left by the bone removal. In time, it would become as solid as the original. The deep muscles were re-approximated with thick sutures and finally, Nathan closed the skin layer as esthetically as possible and applied a sterile dressing.

It was time to remove the drapes that covered the patient permitting Jacob to see again that he had been operating on a whole human being. Jacob requested assistance from Holgers to remove the head clamps and reposition the patient on a recovery room bed. He looked at May McCoy's face and tenderly removed the excess Betadine stains from her cheeks and applied antibiotic ointment in the little holes left by the skull clamp tips. Her face was swollen from so many hours of surgery, her eyes were still not focusing well under the influence of so many anesthetic drugs lingering in her system and yet, she was regaining a sense of being herself, of being aware of her own body, and when Jacob saw her smiling, he knew the operation had really been a success.

The surgery was finished; the patient was now in the hands of the nursing staff. Nathan was physically exhausted, emotionally drained and as usual, he was experiencing severe pain in his neck, shoulders and feet, but he was also completely satisfied with how well the procedure had gone. He walked to the dictating machines, sat down and began recording the procedure. Next, he needed to speak with the family of Mrs. McCoy. It was always very rewarding to tell the good news to worried family members. He was still sitting, half hypnotized by the overall energy drainage when he heard a knock at the door.

Bang, bang !

25

BANG, BANG!!!

Guards were knocking at the doors with the butts of their rifles. It was early in the morning, the first day after Jacob's arrival in the camp. He was wearing the same clothes he had had on for the past week. A line had formed heading into a large brick building, and he could see that piles of clothing were accumulating, and that the people were entering the building in formations of two. At about fifty yards from his line, there was another line of women and children, and they also were shedding their clothes. There were young and beautiful women marching side by side with not so beautiful women, with old women and with children, boys and girls. Jacob could see them, trying to cover themselves with arms too short to serve the purpose, and he could see the sun reflecting in their tears. *Two columns of naked souls advancing slowly into brick buildings*", was the only thought that came to him as he watched outside himself, without shame, without name, his own thoughts being drown by the awesome rumble of arriving trains.

Inside the brick building the heat and humidity were almost intolerable. Soldiers standing in a row shouted at them to advance. Men dressed in prisoners' uniforms began cutting their hair. Not a word was spoken. Piles of hair, lusterless, homeless hair, lay in one corner of the room and were being packed into heavy sacks.

An open door led to a short wide corridor where men were accumulating like sediment in sludge. More soldiers were shouting orders, and he could see two lines were being formed, and people were marched into two long corridors. He could hear the sound of water hoses mixed with shouts and cries and curses and prayers. Like moronic cattle he went where he was told, into a large white tiled room where soldiers with powerful hoses washed them clean of the excrement that had clung to their skin for so many days. And as the dried feces fell from his legs, he felt that the harsh water was erasing his person away and that he would forget his name. Barely moving his lips, he kept repeating "*Jacob Nathan, Jacob Nathan, Jacob Nathan…*" Then, finally, all the naked people were allowed to exit the room, and he found himself amidst hundreds of nude, wet, shame-laden men in a large yard, surrounded by high fences and more barbed wire. And he saw no old men. All the older men in his group had disappeared. Erzon was across the yard. The two friends looked at each other in shame, but they acknowledged with a slight nod of the head that they were still together. It was then that he noticed that the yard holding the women was perhaps a third as full as his, and that only young woman, either strong or pretty, were standing in their dripping shame.

The shout of "*Geht verfluchte Juden – move on cursed Jews!*" brought him back to his place and he marched through yet another gate where he was given a striped, two- piece uniform and a hat. A group of one hundred of them was then herded into a large brick and wood barrack identified by the number BIIb-14 neatly painted on a square piece of wood nailed to the right of the door. Inside, after his eyes got used to the perpetual gloom of what would become his home, he saw a long corridor bisecting the room in two. On either side of the corridor, like the parted waters of the Red Sea, stood a wooden platform holding three tiers of bunk beds without mattresses, just the naked wood. Each sleeping space was defined by a board nailed vertically from floor to ceiling and facing the long corridor, with a number carved at about eye level. In the days that followed he would count dozens of such divisions. In the darkness of barrack number 14 slept one hundred and sixty people.

Jacob was given the sleeping space of Max Klinger, a man in his fifties that was in the process of dying as Jacob had entered the barrack. He was ordered to drag him out and dump him into the "cadaver cart". Max Klinger was not yet dead but there certainly was no life in him, his eyes were open and dry although occasionally he blinked, and although his body felt cold, Jacob noticed that he had gasped for air at least twice. Jacob also noticed that Max had no flesh left on him. The neighbors already had taken his blanket and his uniform away. When Jacob got close to the cadaver carts, he saw dozens of Max Klingers piled on them, gathering flies, and in a twisted way it reminded him of the people gathering at *Michaelkirchplatz* in front of the old gothic church on Sundays prior to the Holy Mass.

To see human beings piled one on top of another, with flies covering their eyes and mouth, with no regard that some are dead and some have not yet died, to hear the cumulative sound of weak grunts, of air leaving the chest for one last time, to realize that all these people were shedding their souls and that one could almost touch them as they fluttered, confused, over the bodies that just instants before had provided a home, is a privilege that comes with great consequences, for no human can be this close to the dying and live to forget. It does not matter that a day or a lifetime has passed, one becomes a witness to infinite humility and solitude, and in being infinite they become a part of God. So, unwittingly, Jacob Nathan became one of God's witnesses.

Jacob prepared his bed on someone else's dying space, and from that moment on he had learned not to question those that appeared to have shed all signs of propriety in the face of extinction. On that day he also got tattooed on the undersurface of his left forearm, this would be the name by which he knew God would know him at the end of eternity and he had in silence called for his God *"Eloheinu, Eloheinu wo bist Du Eloheinu* – My Lord my Lord, where are you my Lord"*.

Watery soup, standing for long hours at attention and physical work soon began to take their toll on the camp inmates. Jacob first noticed the angular features on Herzon's face and then he realized his own body was changing as well. Camp life became a routine, if one can call living in hell a routine. Mornings standing for hours in the middle of the camp while the guards accounted for all the inmates. Then work in one of the camp's factories, either processing clothing materials, or making uniforms, or cutting screws, or the worst, making gravel. And of course, there was also the group in charge of collecting the corpses and of their burial. By late afternoon they were given their watery soup. Then, again they had to stand for hours while they were accounted for. Finally, the prisoners were allowed to enter the barracks and have some time of their own. Then, if they were not too exhausted, friends would talk, some would pray, others would listen to gossip.

It was on one of these early evenings that Erzon told Jacob that he was painting.

"But how can you paint?"

"Jacob, it is not a matter of how I can paint. I must paint".

"O.K. let's say you have to paint. With what?"

"Well, you will be amazed at the things one can use to improvise. I use any paper, white or brown, it does not matter. It can be cardboard, it can be a cement sack, it does not matter."

"But what do you use for painting?"

"I can make a brush by wrapping a piece of cloth or paper or even a stick of wood."

"And what about paints?"

"That's the easiest part. I get black from any piece of charcoal. Other colors are more difficult, and I got to be opportunistic about it. In general, browns are the easiest. I just get them from the earth. The other day I got a red from a candle I found in the trash."

"But Erzon, what are you painting? It is not as if you were going to have an exhibit in the camp."

"Jacob, I told you that I was a kind of expressionist. In a way, it makes it a little bit easier for me." A faint smile showed on Erzon's face, almost a grimace, but with a little dash of sweetness added to the end of his dry lips. "Before, when I painted a flower, I felt the need to darken it, to make it sag and bring its petals down. But now, I don't have to transform the images, I just have to paint the things that I see around me. I am trying to document what I experience, what I witness."

"And what are you doing with your paintings? You cannot keep them around. If the guards find them, they will kill you in a second!" Jacob was really concerned for his friend. He could not lose him, be left alone in the camp.

"I know, I know. But I am not crazy. The first thing I did is to paint small. Forget about large canvases. I don't paint bigger than about fifteen centimeters. And I am burying them wrapped in rags I find here and there. I hope that one day someone will find them." He stopped speaking for a moment, his eyes down, perhaps recognizing that he might not survive. "It will validate my life if some day, years after the war, some people can see what I saw."

"Erzon, my friend, be careful" and after a brief pause, he added "for my sake".

26

In June, Nathan had begun his neurosurgical training and first rotation at Jackson Community Hospital. Rebecca had given him a kiss on the cheek and sent him off to a new adventure, a new beginning. Jacob wore a bleached white, permanent-press's uniform and a pair of soft soled, comfortable leather shoes, a get-up that he would wear during most of his training years. He walked down the front steps of the brownstone and turned to wave goodbye to Rebecca.

Their apartment was only one block from Flatbush Avenue and two blocks from the entrance to the subway station. They rented the third floor of a turn of the century, newly renovated brownstone. Although the area was run down, one could easily appreciate the elegance of an earlier time. The neighborhood had given shelter to a flourishing Jewish community and then, like all organic things, it had died out and decomposed. Now, decades later, life was beginning again in just one single block. The remaining square mile of buildings could best be described as a partially inhabited slum with houses in various states of decomposition and decay. Many had boarded windows and plywood sealed doorways. On the corner with Flatbush stood a one-story building that housed a laundry and dry-cleaning business and a short block from it, was the entrance to the Bergen Street subway station.

The brownstone where Rebecca and Jacob lived was owned by a bald, baby-faced, effeminate Puerto Rican in his thirties named Mario. It seemed impossible that he had almost single handedly rescued the brownstone, but with the help of a couple of friends and the occasional required union tradesman he had managed to bring back the townhouse to its previous glory. Of course, a do-it-yourself job does lack some of the finesse of one executed by professionals, so although all the wood trims had been painted, there was obvious evidence of numerous previous paint jobs that had added, if nothing else, character to the old mansion and there was a clear odor to wet cement wherever brick walls had been left exposed, giving the brownstone the homey feeling of a work in progress. Mario and his significant other lived on the ground floor.

The second floor was never rented during the Nathans' tenure at the brownstone. The fourth floor was rented to the Smiths, a young couple whose habits never ceased to amaze the Nathans. During most days and early evenings Jackie Smith played the piano, an old, short, standing model with rotting wood and peeling veneer. For one and a half years the Nathan's only heard one song, a ragtime composition by S. Joplin. Jackie played the song too harshly, making the same mistakes and interruptions, never appearing to improve on playing the piece. Every time she played it, Jacob anticipated the mistakes and breaks. It had almost become fun were it not for the boring cacophony of sounds badly played on the out of tune piano —absolute proof that repetition does not bring perfection. In the evenings, at around eleven o'clock, the Smith's moved to their bedroom to copulate, and the crescendo of heavy breathing and moaning often woke Jacob up from the deep slumber induced by the constant sleep deprivation imposed by his hospital training routine. In this stuporous state, Jacob desired her: she was naked, covered in sweat, lying on the piano and he caressed her with the ends of the piano keys that stroke her as he played Chopin etudes with passion. Jackie was a small, thin woman, with a pretty face, dark, curly hair and defective feet that made her walk in a slight cross-legged manner. Robert, her husband, was about four inches taller than she, without an ounce of fat on his haggard body. They both dressed in oversized coveralls and frequently smoked marijuana —living relics of the flower children they once had been.

Jacob walked to the corner and descended into the bowels of the earth; placed a token in the machine and pushed his way onto the subway platform. That early in the morning the station was deserted. The subway's ticket office would not open for another hour. The hot wind of the incoming Flatbush Avenue train caressed his soft brown hair combing it back. He entered the half-empty car and stood in silence, hypnotized by the rhythmic screeching of the wheels fighting the rusted tracks. Four stops later he walked up a flight of stairs and found a new landscape of half-abandoned buildings and garbage accumulating on the sidewalks. The entrance to Jackson

Community Hospital, one of the largest hospitals in the world, was just three long blocks to the north.

Rounds began promptly at 7 a.m. The group consisted of the chief resident, two senior residents, two second year residents, Nathan and a rotating intern from another hospital. The head nurse of the floor and three other nurses completed the group. There were no welcoming speeches, no introductions. As if they all had been there since the night before, they began to walk, almost glide, slowly from bedside to bedside.

"Nathan, you will carry the scut work list today", the chief resident had said. After one and a half hours of bedside discussions about each patient, the group disbanded and Nathan was left with the list of things to do. He saw that he needed to take blood samples from four patients and had to place two intravenous lines. He asked one of the nurses where the supplies were and proceeded to gather them in a small wheel cart. With no one to help him, he pushed his way to the first patient on his list.

Mr. Rodriguez occupied bed number 3. He lay there breathing slowly and almost forcefully. He had a brain tumor and was scheduled for surgery on the next day.

"Good morning Mr. Rodriguez, I need to take some blood to prepare you for the surgery tomorrow".

Rodriguez looked at Nathan with his deep-set, dark eyes and without saying a word, extended his long, naked arm –Jacob remembered all those extended arms hanging from the edge of the death cart. So was life for him, at every step he would find an image from a past that made him different from all his fellow companions –as he was watching the death being carted away to be dumped in giant ditches that he had helped dig with unimaginable effort, his American counterparts were watching cowboy and Indian movies and when they were washing and polishing their dads' cars just for the pleasure of it, he was washing and scraping excrements from the wooden floors of barracks under penalty of death. He applied the elastic band around the arm and gently pushed the needle into the bulging vein. Blood began to fill the test tube. Jacob noticed that there was no number tattooed on this weakened limb.

There was no doubt in Jacob's mind that the hand of God was over him during these trying months of training at Jackson Community. For starters, commuting by subway involved some of the most treacherous rides public transportation in the City of New York could offer, especially at the hours Jacob traveled. Wearing the doctor's white uniform and the black leather bag made him a perfect target. The hospital did not provide Jacob with a place to keep his doctor's bag safely. He was forced to carry it during the round trip between hospital and home. Inside the bag Jacob carried one stethoscope, one neurological hammer, a pinprick wheel, one red and one white small spherical targets to test visual perimeters, an eye chart, and a small bottle with perfume to test the olfactory function in his patients. How many people thought the bag might be full of drugs? That black bag must have seemed to some of the elements riding with Nathan on the subway like a red cape to a bull, yet he never was assaulted.

On one occasion, during early autumn, Jacob went to the cafeteria for his evening meal. The food services opened the door at 5 p.m. and this was the best time to go. It was just before evening rounds and before the calls would start to the emergency room, where trauma visits would reach epidemic proportions as darkness gave courage to the violent meek. Jacob got his tray of food and sat at a small table about 8 feet from a window and next to one of the giant supporting concrete columns that punctuated the cafeteria's immense space. In the middle of the meal, while chewing a dried-out piece of meat, Jacob felt as if he had been sprayed with something. He looked up alarmed and found nothing abnormal. He was about to scoop up another bite when he noticed small pieces of glass and cement on his plate. He looked up more carefully and noticed a small round defect on the concrete column about twelve inches from his head. He looked at the window and saw the small hole in the glass that the silent bullet had carved. One more time he felt God had spared his life, although he could not explain why. Somewhere within a three-block radius, also by miracle, a human life had been spared when the bullet that was meant to end it cut through the air one degree too high, missing the forehead by just one inch. The miracle of geometry decrees that a deviation of one degree can be measured to be a small distance when close to the explosive mouth of a gun, but several feet a quarter of a mile away, when force spent, the bullet searches in vain for any target to quench its thirst for blood. This time it had failed.

One early morning, several months later, on the way to the subway Jacob passed by a group of people that had gathered on the sidewalk; he was about to by-pass the bunch but decided to investigate instead. He pushed his way towards the front of the group and to his amazement found a man lying on his back, with a hatchet driven into his forehead; the victim was talking to someone kneeling by his side. Jacob knew he could not do anything for the man at this point, so he inquired if an ambulance was on the way and cautioned anyone from trying to pull the hatchet out.

He arrived at the ward just in time for morning rounds. Another resident was in charge of the scut work list and Jacob looked forward to a morning of study. Just moments after rounds had finished, Jacob was paged to the emergency room.

"Hey, I got a patient for you", laughed the emergency room resident. "The guy probably did not want to carry a grudge and told the other guy to bury the hatched". He was laughing as he gave Jacob the patient's chart. "He is yours now, I'm off to breakfast".

Jacob pulled the curtain to enter the cubicle and was confronted with the same man he had seen lying on the street nearby his home. He spent the morning in the operating room separating the hatchet from the head. Amazingly, the metal edge had managed to get through the forehead bone and had just touched the thick membrane that covers the frontal lobes without damaging the brain. After debridement and closure, all the patient needed was a week of antibiotics. But Jacob knew that just as easily it could have been him lying on the sidewalk with a seven-pound piece of steel sticking out from his skull.

Life during these first years of training followed a rather barbarous routine. On Mondays, arrival at the hospital for 7 a.m. rounds, overnight none stop work dealing with emergencies and late admissions, early morning ward rounds followed by either assisting in surgery or assisting in the clinical chores of the ward or the out-patient clinic, followed by evening rounds, then walking several blocks to get to the subway, forcing himself to believe he wasn't back in a transport cattle-car, arriving home, kissing Rebecca, having dinner, falling into a deep sleep, listening to Jackie banging at the piano upstairs, waking up early to get to the subway to be ready for 7 a.m. ward rounds and start again the cycle. His back ached, his legs ached, and his feet were in constant pain.

Jacob escaped another brush with death. He had been on call that night and was drawing a urine sample on a patient when the beeper summoned him to the emergency room. The nurse pointed to one of the stretchers behind the curtains. Maria Rodriguez was lying on a stretcher, holding with her right arm a towel against her head. She had been hit with a meat cleaver, but fortunately for her, the blade had not penetrated beyond the outer layer of her frontal bone. All she needed was some wound cleaning and suturing. Jacob called for a suture tray and a nurse brought it with no delay. He spent the next forty-five minutes repairing what criminal rage had accomplished in a fraction of a second. When he finished, he gave the patient a prescription for antibiotics and a return slip for suture removal. Before writing his clinical notes on the patient's chart, Jacob decided to go get a Coke from the vending machines in the main lobby of the hospital.   On the way he stopped by the bathroom to empty his bladder –a preemptive move in case he got busy in surgery.

While Jacob tended to Mrs. Rodriguez wounds, the police had brought Johnny Washington to the emergency room. Mr. Washington had been convicted for the brutal murder of a family of five, while attempting to rob their home. He was about to start serving twenty-five to life in a federal prison. At the same time Nathan walked towards the vending machines, Johnny Washington walked escorted by two policemen to the bathroom; he had said he needed to move his bowels. Earlier, he had complained of acute abdominal pain –the reason why he had been brought to the emergency room.

One officer stationed himself outside the bathroom door, the other entered the room with the prisoner. Moments later, Johnny W. walked from the bathroom stall with a semi-automatic pistol, spraying the corridor with bullets as he ran out of the hospital to never be seen again. Before returning to the emergency room, Jacob had been delayed for a few seconds while trying to recover a coin he had dropped in the process of feeding the vending machine. Finally getting his Coke, he snapped the can open and began his trek back to the emergency room. At that moment, before entering the corridor, he heard the gunshots and the commotion. One officer was dead, the other was forever paralyzed from the waist down by a bullet that severed his spinal cord at the level of the ninth thoracic vertebra. That night, Jacob assisted in his surgery.

The continuous feeling of exhaustion was interrupted occasionally by acts of violence. Jacob began to learn a lesson that many Americans have never learned, let alone experience firsthand. Jacob became aware that people –not at war– were violent to each other. Of course, he had been an unwilling participant in the theater of hate and murder and torture that Europeans had displayed towards the Jews, but those had been acts of institutionalized bigotry, even though practiced by individuals. But, here in America, he was privileged to observe a completely different kind of violence. Here, in a country completely at peace, people were killing and maiming each other, even worst, they were doing it at the spur of the moment, with whatever tools they had at hand; thus, a pistol could be used to shoot someone, but just as easily, Jacob saw people injured with a baseball bat, or a plumbing pipe, or a knife, or a screwdriver. And later, when the movement to restrict the sale of guns became a political movement, he would feel soiled by what he had learned as a neurosurgery resident: that people did not need guns to kill, that murder was, after all, in the very soul of the individual. Throughout his life, every time he was beginning to feel at ease with his fellow men, he would remember the day he said good-bye twice to Robert Grant.

It had been a balmy afternoon during the month of December. The night had extended its dark mantle over the city soon after 4 p.m. Nathan was examining Mrs. Rosalie Grant when her son arrived for his daily visit. Robert Grant was about 45 years old, black, about 5 feet 10 inches tall, handsome. He had insisted that Jacob not interrupt his examination. "Doc, you go ahead with what you are doing. My mom needs you more than me", he had said. Mrs. Grant had suffered a stroke and was paralyzed of her left side. Fortunately, she could speak. The patient had been assigned to Jacob and he needed to document the clinical evolution of the stroke daily. In general, he did not like to do patients' rounds during regular visiting hours, but on this particular occasion, he had been in surgery all morning and part of the afternoon and was running out of time. Hence, he was thankful when Robert G. had insisted that he not interrupt his mother's examination. When the clock struck 5, the loudspeaker announced that visiting hours were over. Robert Grant had said good night to his mother and he and Nathan walked down the ward towards the elevators: Jacob to eat dinner and Robert to go home.

Nathan began eating his spaghetti and meatballs as Robert turned the ignition key of his car to exit parking lot number 4. It had not escaped Nathan's eye that the three obese cafeteria city employees were gulping down a large piece of roast beef that they had been carving for themselves. At the same moment that Nathan was served his limited portion of overcooked, gooey spaghetti and watery meat sauce, Robert was backing out of his parking space. The evening was dark and a slight drizzle had begun to fall. It wasn't cold enough for snow. The parking lot exit let to one of the streets within the hospital grounds. There was a stop sign at the intersection. Four cars had stopped and crossed; it was now the turn of the car immediately ahead of Mr. Grant's. But the car did not move. Robert G. waited about half a minute and then he leaned briefly on the horn (a passerby confirmed this to the police). The gentleman driver in front of Robert got out of his vehicle and proceeded to open the door of Robert's car after which he began hitting Rosalie Grant's son on the head with a tire iron.

Jacob was about to take the first bite of a carrot cake when his beeper went off. He cursed and walked to the cafeteria telephone.

"Yes, this is Nathan".

"Doctor Nathan you are needed in the emergency room. Stat".

Jacob ran to the emergency room across the glossy street, completely forgetting about his carrot cake. A group of nurses was busy around the new admission. Jacob approached the stretcher and one of the nurses made room for him. As someone wiped the blood off the patient's face, Jacob recognized the man that had walked with him to the elevators. His forehead was deformed and swollen, his head about a third larger than it had been about 15 minutes before.

Nathan was part of the emergency team that operated on Mr. Grant for most of that night. Surgery evacuated the large blood clot that had accumulated over the left brain of Mr. Grant, but nothing could be done about the extensive contusions that made the patient's brain matter look like scrambled eggs with purple colorant added. As he was applying the head bandages, Jacob knew that his patient would never recognize him or his own mother ever again and he realized that this was as good a time as any to say goodbye to Mrs. Rosalie's son.

Jacob's experiences at the county hospital were profoundly depressing. The wards were populated not only by those unfortunate enough to have a neurological illness, but if someone had been spared from illness, then for sure could not be spared from violence. These were rough times for Jacob. This environment of darkness appeared to involve everyone: the patients, their visitors and the nurses, especially the nurses. What had happened to the image of nightingales, winged angels floating from bed to bed consoling their patients? Overall, nurses were rude, tended to move slowly, to not get involved. Nurses had short fuses and were resistant to instruction or advice. On occasion, Nathan saw a new, young nurse come to the floor and in a matter of weeks turn into a "typical" nurse. But of course, there were exceptions. Some nurses were as good as one could wish and Jacob learned a thing or two from them. Most of them were relics from a past, when acres of farmland had surrounded the Hospital and the dark shadow of the slums had not invaded its pristine grounds. Perhaps, there was no clear explanation as to why people would go into a profession to care for the sick and then turn into cold-blooded, heartless unionized civil servants.

27

Mediocrity and heart hardening seemed to have invaded every nook and cranny of the hospital. Jacob was deeply distressed by it. Hospitals were supposed to heal people, to care for their patients, and even though at the end many did come out in better shape that when they had come in, it was how it was accomplished, rather than the end result that offended Jacob so much. He could make a comparison to a restaurant that specializes in steaks, and that in fact would serve you a large and beautiful cut of meat, but instead of being accompanied by side portions of vegetables and special sauces, it was served as a piece of raw meat in the middle of the plate. One could not say that they had cheated you —there was a steak— but it certainly could have been offered in the expected manner from the kitchen. This is what Nathan observed wherever he went, be it the hospital's kitchen, or the messenger service, or the laboratories and most definitely, the nurses.

On one occasion, just prior to morning rounds, Jacob overheard someone crying. He tracked the faint sobs down to the last patient room at the end of the ward, Mr. Chavez's room. Prior to his admission to the hospital, he had been having a love affair with Conchita Lopez. Conchita was a stunningly beautiful woman, the type that can only result from the genetic mix of several races. Born in Puerto Rico, her family had immigrated to New York during the exodus of the 1950's. New York didn't turn out to be the paradise they had expected. The family ended up on welfare, living in a slum in upper Manhattan. Conchita had met Rufino Lopez on the day of a Puerto Rican religious celebration in Central Park. A week later she left her family and moved in with Rufino to a dilapidated apartment somewhere in central Brooklyn. Lopez turned out to be a rather jealous, violent and abusive man.

Six months after moving in with Rufino, Conchita met Jorge Chavez. He was not only very handsome but had a soft and gentle manner. At first, they were just friends. Conchita told him about her life and how gloomy it had turned out. With time, however, the relationship became physical, and soon they were making love and were deeply in love.

Rufino began to suspect his wife's infidelity and on one occasion he followed her to Jorge's apartment where he surprised them in bed. Without any noise or fanfare, he drew a 22-calliber revolver and shot at them six times. Only one bullet found its target. Unfortunately for Chavez, the bullet entered his spine at the level of the third cervical vertebra, paralyzing him immediately. Mr. Chavez was rendered incapable of moving any muscle in his body below his Adam's apple. He had been brought by ambulance to the emergency room where x-rays confirmed the destruction of the third and fourth vertebrae of his neck and that his spinal cord was completely severed. He would remain paralyzed for as long as he lived.

After admission, it had been determined that the best course of action was to place him in skeletal traction. To accomplish this, a 7-pound weight was hung from his skull using an attachment similar to old-fashioned ice tongs. Mr. Chavez lay in bed day and night with a pair of metal tongs screwed into his skull, totally dependent on nursing care.

Entering Chavez's room had never been easy for Jacob. It always had an effect akin to peeking into hell. As he approached the room, he took a deep breath and entered. Chavez was crying, tears rolling down the corners of his eyes. Jacob asked him what was wrong and if he could help. Mr. Chavez replied in that characteristic shallow, almost atonal murmur spoken by people with limited function of breathing muscles:

"It's the damned flies. They crawl on my eyes and on my lips all night long. I ask the nurses to keep them off of me, but they never come back ". He sobbed a few more times.

"It's like being eaten alive, doc."

The bed sheet by the sides of his head was completely soaked in tears. Jacob promised him he would speak with the nurses. He left the room and cried as he walked towards the nurses' station.

But hell had not finished yet with Jorge Chavez. One of the problems with an injury to the spinal cord at the level that Chavez had his severed is that it disrupts the nerves controlling normal breathing. What had been effortless and automatic before, was now a very laborious task. Therefore, it was necessary to perform a tracheotomy on Chavez in order to connect him to a respirator. Without a respirator, Jorge would soon develop respiratory insufficiency, pneumonia and death.

On the day the tracheotomy was to be performed, Jacob implored the chief resident not to go ahead with it.

"Come on John, let him die"

"No, it is our job to keep him alive. It is our job to do the best we can for the patient".

"Yeah, but the best thing for this patient is to die. Don't you see, flies are laying eggs on the dampness of his eyes and he cannot do anything about it".

"No, we do him today, first case in the afternoon; it is a good case for junior practice".

"He will rot with bedsores".

"It's good practice".

Jorge Chavez's fate was sealed. From that moment on, not only was he paralyzed, but mute. He was to be buried alive in a hospital bed at the mercy of the nurses. And as time passed by, Jorge's back and hips and legs began to rot with bedsores, with that ever-present stench, proof positive that the patient was not getting adequate nursing care. The flies could feast on him. Had God also abandoned him?

The internal messenger service was in even worse shape than the nursing department. At least, nurses had formal college training, this of course was not a requirement for messengers. It was clear to Jacob that the hospital's hiring policy for messengers was the direct result of pressure from the neighborhood's social-welfare leaders.

Not requiring any education or ability, messengers often lacked social skills, or sense of responsibility, and went their way pushing empty gurneys at unsafe speeds, racing along hospital corridors, damaging the gurneys and scarring the walls. Often, Jacob had to improvise with adhesive tape to keep the side-guard of a broken gurney upright to prevent a patient from falling off. Or the gurney's wheels would vibrate, shaking patients that surely did not need to be shaken on their way to surgery. When patients needed to be taken for tests on wheelchairs or stretchers, the messengers often left them unattended for hours along the hospital corridors.

During transport, respirators would have their tubes and attachments banged and kinked, or even worse, ripped off. Blood and urine samples waiting in designated pick-up drawers would be collected too late, or never delivered to the laboratory. On many occasions tests tubes with blood and the patients' identification tags were found lying on Coney Island and Brighton Beach and in parking lots of supermarkets, still in their original wrapping and carrying basket. The service was so bad, that Jacob and most of the interns and residents would, more often than not, carry out the duties of the "messenger service" themselves for the sake of their patients, adding one more chore to their already exhausting task.

But Jacob was not easily discouraged. He had decided to become a neurosurgeon and that, he would accomplish. However, as if things were not bad enough, Jacob eventually realized that he had no choice but to change teaching programs.

Half of the neurosurgical residents were from Middle Eastern countries, which he did not mind. But that soon was to change one quiet evening. Nathan remembered the event like if it had been yesterday.

"Are you going to eat?" Inquired Mohamed Ahlmoudi, a third-year neurosurgical resident. They were standing by the nurses' station, checking on the most recent laboratory returns. Jacob looked at his watch and was surprised that being half past five in the afternoon there had been no calls from the emergency room.

"I guess so. Hope no one beeps me", Jacob replied and the group of aspiring neurosurgeons walked through a light snow, across the street and small park, into the cafeteria. The doctors' cafeteria had been closed about a year before, during one of the city's failed attempts to cut expenses. Now doctors had to stand in line with all the rest of the personnel as well as the visitors. Sometimes the line was so long that Jacob was paged before he even got to see what was on the dinner menu. On that particular December night, the line was short. They got their dark-gray plastic trays and walked along the narrow path collecting the selections they made from the menu written on a small blackboard hanging from a column next to the entrance to the cafeteria. Jacob remembers that on that night the choices were: meatloaf with mashed potatoes, or spaghetti with meat sauce. As they approached the food containers, they could see the cafeteria employees inside the kitchen area, gorging on large slabs of roast beef.

The four colleagues chose a table as far from the kitchen as it was possible.

They ate in a hurry, as was the custom in case one was called in an emergency. As they finished eating, their silence was replaced with lively conversation.

"So, what are you up to, Mohamed", inquired Jacob.

"I am finishing my Neuropathology rotation", he replied.

"How is Johnson? Is he a good teacher?"

"Oh no, I am not taking it here, I am going to Columbia", referring to the Neuropathology program at Columbia University Medical School.

Jacob was interested: "To Columbia! That is a good program!"

"An excellent program", Mohamed replied.

It was at that point, at the end of a good meal, in the middle of a snowy winter night, that Farouk intervened:

"Yeah, a very good program. Only bad thing is that it is full of Jews."

"Yeah, when I did my neuropath there, I had Goldstein as my proctor, it would have been perfect if he hadn't been a Jew", interrupted Khatib.

"What is it with the fucking Jews; they are always where the good programs are", interjected Mohamed.

Jacob felt his brain moving faster than the food churning in his stomach. He did not know what to say. From the conversation it was obvious that his three Iranian colleagues had no idea he was Jewish. They had assumed he was

German. He thought to take a stand, but then decided that nothing would be accomplished by it. These people were intelligent, learned, and yet, could not accept that the "program" was good because of the professors that taught in it, and in this particular case, the world-famous doctors who happened to be Jewish. The Holocaust was over. That is what Jacob had thought for many years – at least since he had finally ventured out from the deep depression that enveloped him after the liberation. He had thought, or wanted to believe that Jew hatred was over, that it had been an aberration, a mistake made by an entire continent, but that with the end of the war, it had been over. The war had finished with bigotry. Of course, he had witnessed hate and abuse after the war. He knew of many Jews that were killed when they returned to their hometowns, as the doors of the concentration camps had opened freeing them, but Nathan had interpreted these killings as acts committed by the leftover riffraff. He had thought that some of the killings were motivated by greed –that after having taken Jewish property illegally, people were not willing to give it back to their rightful owners and taking advantage of the reigning chaos, had recurred to murder—rather than by anti-Semitism. But now, looking at his Iranian colleagues across the dining table it suddenly clicked in his mind that he had been deluded, duped perhaps willingly, in trying to think the best of mankind and that he was going to live in a better world than before. At that moment he made the decision to leave Jackson Community and enroll in some other program. All the inhumanity he witnessed day after day had not pushed him away; it was the ignorance of three bigots that had pushed him to make such a decision.

When Nathan got home later on, he related to Rebecca the experience he had at dinner with his three neurosurgery colleagues, they both agreed that life amidst Jew hating Iranians was not going to be a pleasure. They sat down and went over a list of desirable neurosurgery programs. It was clear that they would go wherever there was an opening. Things were complicated by the fact that he was not requesting admission as a first-year resident but as a second-year resident, and that significantly limited the probability of finding an opening in any teaching program.

Jacob began calling neurosurgical departments throughout the nation. None had an opening. Things were getting pretty tight, when it occurred to him to phone the Neurosurgical Department at Raimondi-Dupertin in the Bronx, a Jewish Institution.

"Yes, we do have an opening for a second-year resident", replied the secretary's voice on the telephone.

"Our second-year resident got divorced, suffered a nervous breakdown and left unexpectedly".

Jacob could not believe his luck. "Please, I am asking you not to fill that spot before you interview me", Nathan pleaded, feeling a knot in his stomach.

"Very well. Can you come next Monday at

7 a.m.?"

"I'll be there".

And so, it was that Jacob Nathan saw once more the hand of God shading him from too much harm. But the irony did not escape Jacob, that on this occasion, as on numerous other occasions in the concentration camp, a little goodness in his life had come to him by way of someone else's misery.

28

These were happy times for Jacob and Rebecca. Happy times needed to be shared with friends and Jacob had only one friend.

"Erzon, why don't you come for dinner next Saturday? Let's say six o'clock. It will give us time to talk."

"Jacob, as always, it will be a pleasure. Regards to Rebecca."

Erzon was one of those few artists that happened to be punctual –perhaps his Germanic background. He had managed to survive the camp and the immediate post war period. Several of his friends, including Leib had made it through the camps just to be murdered by anti-Semitic crowds during the first months after the war was over. But he, like Jacob, was a true survivor.

After recovering for a few weeks in a camp for displaced people, he had been sent to Sweden and after a few months, to England. Erzon could not take the continuous dampness of his small apartment in London nor could he live knowing that he belonged to a group of people that would never be accepted as an equal and not for being Jewish, but for not belonging to an appropriate social cast. England's skeleton was based in royal history and he was as removed from it as one could be and still remain on the same planet. As the artist that he was –albeit not yet realized— he saw himself totally incompatible with the very same society that had extended him a welcome. He needed to go to America, the land of opportunity, where royalty was not hereditary but self-made. Reams of application forms and months of waiting eventually paid off, he was able to immigrate to New York.

To survive, Erzon got a job as a window dresser for second-rate stores in lower Manhattan. He wanted to be artistic and the storeowners wanted him to fill the windows with merchandise. He could hardly take it, seeing those display windows filled to the hilt with leather bags, or shoes, or clothing went entirely against his artistic taste, but the owners were not interested in beauty, they wanted passersby to see what was inside the store, not artistic arrangements; the lower-Eastside was not ready for artful window decorations. But, as he repeated to himself over and over in his solitary apartment, "*it does pay the bills and the art supplies as well.*"

Little by little, he accumulated enough paintings to begin exploring for a gallery. Of course, he had no experience. He had been too young in Germany to realize that there was a big abyss between painting and showing. Now, in America, he was learning it the hard way. Soon he understood that he needed a connection – someone to introduce him to a gallery owner or director– even though he was a loner. Up to this point, he had been too naïve to realize that creative works were not judged by their content but by their cover –at least in most cases. He was not aware that a few art critics and gallery directors controlled artistic taste in America; he was not aware that there were very few people of means that did not need of an artistic homunculus telling them what to buy and what not to. He was too naïve to comprehend the deep chasm that existed between those that created art and those involved in the business of art. A deep disdain and contempt existed, as if galleries and museums resented the very hand that fed them. Erzon could not possibly enter the visual field of these "gate keepers of the arts" to be noticed. Nevertheless, if painting was a matter of self-expression, showing became a matter of self-preservation. He began to attend gallery openings, to mingle with the crowds, to start conversations with onlookers. It was in this manner that he first made contact with Robert – "just first names please." That's how Robert had established their relationship.

Erzon met Robert at an opening for a Dutch artist at the Mandell-Horowitz Gallery on 57th Street. Minimalism was trying to make its twelfth comeback in fifty years. The walls were covered with large canvases colored in various pastels, without any trace of brushwork. Evidently the color had been applied with a spray gun. The gallery director had chosen to exhibit them in a sequence that followed the colors of the rainbow. Art critics walked with their little notebooks at hand, while the general audience following the infallible dictum of the naked emperor's clothes glided from one painting to another with their jaws slack open and Champagne at hand. Erzon could not be moved by these paintings and he certainly could not be wooed into behaving like the rejoicing culturati. He was shaking his head when he heard someone addressing him.

"So you don't like these paintings either." It was Robert.

"No, I am afraid I cannot see the virtue in them".

"Well, don't feel bad. Most of these people don't like them either, but they don't know it yet."

The two of them laughed.

"My name is Robert."

"And I am Erzon".

"Wonderful! Just first names please."

They left the gallery together and talked for most of the night, first in a café by Washington Square and later on a bench by the park. It was clear that Robert was homosexual. That first contact did stir repressed memories in Erzon's mind. For reasons he could not explain, that first night, he told Robert things he had not dared even think about during these last years after being rescued from the concentration camp. He had told Robert how he had been chosen by one of the SS-guards as his sex object. Although homosexuality was blacklisted in Nazi Germany, it was rampant within the Nazi ranks. Your life depended on guarding well the secret. Guards saw in young prisoners a way to express their brutality and at the same time a way to exert their homosexual fantasies without fear of exposure – betrayal meant death. Erzon had been chosen by a guard. It had been a horrible experience, but one that at the same time came with a silver lining. He would remain alive as long as the guard wanted him to remain alive. And even though Erzon had never experienced any homosexual tendencies or desires, he in fact had become, for all practical purposes, homosexual. He had never spoken to anyone of this experience, not even to his best friend in the camp, Jacob Nathan. And now, he had felt the compulsion to tell it all to Robert and when the morning sun began to erase the night stars, they were exhausted, but with the new day, a deep friendship had been born.

After the war, Erzon had suppressed this episode of his life. Now, triggered by a series of empty canvases, by a feeling of unfulfilled artistry, by the need for companionship, and by the company of Robert at that precise time and place, he had emptied his heart out. Robert, a sensitive and intelligent art graduate from NYU had listened to his new acquaintance story with fascination and revulsion.   He had first approached Erzon because of physical attraction, but now, he could not make a pass at him. And yet, between the two, a friendship developed, so deep, so strong, like seldom friendships can be and sadly often they are not. It was different with Nathan; the two of them were blood-brothers, not their blood, but the blood of thousands of inmates during those horrible times in the concentration camp. They were twins in the way they had responded to fear, to hunger, to despair and to hope. With Robert, Erzon felt there was a bridge to an inner peace, to beauty, to solace. The two could enjoy a cup of coffee amidst the noise and pollution of the city and feel as if they were watching a sunset over the Pacific Ocean, silent but for the distant sound of the waves braking over the coastal rocks. Robert became Erzon's promoter in the art world, his guide and advisor, opening doors for interviews that soon resulted in admission to the inner sanctum of artists represented in galleries. People were actually buying his paintings enabling him to quit his window dresser's job. He became a New York artist.

One night, during the opening of Erzon's latest expressionistic paintings at the Moore-Gurevitz Gallery in Soho, the inevitable occurred. Jacob and Rebecca doing gallery rounds, decided to explore one more gallery. As they read the poster on the entrance to the gallery, their hearts skipped beats and galloped with uncontrolled excitement. Was this his Erzon? The one Jacob thought had died on liberation day? The one he had mourned for months. Jacob had not felt happiness during those times because he had mourned his friend –the sight of two people shaking hands just reminded him of what could have been, and the missed joy of what could have been is immense. Jacob tightened his hold of Rebecca's hand as they entered the gallery feeling simultaneous foreboding and elation. Rebecca had never met Erzon, had never seen his paintings, but Jacob immediately recognized that raw power, the expressionistic style, even though it clearly had changed and evolved from the paintings he had seen in the camp. The gallery was filled with people and it took some time to move through the crowd. He was sure Erzon was there. The two friends had grown older, more mature, the haggard faces –the last registered image of each other– had healed without apparent scars, but the moment their eyes met, they felt the jolt of instant recognition; the large crevasse, the void of years of separation, was instantly closed as they ran and embraced and cried and laughed. Now they would renew their interrupted friendship. There would be no more wars to separate them.

Afterwards, Jacob told his friend all the gory details of his hospital experiences. It was almost as if Erzon was learning medicine by proxy. And of course, even though Jacob could not draw, Erzon's tales about his experiences in the underworld of the arts made Jacob an artist honoris causa.

At six o'clock on Saturday, the doorbell rang. It was Erzon. Jacob let him in and Erzon climbed the stairs to their apartment. Rebecca had prepared all sorts of appetizers and a bottle of chilled wine awaited on the living room table.

"So what's new?"

"You won't believe it, Erzon, but you know how disappointed I have been with my situation at the hospital. Well, I have been accepted at Raimondi-Dupertin in the Bronx, a Jewish medical school!"

"Mazel Tov", shouted Erzon and lifting his glass of wine "L'Chaim".

"L'Chaim!" replied Rebecca and Jacob and they proceeded to tell him how it all had come to be.

29

The slope of the trail had become steeper and Nathan observed his breathing demanding more attention realizing how much age had taken away from him. The air was bright and crisp and two ravens sat atop a large Piñon tree, cackling away. He produced a flask from his back pocket, twisted open the cap, and drank the pure crystalline water that had come from his own well. Its source lay seven hundred and fifty feet below the surface of the earth. Jacob Nathan wondered if the bottom of this water well was as dark as his days at high noon!

"Why, why God *Adoneinu* did you let it happen?"

"*Wo warst Du* –Where were You?" Jacob shouted.

The two black birds flew away disturbing momentarily the silence of the mountain forest with their hissing wings. He could see the darkened dorsum of one gliding raven with its powerful shoulders and the cerulean blue-black feathers, wings extended over the rugged landscape; the second raven keeping its distance, never too close and never too far apart, tracking the invisible and whimsical path of elegant sweepings of its partner daring the current in the winds.

Jacob could see the ravens from his pedestrian perch along the worn path over the spine of the mountain until they disappeared between the blue of the sky and the intense green canopy of the climbing horizon. He felt envious. He was crawling and they were soaring. At the same time, he felt that if nothing was as it seemed, he, at least, had had the privilege of seeing them floating on gusty winds, dancing and flirting with death. It was now time to go back to his walk, to his pedestrian path along the ruffled trail.

30

Jacob's neurosurgery training lasted six very long years. The hospital became a prison, albeit one he could walk in and out at will. Urban plans compete angrily for space, leaving few trees standing around the massive buttresses of the healing walls. And yet, nature survived even under these harsh conditions. Without neighboring competition, trees would branch with exuberance, becoming a heaven for all kinds of furred and plumed city dwellers. And under the protective canopy, grass managed to survive, softening the concrete halo and its geometric white parking lines surrounding the hospital. Often, he would look through the windows at the birds on the ground below, collecting breadcrumbs or small pebbles or perched on the branches of the trees or the ledges of nearby buildings, basking in the sun. Sometimes he felt the birds were the only contact he had with the outside world. He had done it at the camp, when he had felt he was losing the concept of freedom; he had looked at the birds.

There were times when the only living beings appeared to be the small birds that often would waddle in the water trapped in the imprints of feet in the mud. Sometimes Leibish and Jacob would imagine that there were secret melodies written by the tiny birds sitting along the barbed wire –converted into a musical staff— that surrounded their lives. The war had been harsh to all, even to the birds.

Now, in freedom, he felt unnecessarily separated from his wife. He felt guilty for sleeping during the few hours he was at home, instead of sharing them with Rebecca. Even when awakened by the moans of pleasure of their neighbors upstairs, his momentary excitement soon gave way to sleep. The situation did not improve after the first week at the Bronx program, when he realized that the chief resident would delay starting evening rounds, even if all was stable with the patients and there was nothing special to be done. It became clear that both Goldberg and Siegel did not care to go home too early. The fact was, they were avoiding their wives. It was plain and simple: the later the evening rounds were started the less time they would have to spend at home. After arguing unsuccessfully for earlier rounds, Jacob just resigned himself to their schedule, and he watched the birds cavorting and hopping and flying freely outside the windows of his hospital prison.

The nurses at John Fox Municipal Hospital were not too different from the ones he had encountered in Brooklyn. Fortunately, the program also involved rotating at Raimondi-Dupertin University Hospital, where the nurses fitted better the pattern one would expect of the saintly nightingales. This, of course, made it even more difficult to swallow the callousness of most of the nurses at the other hospitals.

This contrast between good and evil had an unexpected effect on Nathan. He began to feel an attraction for the nurses at Raimondi-Dupertin. First, he was attracted to their eyes, seeing how they looked at their patients. During surgery, all he could see of the nurses were their eyes, the rest being covered by layers of sterile surgical garb. He began having fantasies. He imagined their bodies under the surgical gowns and tried to put them together with those eyes. He felt continuously guilty for having these thoughts and at the same time not being with Rebecca. His flirting was reciprocated by some of the nurses, perhaps sensing that he was just flirting, that his soul belonged to someone else. And his fantasies remained fantasies, even though he always wondered about what could have been but never was.

But Raimondi-Dupertin was not a permanent base and Nathan had to return to the JF Municipal Hospital. On one occasion, after a particularly strenuous day, he needed some sleep, and as if God had listened, on that Tuesday night there were no calls from the emergency room. Jacob went over the evening scut work list, checking that all that had been requested during the evening rounds was done. At 8 p.m. he sat at the beaten-up desk in the doctors' lounge and studied the last issue of *The Journal of Neurosurgery*. He underlined the important parts, not so much to be able to find them again, but because in doing so he automatically memorized them. By 10 p.m. he could not stay awake any longer and opened the convertible sofa, placed a clean sheet over the heavily worn mattress, did the same with the stained pillowcase and collapsed.

"Doctor, doctor!" Jacob heard the knock and the voice of the nurse. He could hardly believe it. The watch indicated 11:05 p.m.

"Yes".

"It's nurse Mullan. The i.v. on Mr. Rogers infiltrated. You need to start a new one".

Jacob sat on his bed, slightly woozy from the deep sleep he had been ripped away from. He slipped into his shoes and left the room. He walked to Mr. Rogers' bed and checked the intravenous line. Indeed, there was no flow that could be seen in the translucent plastic tubing. The entrance point of the catheter into the patient's skin was swollen and moist, oozing saline solution. Mr. Rogers was a 300 pound, fifty-year-old unlucky guy who had fallen from his bed, hitting his forehead against the night table, causing his neck to snap back. On the following day, a friend had found him on the floor next to his bed. The myelogram done on the day of admission had shown severe osteoarthritis of the cervical spine with significant narrowing of the spinal canal, enough to squash the cervical cord as his head snapped back during the fall. He had become a complete quadriplegic, unable to move anything from the shoulders down.

Nathan walked to the nurses' station and got adhesive tape, alcohol swabs and a Medicut-Needle-Set to start an intravenous infusion at a fresh site.

"Mr. Rogers, you will feel a little pin prick, I am placing a new i.v. line" he said, knowing well that Mr. Rogers was not listening to him. He had suffered a respiratory arrest the week before and was now comatose –thank God for small favors. Jacob looked with expert eyes for a new site. He was looking for a piece of skin that had not been stuck before, that was not swollen and that had a vein visible near its surface. The left arm was swollen, in part from the paralysis and in part from the extravasation of the intravenous fluid. On the right arm there was one vein showing on the dorsum of the hand. "The last vein here", he thought. He applied a tourniquet around the forearm, cleaned the skin with an alcohol swab and introduced the needle into the vein on the first try, releasing the tourniquet immediately. He secured the needle to the plastic tubing, connecting it to the bottle of saline and after proving to his satisfaction that it was working properly, he taped the assembly securely to the skin and opened the flow to 100 drops per minute, wrote a note on the patient's chart detailing what had been done and went back to sleep in the doctors' room. It was now 11:45 p.m., he had been robbed 40 minutes of sleep.

Knocks at the door.

"Doctor Nathan, Doctor Nathan, need to tell you that Mr. Rogers lost his i.v. again".

Jacob could hardly believe it –he had been flying with his own pair of wings over tall trees, some effort in flapping and then gliding silently; it was beautiful, it was peaceful– that he was being disturbed again.

More Knocks.

"Doctor Nathan, Mr. Rogers lost his i.v. again".

"I heard you the first time". Jacob could not hide the irritation in his voice.

He looked at his watch and realized he had slept about an hour. The voice of nurse Mullan somehow sounded hideous. Jacob tried to regain some degree of wakefulness. He got his shoes on and exited his room just in time to see the corpulent figure of nurse Mullan disappear into the nurses' lounge from where the sound of music and conversation and the smell of pizza emanated without regard for the patients. He again gathered the necessary implements and marched to Mr. Rogers' room. There he was, all 300 pounds of swollen, comatose, quadriplegic human being and sure enough, the site where he had placed the last intravenous catheter was swollen and humid. How was it possible, he wondered, how could the patient lose his i.v. again? This time there were no other sites in his arms and he was forced to place the new i.v. on the dorsum of the patient's right foot. He did not like it. He knew that intravenous lines in the legs were more prone to produce phlebitis than those in the arms, but at this point he had no choice. When he finished, he wrote a note in the chart and went back to his room. It was now 1:40 a.m. Still no emergency room calls, for sure he could get some sleep.

The voice of nurse Mullan resounded in the cavities of Jacob's skull like the Angel of Death. He had been dreaming again, flying by just extending his arms into the wind, a few arm flaps and then soaring over the cityscape. It was the Berlin of his youth and all was surrounded with a beautiful silence, only the wind noise as the air rushed by his face.

"Mr. Rogers' i.v. is not working", she bellowed from the corridor. Nathan was furious. He knew that this time he would have to do a Cut-Down procedure on Mr. Rogers. He would have to actually cut the skin and soft tissues and find a reasonably good size vein and insert into it the plastic intravenous catheter. Given the tremendous obesity of the patient, he knew it would not be easy to find a suitable vein in a sea of fatty tissue. This time it was going to be a one-to-two-hour procedure depending on his luck.

Jacob addressed nurse Mullan as calmly as possibly, even though by now he was experiencing a pounding headache.

"How in the hell could this patient lose three i.v.'s in one night ?!!"

"Well, he keeps pulling at them!", she replied.

There was nothing Jacob could do. He realized he was talking to the Devil himself disguised as an overweight, over paid, parasitic city worker, incarnated in the shape of a female nurse. No, this was no nurse, this was a monster, a grotesque human dressed as a nurse, given the right to torture patients by the Borough of Bronx, New York. Here, in front of him, stood a person that was claiming that a fully comatose, complete quadriplegic human being was pulling at his i.v. lines. If true, this constituted a miracle, perhaps in due time, two thousand years from then, a new religion would thrive based on this spectacular event.

Nathan went to his room and, exhausted, extended his body over the sofa-bed without bothering to take his shoes off. It was now 4:30 in the morning. He was awakened at 6:30 a.m. by the noise made by the night nurses as they, preparing to leave, were handling the care of the patients to the nurses of the morning shift. Jacob went to the bathroom to freshen up and be ready for the new day. In his mind, it was clear, that there had been no miracle, rather, nurse Mullan had tripped and disconnected Mr. Rogers' i.v. every time she went to check and turn him in bed. What hurt him the most was the thought that someday she would retire with a full pension –but after how many Mr. Rogers!

By the end of 1963, Jacob had witnessed the divorce of one of the residents, Siegel. It certainly had not come as a surprise to anyone. For months Siegel had been avoiding going home until late at night, in the process forcing Jacob to do likewise. His routine of starting afternoon rounds at 6 o'clock was just so that he would not get home to his "princess", as he would call his wife. Worst of all, there were two children in the middle, but it seemed to be of no importance to Siegel. He was a good-looking man, with an old, childhood linear scar over his left eyebrow, probably a bicycle fall. He smoked as often as he could and had dark, dense, short wavy hair. On more than one occasion Jacob saw him seriously flirting with some of the nurses. He was quite knowledgeable in neurosurgery and possessed a good surgical technique. In years to come, Jacob would remember that on his first Monday morning conference, Siegel had presented the case of a patient who had been operated on the wrong side of his spine by one of the attending neurosurgeons. By coincidence, on the last Monday morning conference of his own training, it had been Jacob's turn to present the case of a wrong-sided surgery by that same attending physician. The world played tricks beyond anyone's control. That particular physician was, in fact, a superb surgeon who had committed two errors that served as brackets to Jacob's training.

In any event, Jacob believed that he and Siegel had a good relationship in spite of his senior resident's difficult character. They would also share the same coup of destiny when their professor, chairman and mentor, Doctor Karlsman committed suicide. Two years after completion of Siegel's training and one year after Jacob's, Michael Karlsman had died. Jacob had gotten a phone call from the secretary of the department.

"Sorry to call you with these sad news, but Professor Karlsman is dead". The secretary had been as brief and direct and callous as always.

"What do you mean 'is dead"!

"It is a long story, but basically, he did not come for his Wednesday Surgery and he did not come for Thursday's Neuropathology conference. Bulgar was assigned the chore of looking for the missing Karlsman. Not finding him at any of the hospitals, he went to his home and found him dead, sitting by the kitchen table, slumped over it; an intravenous line with Potassium Chloride neatly implanted into the dorsal vein of his right arm".

Jacob had hung up the phone, remaining motionless on the living room couch. He began to cry. Rebecca knew not to interfere. She knew he would tell her about the call after he calmed down. It always had been like that. And after a while:

"It is about having lost a father twice", Jacob spoke almost to himself. It already felt as an old memory, even if it had just happened. He saw himself glancing from his own window into Karlsman's kitchen window, sitting incognito, protected by layers of glass, unable to hear through the panels of transparent crystal the needs of his professor feeling the impotence of watching his old mentor sitting on the other side of a mountain of memories, melting down, eroding away –the darkened kitchen where he had died waiting for a visitor. And he also imagined looking through an even darker window at his own father –his first professor, who had taught him to read and write and mend wounded books– being taken away, along with his mother, to the certain death that Germanic discipline brought to defenseless people as they cleansed Europe of the Jewish varmint. But the glass was too dark to look into his parents' eyes just before they died.

"It is about having lost a father twice", Jacob repeated.

"It is about having been taught the skills and nuances of neurosurgery by a kind man and while doing so, conversing about philosophy. It is about having been the teacher of so many doctors and dying alone over a kitchen counter thinking that there was no option better than death. It is about him thinking there was not a single friend he could call upon". Jacob felt his stomach churning, he felt emptiness, guilt, shame. Why Karlsman had not called him? He knew Jacob admired him; he knew he was his friend. Is this how it is? Is this how death acts, by surrounding its victims in a cocoon of isolation so thick that no light, no hope can get in? Hundreds of miles away, Siegel would be thinking along those same lines. The two of them had been the favorite students of Karlsman and now that they had failed him in life, he would fail them in death.

31

He had lost a father twice in his lifetime. Once, many years before, to a system that demonized Jews. How easy it had been to kill old men with beards, with long black cassocks and a compulsion to read and be kind to others. Jews were disproportionately represented in all the major professions, from lawyers, to physicians, to musicians, to physicists. This certainly had helped to fuel the hatred. It had taken less than a decade of propaganda before the German People were ready to close their communal eyes to injustice and genocide. But Europe was prepared for a Holocaust. Europeans had been undergoing brainwashing since the Fourth Century; since the Holy Roman Emperor Constantine had started a movement that required a shadow-people to contrast the path of light that preached love, and in order to succeed had adopted violent retribution for those that stood in its way. And so, after several crusades, after countless heavenly inspired writings and edicts, after a sacred inquisition that lasted for centuries, after having built ghettos for the surviving shadow-Jews, the Europeans were taking their next logical step: that of cleansing the continent –and perhaps the world– of those perfidious Jews. Jacob's parents had become the object of scorn. In an instant they had metamorphosed from a loving family in a tightly knit society, into corpses that became a source for hair, gold teeth fillings, and clothing – and even soap. In a matter of minutes, they had turned into material for disposal, a major hold-up to the German realization of their Final Solution and their sublime Third Reich. Jacob could see without having seen, how those stained fingers that had healed so many books and manuscripts and those maternal eyes were now decomposed somewhere in the middle of the countryside, perhaps next to a lovely clump of pine trees feeding from the enriched soil that had become Europe during the war. He remembered his father telling him as his fingers expertly mended back to life old, wounded books:

"Life is nothing but a series of anecdotes. And remember, Jacob, a good life in the end, is nothing but a good book".

Now, Karlsman was dead. He had been a victim of isolation and insensitivity on the part of his colleagues. He too had become in the end, different from the faculty over which he presided. His sensitivity to human concepts had taken over his life.

"Jacob, you will succeed in life", Karlsman had said in his quiet manner while delicately dissecting around an aneurysm at the base of the brain.

"You will succeed because you are writing your own destiny".

Now, those sad blue eyes and those expert fingers where decomposing as the legacy he had left to the world of neurosurgery was going to be forgotten. He had died alone and had left

Jacob alone once more, because death, no matter how public, always is a lonely affair.

If there was one thing that Jacob had learned during the years of studying neurosurgery, it was that the field was very competitive and that anti-Semitism was rampant in many institutions of higher learning. In fact, the very medical program in which he studied had been founded, in part, to compensate for this peculiar phenomenon, thusly, opening the doors to Jewish doctors. In addition, young neurosurgeons had two options upon graduation, either going into private practice, or going into academia. Those trained in a top-notch academic institution saw private practice with somewhat negative eyes. Nathan had thought to go into academia: To teach and do research, as he had wished long before in Berlin.

32

"**He**y, Jacob…Jacob", Shlomo had whispered into Nathan's ear in the middle of the night.

At first, he had thought that an angel was finally calling him. During the few seconds it took him to become fully awake, he had thought that the Angel of Death had flown by him. He had felt the faint current of air over his right ear. "Jacob, Jacob" he had called. But then, he realized that it was Shlomo that was calling him. What was he doing here away from his own barrack?

"What do you want? They will kill us", he whispered.

"No, Jacob. They need you in the next barrack. Shimen is sick".

"But I am not a doctor ".

"No, but you wanted to be one", Shlomo answered with infinite eagerness in his voice.

"Come, Shimen needs you."

During the early morning hours, the two of them had crawled out of No.14 barrack, so close to the ground that they scratched their faces on the frozen dirt –guards were always eager to kill prisoners and this would have given them the perfect excuse. Sometimes, prisoners that had disobeyed the camp orders would be tortured and then killed in front of the other inmates that in turn were forced to stand for hours and watch as their friends were hung from their necks until they died. Jacob had seen it. He did not want to become one of them. The lights of the camp reflectors had swung close to them several times, but Shlomo appeared to know how to move within the camp confines. Jacob felt that his life was soon going to be over. His heart was fluttering so strongly that he could listen to it, mixed with the sound of air escaping his lungs.

When they entered Shimen's barrack, they were welcomed by the stench of rotting flesh. In the dark, they were escorted by several inmates to Shimen's bunk bed. He was shivering, his eyelids were closed and his skin was cold and clammy and completely covered in sweat. His left leg was swollen and it clearly was the cause of the stench. There was a large ulcer, covered in yellow pus. Jacob saw maggots moving in the tender wound. What could he do? He had not taken a single medical course. His future had been interrupted by the thunder of powerful knocking on his father's door.

"Hi, Shimen. Can you hear me?"

Shimen did not react. His breathing was shallow and fast. The ulcer had eaten part of his foot and had advanced to mid-calf. The skin around it was discolored blue. Serum escaped the edges and wet the boards of his bunk bed; it had that characteristic odor of burned sugar.

"What can you give me to clean the wound?"

"We have some water and some rags." Shlomo acted as he spoke. Jacob submerged one of the rags in the water and applied it to the wound. At first very delicately, not knowing what to expect from Shimen, but since his patient did not react to the gentle debridement, Jacob proceeded to rub off the pus and the maggots from the festering site. Then he added:

"I think it is better to keep it covered and change the dressing at least once a day" –he was already giving medical orders.

"I have to go back to my barrack. Someone has to take me there."

This had been Jacob's first medical consultation. He did not think he had done much for his patient. As Shlomo returned him back to the entrance of his barrack, he extracted from his pocket a piece of dried bread and gave it to Jacob:

"It is in payment for what you did", he said. "Take it, you well deserve it". And he disappeared into the darkness.

33

Studying neurosurgery for six years, going to national conventions, talking with residents from other programs, had given Jacob certain extra-curricular information as to the nature of the beast, the beast being those special neurosurgeons heading their departments, better known as professors and chairmen. The picture was not a pretty one. There was an eight out of ten chance that the chairman of the department in charge of one's destiny would be a sociopath. The tales abounded of residents being fired from their programs because they got married without consulting their professor. Tales of intrigue and envy and hate, tales of abuse of power, there were so many tales. How many times he heard stories of a surgery to be performed by an attending physician that ended up being performed by the chairman, just because he wanted to do that particular case. How often he had seen the backstabbing during clinical conferences when one professor would come and whisper in his ear some embarrassing question to ask of the presenting attending. How many insults and abuses he and others had taken from their professors, serving as displacement targets for their frustrations. Somehow he knew, that at some point in his career, he would sorely miss the protective hand of Professor Karlsman. His tears were full of sadness for his old teacher, but they also tasted bitter for he knew he had lost his protection against future abuses, his defender in shining armor. In order to survive as a young professor, one needed the protection of the old master, the person that could confront and correct any inequity being committed against his former students –no different than a young lion cub losing the protection of its mother against the other members of the clan.

Jacob was visited again by that feeling of terror twisting his entrails, listening in the silence of the surrounding night to the pounding of his heart against the cold, dusty ground as he returned to his barrack. Who could know the pain he suffered in the silence of his secrets? He dared not cry any more for fear that his tears would burn trenches on his face, trying to hold his breath to erase the memory of the putrid scent of Shimen's leg.

On occasion, the gloom of hospital work gave away to some peculiar incidents that helped him survive those years of pounding tragedies. Jacob still smiled when he remembered the story of the Smiths. John Edgar Smith had been 52 years old when he suffered a stroke and was admitted by the emergency room doctor to the neurosurgery service, while the residents were busy in surgery. By the time they discovered that he should have been admitted to the neurology ward instead, it was too late. It would have been more effort to transfer him than to just treat him and so, the patient was assigned to Doctor Jacob Nathan. The history had been rather straightforward. Mr. Smith had suffered of high blood pressure for several years and in spite of knowing it, he had failed to follow medical advice and resisted treatment. Mr. Smith was black and 20 percent above the recommended weight for a man of his height. He was a perfect set up for a stroke. On the morning of the admission to the hospital, he woke up, had breakfast and sat in his recliner chair in the living room of his home, where his wife found him two hours later, somnolent and capable only of moving his right side minimally and with great effort. An ambulance was called and Mr. Smith was taken to the emergency room of John Fox Municipal Hospital.

When Nathan got to examine Mr. Smith, he in fact confirmed that the patient was experiencing a right hemi-paresis. The differential diagnosis included stroke from embolism, stroke from hemorrhage, possible ruptured cerebral aneurysm, and arterial-venous malformation. A cerebral angiogram ruled out the last two diagnoses, and a spinal tap showed no signs of blood in the cerebrospinal fluid. The diagnosis of a stroke secondary to arteriosclerosis and hypertension was made. Now that Nathan had established the how and why, it was necessary to establish the where: where was the brain lesion located –just as a musician can place a musical sound on an exact spot in the musical staff, so neurosurgeons can place the site of damage within the brain by the symptoms and signs a patient might offer. Jacob reasoned that the lesion could be in the left internal capsule, interrupting the motor flow and explaining the weakness the patient was experiencing on his right side. However, placing the lesion at this location could not explain the speech deficits that Jacob found during his examination. A deficit in language would place the lesion not in the capsule but in or close to the cerebral cortex, more specifically an area in the temporal-parietal lobe that mediated language.

It was clear to Jacob that Mr. Smith's examination demonstrated an expressive dysphasia: a paucity of sentences, with difficulty in finding words to express himself, and with use of neologisms to fill in empty spaces in the sentences he delivered. Such language deficit indeed placed the lesion secondary to the stroke right smack in the temporal-parietal area.

When Monday Morning Neurosurgery Conference came, Jacob had to present the case to the interns, residents and faculty. He was nervous but confident that he had done a good job. After a brief presentation of the history, Jacob asked that the patient be brought to the conference room. Mr. Smith was brought in a wheelchair. Some of the attending physicians examined him while others asked questions of the patient. Shortly after, Mr. Smith was wheeled out of the room.

"It is an interesting case", said Doctor Donskoy.

"The patient has a clear-cut hemi-paresis, but it is accompanied by a most beautiful expressive dysphasia."

"An electroencephalogram will confirm the clinical localization of the stroke" added Professor Kline.

Jacob's stress level diminished by leaps and jumps and he felt comforted that his work-up had withstood the scrutiny of the conference. At noon, when the presentation was over, he left and walked in the direction of the elevators but changed his mind and decided to visit once more with Mr. Smith. He found him in bed, surrounded by what were clearly some friends and members of his family. It was a perfect opportunity to find out more details about how the patient had developed his dysphasia, before or after the paralysis. So he approached the group, noticing that they were talking and laughing, he politely interrupted the conversation.

"Hi, I am Doctor Nathan, I am in charge of Mr. Smith".

"Oh, hi. . . doc" replied the visitors in unison.

"Who is Mr. Smith's closest relative"

"I. . . I am. . . I's. . . I's his wifes" responded the lady with a sweet face in the red dress.

"Could I ask you a couple of questions?"

"Su-Su-Sures you caan", she replied.

"When did you notice the change in speech in Mr. Smith?"

"Hmmhuum. . . wha. . . whas you mean? Whas Hummh change?"

After a few more questions Nathan began to realize his error.

"Well, thank you very much for your information" he said, remaining by the bedside, for a few seconds while he overheard the group chatting. It was then that he fully understood that they all were talking like Mr. Smith, and that he needed to change his diagnosis with respect to the location of the brain lesion back to the internal capsule site, otherwise he would have to assume that all the members of Mr. Smith's family were affected by the same stroke. He smiled and then laughed as he walked down the stairs to the main floor and towards the dining room, he had learned that culture had superseded neuroanatomy –his arrogant knowledge had been humbled.

In retrospect, the years at John Fox Municipal Hospital flew by like a bird on a stormy afternoon. But as they were happening, they seemed to move with the speed of slow eternity like during the last minutes of a drowning. Most of the time, perhaps as much as one third of it, was spent doing the chores that others should have done but didn't. Mornings after rounds were dedicated to collecting the blood samples written on the scut work list. Then, for fear that they would never get to the laboratory, Jacob would carry the samples himself. Needless to say, the results from the lab were supposed to come via the internal messenger service as well, that is to say that Jacob, in order to insure having the results on time, would pick up the lab reports himself and bring them to the nurses station, hand delivering them to one of the nurses that was always there on a break.

A great deal of time was spent placing intravenous lines into patients, a task that was normally practiced by nurses in other hospitals throughout the world but that at municipal hospitals in United States had been claimed as a victory for nursing when they were able to shift that particular chore to the doctors in training; the same was the case with introducing urinary catheters and obtaining urine samples. The reports from radiological testing were also sent by way of the messenger system and consequently Jacob and his classmates had to either go in person to pick up the report slips or call on the phone for a reading. Either way, the radiology secretaries kept them waiting as if there were a perverse conspiracy to waste doctors' time in municipal teaching hospitals. And finally, to assure that a patient was at the place he or she needed to be at the prescribed time, there was nothing as reliable as the manpower provided by doctors.

The remaining time left was spent interacting with other physicians during rounds and in specialized lectures, like the Monday Morning Conference, and the Thursday afternoon Neuropathology Conference, or the Friday afternoon Neuroradiology Conference. That left just enough time to assist in the operating room for a few hours a day, that is, when there was no Outpatient Clinic.

The Outpatient Clinic provided clinical follow up for those patients seen either at the emergency room or discharged from the wards. It was a very important part of the service and of the learning experience, and yet, it had a most definite negative aura around it, perhaps in part, because in a surgical specialty, doctors prefer to be in the surgical suites, either observing or performing surgeries. In addition, surgeons tend to put a lot of effort into surgery and the remainder of the treatment becomes almost an anticlimax, even though they know it is an important part of the overall picture. But in addition to these factors, the clinic was full of patients who had nowhere else to go and remained like ballast, year after year after year, in the system. And of course, the clinic had its handful of peculiar, odd-looking, even grotesque patients that were assigned to the newcomers as a rite of passage, an initiation.

Not long after his arrival to the Bronx program, Jacob was sent to the Clinic. Clinic days were held on Tuesday afternoons and Thursday mornings. Jacob had heard much about it, enough to be suspicious of anything he was told by the other residents. But on that first Tuesday at the Clinic, he had no idea of the things he was about to see.

Goldberg was in charge on that day. After shooting the breeze for a while he said:

"O.K. let's start clinic. Jacob, you take Willie".

Jacob went looking for the chart. He found a two-foot-high stack of paper with a coversheet that read: "William Spaulding Gonzales". The various folders held by rubber bands were falling apart. Jacob grabbed a cart and rolled the chart into one of the examining rooms that served also as offices. Each office cubicle was about eight by ten feet. Along one wall there were a small metal desk and a swivel chair, and against the opposite wall a wooden table topped by a foam mattress that served the dual role of both sofa and examining table. He began reading about Willie.

Willie had been first seen in the emergency room after he had suffered blunt head trauma secondary to a fall from a bicycle at age 10. He had lost consciousness immediately after the fall. He had suffered generalized seizures for many years, probably secondary to the meningitis he had when he was four and a half years old. At that time, he had stayed in the hospital for almost two months, requiring intensive care and a prolonged course of antibiotics. Several weeks after his discharge, he had become very somnolent, impervious to all efforts to wake him, giving his mother a major scare. She brought him to the emergency room and was admitted with a diagnosis of Obstructive Hydrocephalus secondary to the previous meningeal infection. An emergency shunting procedure had been done. He received one of the first Xylastic shunts ever developed. The child did well after that, except that he continued experiencing the seizures. Four years later the Children's Charitable Foundation of the Bronx gave him a bicycle for Christmas, and a week later he had fallen from his bike, striking his head against the pavement. On that admission, Willie was unconscious, paralyzed of the left side and had a large and unreactive right pupil. An emergency angiogram had shown significant mass effect on the right compatible with a Subdural Hematoma. He was taken to surgery and an emergency craniotomy and evacuation of a massive subdural blood clot was accomplished successfully. At that time, it was noticed and duly written in the chart, that Willie might "have suffered from Arrested Hydrocephalus when he was an infant, given the rather large circumference of his skull. A factor that did not contribute to the second Obstructive Hydrocephalus he suffered as a consequence of the meningitis years later". In any event, Willie recovered little by little and began opening his eyes and recognizing family members a week after the surgery. In another week he began regaining movement of his left side. Then, on the eve of a transfer to a rehabilitation facility, he had spiked a fever and become comatose. His white cell count was 35,000. There was slight drainage of pus from the surgical wound. An emergency craniectomy with removal of an infected bone flap was accomplished. He remained on antibiotics for another month and again, began recovering. Since then, a year prior to Jacobs encounter with Willie, he had been followed at the Outpatient Clinic by the residents in training, more specifically by the juniors. Jacob asked the nurse to bring Willie. He had no idea of what he was about to see.

Willie entered with his mother. He was about normal in height and weight. He was wearing a football helmet, a Los Angeles Rams football helmet. From under the helmet, large clumps of abundant black hair jutted out. Jacob made the standard salutations and then asked that the mother remove the helmet.

Jacob should have known better, but it took him by surprise. To begin, it was not a child's helmet, but rather a large adult helmet.

171

Secondly, it did not cover fully Willie's head, rather, it sat like a cap on top of his gigantic head. The mother, as a matter of fact, removed the helmet, revealing a large hole where Willie's right brain should have been, covered by a thin layer of skin with small pockets of hairs. Along the upper most corner of this massive defect, a small larva of a maggot crawled between two holes in the skin. Willie's mother acted as if she had just removed a school cap from her son. Jacob excused himself and vomited on the floor of the doctors' bathroom at the end of the corridor. When he returned, he passed by Goldberg's examining room and saw through the corner of his eye the smile on his senior's face.

Willie's bone infection had made it impossible to repair the skull defect; his hydrocephalus had made the brain collapse under the normal atmospheric pressure, the skin served as a circus tent, covering like a wet blanket from one edge of the bone to the next. At the edges, where the skin was tight against the bone, there were pressure sores where flies would land on occasion. Jacob cleaned the wound with peroxide and Betadine and applied the helmet with the attached wig back on Willie's head. On the chart, there is a note from Doctor Jacob Nathan that mimics all the previous notes:

"2 p.m. Willie continues in stable condition. Return to clinic in 2 months. Dilantin prescription renewed. J. Nathan, M.D."

Clinic days were boring most of the time, but sometimes great lessons were learned from seeing these patients. Jacob remembered the case of the man who wanted to meet and thank him for all that he had done for him.

José Raymond was walking under the elevated railroad tracks when the brake shoe from a wheel of a passing subway hit him right on the top of his head. Needless to say, he passed out immediately. The paramedics brought him to the emergency room where Jacob met him for the first time. Mr. Raymond was in a state of agitated stupor. He was unaware of his surroundings, did not reply to questions, continuously picked at the blanket with which he was covered. The exam did not show any focal abnormality with the exception of several small contusions to the scalp by the top of his head. An angiogram had not shown any major shift of brain structures and it was decided in consultation with Doctor Goldberg, the chief resident, to place the patient under observation. During the following days, José remained somewhat agitated but became more responsive. He knew where he was, who he was, but had no idea of what had happened to him. Then, on the fifth day, during Jacob's night on duty, Raymond became unresponsive. The exam demonstrated a slight left sided weakness and his right pupil was a tad larger than the left. Jacob recognized that these changes were probably the result of a bleed into an area of previous brain contusion, and that it would be important to determine if surgical excision was in order. He called radiology and asked for a stat cerebral angiogram and then phoned the senior resident on call.

"Hey, Ken, it's Jacob, I got a case for you"

"What's up", replied Doctor Siegel, not quite fully awake. The night-table clock indicating it was 2 in the morning.

"Do you remember José Raymond, the guy hit by the subway brake? Well, he is going down the tube. I ordered an angio, which will be done in about an hour. I think we should reserve the O.R."

"Sounds good. I'll be there in about 45 minutes", and he hung up.

By the time Siegel got to the radiology department, the films were coming out. There was no distinct shift as both Jacob and Ken were expecting.

Siegel said looking at the films against the milky white screens:

"I think we should go in and suck all the contused brain".

Nathan was cautious: "But if we do, where are we going to operate? We have no clue as to where the clots are. I think we should give him Mannitol, dry him up, and sit tight. If he gets worse, then we can go in anyway".

"O.K. Let's intubate him and put him on Mannitol and also place a catheter so we have an idea of fluid balance", Siegel said and then with a smile, he added:

"But his life is on your hands".

Jacob knew that to be the case. He also knew that to just open the patient's skull and suck some contused brain was going to result in more neural deficits, and as long as the swelling would go down soon, he could spare lots of healthy brain for Mr. Raymond's future use. The patient was transferred to the neuro-intensive care unit and they began the countdown. Sure enough, 36 hours later, José began waking up. From then on it was continuous improvement day after day after day. By the second week after admission, José was completely coherent; he had regained the strength in his weak arm. Jacob often visited him, for he considered that this had been his first truly saved patient –not counting Shimen with his rotten leg. The patient and his family were well aware of what had transpired and were very thankful to Jacob. On day 24 after admission, Raymond was discharged home, with an appointment to return for a clinic visit a month later.

When Jacob saw the name of Raymond among the clinic charts of that afternoon's appointments, he was glad. Finally, José Raymond and his wife walked into the exam room. José was very friendly and enthused about meeting the doctor that had saved his life. According to his wife, José had done wonderfully since his discharge from the hospital. He had related perfectly well with all visitors and family members; he behaved normally. And yet, about a week prior to that day's clinic appointment, during lunch he had asked what had happened to him; he had become aware of himself. From that day on, he had become his old self and had no memory of any of the events that had transpired from the time of the accident to that instant at lunch. He had then expressed his desire to meet the doctor that had saved his life. Jacob was glad to meet José again. He determined that indeed he was fully recovered. He gave him an appointment to come back in two months and he saw them out to the waiting room.

Jacob mulled over what he had learned from Mr. Raymond's case with great enthusiasm. It had been a magnificent demonstration of what the brain could do. For more than a month's time, the patient had acted perfectly normal, and yet, he had not been normal. It was as if he had been living within a parenthesis and that after some healing time, the parenthesis had been closed and the real José Raymond had returned to his normal life. Jacob loved the way the human brain worked!

On another occasion, Jacob had to admit to the private service a patient of his professor, Doctor Karlsman. It was a very sad case. She was a thirty-two-year-old woman, mother of three. Three months prior to this admission, an operation had been performed to remove a tumor from her right breast which had proven to be cancerous. She had recovered well form the surgery and had completed a course of radiation therapy. Then, the afternoon of her current admission, she had suffered a generalized seizure. The attending general surgeon had asked Doctor Karlsman to see her. Karlsman had phoned Jacob asking him to admit the patient and schedule a bone scan for the following day and also an angiogram.

"Dr. Nathan, Mrs. Anna Taylor, your admission for tonight is in room 424".

Jacob gathered the neurological hammer and his pinwheel and headed for room 424 along

THE LAST WITNESS

the long corridor.

34

As he walked, the corridor got darker and narrower and full of people. The people did not know where to go, what to do. They were herded to the platform of the train station. The town's people were pointing with their fingers and were laughing at them. The guards were shouting obscenities and orders. Women walking like in a trance as if they had been awakened from deep sleep. Men, disheveled, staring at their shoes, ashamed to look into their wives' eyes, not knowing how to protect them. They were wearing winter coats in the middle of the summer. Some were carrying luggage, others carried their belongings wrapped in a bedsheet. The noise was intolerable, the heat oppressive, the air difficult to breathe, and then he saw her. Like an apparition, floating in the air, apparently unconcerned, separated from all the turmoil that surrounded her; she stood with her long blond hair and the small jasmine hair pin, with her blue-green eyes and soft oval face and pearly skin, blushed cheeks, long neck and slim and well-shaped body, wearing a light silk dress. He walked toward her, his eyes locked on hers, feeling only the shortening of his breathing and the increasing heart rate.

"My name is Jacob Nathan. I am entering medical school in Berlin", he said without even thinking what he was saying or why.

"I am Anna", she replied in a voice that

reached him like an angel's whisper, dissecting through all the noise and chaos.

"Do you want to travel with me?"

"Yes", she had replied.

Jacob offered his arm and Anna took it and for the next several days they remained attached to each other, their embrace made even tighter by the constant pushing of Max, Frieda's husband, and the other passengers in the cattle car. And then, the rhythmic lullaby of the train's wheels against the hard rails began to slow its pace, and then, silence. The trip was over and the single sliding door of the cattle car had opened and the light had entered into the cavernous death trap that had become the transport to the concentration camp. People filled their lungs with fresh air that had the aroma of paradise, in contrast to the filth they had breathed in and out, with the stench of death in the darkness of their prison transport car. Camp prisoners dressed in striped uniforms placed a heavy wooden ramp against the threshold of the door. Many began walking the ramp, too weak to jump. Jacob and Anna jumped together from the railcar not really knowing what was to happen to them. They were confused, the barking of dogs, the soaring notes of Wagner's music, –or was it Beethoven's?– the noise of the thousands of people wondering, questioning, trying not to lose the proximity of their loved ones. Then, a soldier approached them shouting at Jacob to go with the men and pushing Anna towards the women. The ground was uneven and wet from a recent rain, Anna fell, the guard began shouting at her, she tried to stand up and fell again, the guard kicked her in the stomach, she vomited. The guard backed up one step, drew back his rifle and with a single swooping thrust, pierced her head with his bayonet.

35

Jacob opened the door of the room and confronted Anna. Anna Taylor was an attractive woman who appeared slightly older than her chronological age, no doubt because of her recent bout with cancer. She was well dressed, and her jewelry indicated that she was from a well to do family. She was polite and cooperative and answered all the questions Jacob asked of her, questions typical of a neurological exam. Jacob then proceeded to examine her. He noticed she had a slight flattening of the nasal fold on the left and had a slight increase of the deep tendon reflexes on her left side. When asked to keep both of her arms extended in front of her, Jacob noticed a minimal downward drift of the left arm. He then proceeded to examine her vestibulo-cerebellar function. He asked her to follow his index finger with her eyes without moving her head as he in turn moved his hand from right to left, back and forth. To his amazement, she would not move her eyes, even though he asked her to do so over and over, instead she argued that indeed she was following his commands.

"Follow my finger with your eyes", he said, "do not move your head or neck, just your eyes"

"Yes ".

"Do it. Follow my finger"

"Yes, I am following it". But in fact, she was not.

Jacob finished his examination, wrote a

history and physical in the chart. Wrote the medical orders that Doctor Karlsman had requested, placed the patient on steroids to decrease brain swelling around a possible metastasis from the breast cancer and then proceeded to complete the other unfinished work assigned to him during clinical rounds that day.

The following morning, during rounds, he presented the case to Doctor Karlsman. By then, the steroids had taken effect and Ms. Taylor was greatly improved, with no neurological deficits. It was during that morning's examination that the patient asked Nathan why, the night before, he had repeated so many times in so loud a voice that she should follow his finger with her eyes. Jacob was surprised at her remark and explained to her that in fact, she had not moved her eyes. The patient insisted she had been doing exactly what he had asked her to do. This was an interesting phenomenon that Jacob never forgot and never got to write a scientific paper about, and yet, he thought it was one of the most important clinical observations he had ever made: that the human brain is so well organized that each part assumes the rest is doing their duty. Certain behaviors are simple and automatic and the central processor would not dream that an order issued is not an order fulfilled. Of course this is achieved during infancy after years of practice and maturation, establishing new connections between nerve cells. Certain behaviors become completely automatic so that the brain does not have to bother with telling one foot to move after the other while walking, for example. In the case of Anna Taylor, the nerve paths between the brain region that was receiving the order to follow Jacob's finger with her eyes and the muscles of her eyes had been temporarily interrupted by the swelling, but the brain as a whole had assumed that she was complying with such a simple task. A magnificent example of the delegation of tasks by a central command network: the soul was compartmentalized! Observations like this were as beautiful to Jacob as a magnificent sunset over the Jemez Mountains.

The world of neurosurgery is indeed a strange one, obscured and mysterious to outsiders and often brutal to those who inhabit it. Archeological digs in Peru have provided evidence of cranial trephinations performed on people thousands of years ago. Some skulls showed sharp edges around the trephination indicating that the persons had died before there was time for the bone to heal. Other skulls clearly had smooth rounded edges around the trephination, clear proof that they had survived the procedure and had gone on to heal. During the following thousand years neurosurgery made relatively little progress. Illustrations from the Middle Ages reveal that man never ceased to operate on the brain. However, the level of sophistication of these surgeries was clearly rudimentary. It was not until the 20th Century that a big jump in the evolution of neurosurgery took place, and in great part thanks to the contributions of one man, Harvey Cushing.

Neurosurgery procedures were being

performed all over the world, but because of the concentrated efforts of Cushing, neurosurgery was reborn as a distinct and separate branch of medicine, and it was reborn in America. Neurosurgery was so young, that two of Jacob Nathan's professors had been students of Cushing.   From its inception in the early 20th Century, neurosurgery rapidly developed into a complex and diverse surgical specialty. Cushing had made extensive contributions and his students expanded the field further. The third generation felt comfortable within the specialty and by the fourth generation, modern neurosurgery was fully established and continuing its normal path of evolution.

But just as the science of neurosurgery had sprung forth from Cushing, so did the psychological stigmata that plagued those who practiced it.   Perhaps as a result of the times in which he lived, perhaps in combination with his own personality, Cushing was a stern and abrasive man. Jacob had seen one of the few movies made of Doctor Cushing. It was a short clip filmed just as the famed doctor was finishing one of his surgeries. He had walked out of the operating room into an expansive corridor where a dozen or so of his disciples and staff where waiting for him. Cushing stood alone. The small crowd stood around him, but about seven feet away from him.   Jacob judged by their body movements that they all were eager to do something, or expecting to do something, like trained dogs ready to please their master. But Jacob saw nothing happening until the instant when Cushing signaled with a slight, almost imperceptible nod of his head, then, the most senior member of the group, extracted from the pocket of his white doctor's lab coat, a silver cigarette case, opened it and walked with his head bowed towards the master. Cushing picked up a cigarette, which was lit immediately by the same man, he inhaled and puffed out the smoke and smiled. At that instant, all the tension demonstrated by the group vanished, and they began chatting, but the halo of several feet of clear space around Cushing remained. The film ended. Jacob was mesmerized. The scene was a copycat of the behavior demonstrated by gorillas towards the silverback, dominant male, except that gorillas do not smoke.

Jacob had learned from Doctor Feldberg, a neurosurgical son of Cushing, that no one spoke to the master before being spoken to; that no one got married unless he permitted such an action. Workdays began before dawn and ended long after the sun had set. Any action interpreted as insubordination was punished by immediate dismissal from the training program. The students of Cushing, whether they admitted it or not, had been psychologically battered and abused, and like the children of abusive parents, they in turn became abusive with their students. Variance of opinion was not tolerated; rigidity was the rule. The world of academic neurosurgery was infested with scarred sociopaths. Pleasure was to be found in knowing the inherent superiority of neurosurgeons over other physicians, and pride in accepting the excessive demands and the pain they produced among the followers of this sublime specialty.

In between pushing stretchers, executing scut-lists, carrying blood samples to the lab and placing and replacing intravenous lines and urinary catheters, Nathan needed to make time to go to the operating room and observe and assist in surgeries. During all the years of his training, Jacob was always supervised in the operating theater. During these cases, Jacob made lasting mental notes about what to become and what not to become as a surgeon, for each of his professors had a characteristic professional style and quite different surgical abilities.

After Friday morning rounds Jacob usually assisted Doctor Baum. His surgeries were immaculate. Baum was delicate in his movements and a master of the microscope. Operating with him was a true pleasure: his technique was bloodless and Jacob could appreciate fully the anatomy of the nerves and the brain. But one thing was to know Baum in the operating room and another to deal with him outside the confines of surgery. When the surgical pajamas were replaced by street clothes he turned into a mean and cheap person. His wiry build was the perfect fit for his oversized shoes, polyester plaid pants and cheap plastic frame eyeglasses that distorted his eyes just enough to give him a mean look. His nasty streak would surface with the least instigation. He was demeaning towards interns and residents, often confronting them with shouts and insults. He accused residents of lying when he had forgotten to order some special test and was lacking the results during rounds. He needed to blame others, never himself. And yet, during surgery, he was kind and generous with his wisdom. Jacob learned from Baum all kinds of things concerning the surgery on the back of the head and its contents: the delicacy of the cerebellum and the unforgiving nature of any surgical errors, the techniques to manipulate the nerves that originated from this region and techniques to free them from the tumors that often sprung from or surrounded them.

Some afternoons Jacob, as part of the Spine Clinic, had to assist Doctor Wisseman. In many ways he reminded Jacob of a teacher he had had in grammar school. He was a sensitive, kind and intelligent person, who lacked self-confidence. This made him hesitant and meticulous during surgery, continuously questioning every move he made, making the procedures somewhat tedious. But aware of his shortcomings, Wisseman would not deal with problems that were beyond his scope. The world of academia permitted him to survive within its protective cocoon. In the future, Jacob would remember Wisseman's wisdom and his capacity to judge himself when confronting very complex surgical problems. "Remember, don't grab if you cannot hold on", he often said to Jacob.

If Wisseman's theorem was "don't grab if you cannot hold on", Doctor Kleinstein's was "grab as much as you can and don't bother with the consequences". No one liked to assist in Kleinstein's surgeries that often took eight, even twelve hours. It wasn't just because the problems were difficult, they indeed were, but because Kleinstein was a bad surgeon. Sometimes a surgeon possesses good clinical sense but bad surgical technique, sometimes it is the other way around. But Jacob found that Kleinstein was neither a good clinician nor a good surgeon. Most of his patients had complications; most were not helped. The sight of people with pus coming out of the side of their heads was very bothersome to Jacob. It got so bad that at one point, risking his own career, he wrote a note to Doctor Karlsman, the chairman of the department, exposing Kleinstein.

"Dear Prof. Karlsman:

There is a passage in the Bible that cautions against the sin of passivity. It says that he who observes someone raising a knife to strike another person and does nothing to prevent it, is as guilty as the person committing the crime.

I cannot stand it any longer. Please do not retaliate against the messenger. I am writing to let you know that Doctor Kleinstein's patients are suffering a rather high rate of complications and deaths. Please look into it.

Sincerely,

Jacob Nathan, M.D."

A few days later Jacob was called to the chairman's office. Clinical rounds had just finished when he was approach by a secretary with the summons. He had followed her like a punished puppy, down the long corridor, past the reception office and into the professor's sanctum.

"You know, things are not always black

and white", the chairman said. He was sitting behind a desk completely covered with patients' charts. His pipe was resting on a two-pipe rack and was the only non-clinical object on the surface of his desk.

"I know that, Doctor Karlsman, but I think this is way beyond subtle shades of gray". Jacob was somewhat nervous, not knowing if these were his final hours in the teaching program. He continued:

"I don't know how long or how many patients will have to be butchered by him before the word gets out there to the community". Jacob was referring to the Scagoonnah County inhabitants from where most of Kleinstein's patients came and few returned.

"Jacob", the throaty voice of Karlsman was steady, his blue eyes looking at him with kindness, almost with envy. "Jacob, what you are doing is a brave thing, but one cannot act always as one wishes. The gray I am referring to is not in the crime, but in the legal aspects of it. A crime may be black and white, but lawyers soon will make it look gray, more so when dealing with brittle patients. Being chairman is not an easy job. Sometimes we have to tolerate a certain amount of imperfection".

Jacob understood. He had seen Karlsman's eyes, full of knowledge, full of passion and at the same time sad, like sometimes is a field of wheat when caressed gently by the winds on cloudy days. Nathan knew that sometimes it is better not to attempt to move a mountain. Instead, he began to assist Kleinstein more often, attempting to decrease his professor's surgical errors and learn from them.

On occasion on Tuesdays, Jacob was called to assist Doctor Wistorowski. Although he had not been a student of Cushing, he had studied with some of his students. He was a repository of old surgical techniques. During his surgeries he often commented on the how and why of the maneuvers he was performing and in so doing provided Jacob with living testament of the recent history of neurosurgery. In addition, Wistorowski had confidence in Jacob's ability and the two of them shared a healthy relationship. Wistorowski was the only one of Jacob's professors who did not resent being shown a new trick in a surgical technique by his student; if he saw its usefulness, he incorporated it into his own repertoire.

And of course, there was Professor Karlsman with his blue, intelligent eyes and his propensity to philosophize. Jacob had certain ambivalence assisting him. He liked the way he studied and approached cases. He liked his efficiency and his technique of dealing with delicate parts of blood vessels and brain, but he disliked how once the delicate stuff was completed, Karlsman would become somewhat careless with the more pedestrian aspects of the surgical procedure. It was as if, after hours of dealing with matters of life and death, when it came to closing the surgical wounds, pedestrian details did not matter any longer. On more than one occasion Jacob had to correct the closure so that tissues were in their correct anatomical relationship.   And this too, was a lesson for Jacob.

One Monday, just before the Morning Conference was to begin, Jacob was called to the office of the chairman. He found Karlsman trying to calm down Doctor Feldberg. Feldberg had been one of Cushing's students. The old man was fuming and when he saw Jacob, he began to insult him, to call him ignorant, to accuse him of trying to undermine everything he stood for. Jacob, of course, had no idea of what he had done to the old man to bring on the insults. When Karlsman was able to calm Feldberg, Jacob learned the details of his transgression. As it turned out, on the previous Sunday, during rounds, Nathan had found one of Feldberg's patients with the original bandages still covering the wound some seven days after surgery. Jacob had removed the dirty dressing just to find, to his surprise, a second dressing firmly in place over the surgical wound. He had left that one intact. It had been Feldberg's absolute and unmodifiable routine for at least three decades, if not longer, to apply two surgical dressings, one on top of the other and to remove the more superficial on the eighth day after surgery. Jacob had broken his law by removing the top dressing on the seventh day.   None of the other neurosurgeons applied two dressings. Indeed, most of them removed the original dressing on or about the third post-operative day, some would keep it for only one or two days!

Another peculiarity that Jacob observed, involved the change in personality that occurred among all his professors once a surgery was under way.   This was an amazing experience. No matter who the surgeon was, or how simple the case, once they had scrubbed and gowned, Jacob could sense great tension inside the surgeon as if a biological storm was brewing. They became intolerant, rigid and aggressive, at the same time they were showing fear and doubt.

Judy Morton had been admitted via the emergency room. She was diagnosed as having a subarachnoid hemorrhage secondary to a ruptured aneurysm. She had been a healthy and attractive, married woman. On the morning of her admission, she and her husband had had sexual intercourse.   A minute later, still kissing, she suddenly experienced a horrible, fulminating headache.   She had just told George, her husband, that she had the worst headache of her life, when she lost consciousness.   Soon after admission, she underwent a cerebral angiogram that demonstrated a bleb the size of a pencil eraser, originating at the junction of the internal carotid and posterior communicating arteries at the base of the brain. During the following ten days she had regained consciousness and was now ready for surgery. The surgical procedure was quite simple, in principle. Simply, expose the blood vessel bleb and apply a special clip over its base to isolate it from the remaining normal vessel from which it originated.   Patients of this type had to survive several dangers. First, there was the danger of a re-bleed while waiting for surgery –these second bleeds usually resulted in death. Then, assuming that she did not re-bleed while awaiting surgery, there was the imminent danger of a bleed during surgery, and if it happened before the surgeon had control of the base of the aneurysm, the person usually died, if it happened while exposing and dissecting the base of the aneurysm, the patient's chances of survival increased dramatically if, and only if, the surgeon did not panic.

Judy Morton had become the patient of Doctor Kleinstein. The induction of anesthesia had gone smoothly, without any apparent problem. Her blood pressure was kept on the low side of normal to minimize an early rupture. Jacob was designated as Kleinstein's assistant. Jacob had shaved all of Judy's hair at her request. The scalp had been scrubbed sterile with Betadine and a question mark shape incision had been made just behind the hairline on the right. Using the new craniotomy drill, several burr-holes had been connected with the sawblade and the brain at the base of the forehead had been exposed. Opening the skull in this way minimized brain retraction maximizing future brain function. Self-retaining retractors had been applied and after aspirating some cerebrospinal fluid, Doctor Kleinstein was beginning to clear the fine membranes and residual blood clots that surrounded the aneurysmal bleb. So far, Kleinstein had not exhibited any unusual behavior. He was following the normal pattern of arrogance and doubt. This part of the surgery had to be performed using a microscope, a part of the procedure that had become more and more accepted as its benefits became clear.

Without taking his eyes from the field, Kleinstein demanded:

"Give me the # 4 dissector".

His left hand held a small suction probe. With the dissector in his right hand, he began teasing away some of the membranes around the aneurysm. Then, suddenly, like an explosion, all became red. Jacob jumped back, then realized that all was happening inside the patient's head. He looked first through the microscope and saw only a sea of red blood growing every second. He took his eyes from the microscope and looked at Kleinstein. He was immobile, his forehead covered with sweat, not even blinking. Jacob saw pure panic in the eyes of his professor. He realized that in a matter of moments Judy Morton would be dead.

"Give me a medium suction!" Nathan shouted at the nurse passing the instruments. Without delay, he introduced the suction in the general direction he remembered the aneurysm to be. In about ten seconds or so –an eternity– he saw the dome of the aneurysm.

"Jack", he said. "There is the dome, get the curved aneurysm clip and follow my dissector".

Kleinstein broke from his frozen state and followed the instructions Jacob was giving.

"Good. I am going to go a little deeper with my suction and retract the dome. As soon as you see the neck of the aneurysm, just apply the clip". Jacob was astounded at the sound of his own voice. A moment later, Doctor Kleinstein had applied the metal clip at the base of the aneurysm, all bleeding had stopped. All was in order. It was time to irrigate out all remaining blood with saline solution and close the wound. The patient was going to do just fine.

Nathan had reacted in a matter of a few seconds and had talked his professor through the moves that needed to be done. He wondered why his professor had frozen during surgery and he patted himself on the back for having rescued him. Only after he graduated from the program and became himself the surgeon in charge, only when there was no one supervising him and he was the supreme authority during the procedure, only then Jacob understood. Every moment of vacillation, of panic, of anxiety that he had observed in his professors he experienced the very first time he entered an operating room and realized he was there alone. The responsibility to have someone's life depending on one's skills and knowledge could not possibly be understood, but by those who have experienced it. On one's shoulders weighs a human life, attached to memories, with connections to other human beings, parents, friends, husbands, children, all of them depending on the surgeon's skills. When all was going well, Jacob could be arrogant, perhaps somewhat pedantic, but this was simply a defense mechanism against the insecurity that is there, ever present, no matter how good he was as a surgeon. But when things went wrong, then, in a matter of instants his chest filled with a sense of desperation as if the lungs were not big enough to breathe, becoming conscious of the pounding sound of the blood vessels against the temples and behind the eyes, it was as if the world was going to end and he alone was there to prevent it from happening; he and no one else. This is how intense the relationship between patient and surgeon is –different from those that had practiced suturing techniques on Nathan's back decades ago in the camp's hospital.

Years after he completed his neurosurgery training, when he was fully established in the practice of his profession, Jacob was again reminded of the sociopathy that was so rampant, especially among the third and fourth generation neurosurgeons. It happened at one of the annual meetings of the Congress of Neurological Surgeons. As was customary, a Gala night took place midway through the convention. This was an elegant affair, with a sit-down dinner for about 600 neurosurgeons. After dinner, the guest of honor, a senior faculty member from Duke, delivered the "Invited Lecture". As part of his recollections and treasured moments from the past, this man told the following anecdote:

". . . As you know, I was not privileged to know Harvey Cushing, but I did meet several of his students. Some were my professors. Throughout these years I have followed the norms established by them in my dealings with my students and patients. I know my students think I am demanding. Well, I do ask that morning rounds take place at four-thirty. The doctors in my program must be there on time or not at all. It is hard work, but it carries its own rewards." Jacob's mind rushed searching for the rewards of starting rounds before the sun had shown its face but could find none. He just imagined what it would do to family life.

Then, perhaps to spice his lecture, the guest of honor changing his voice became somewhat less pedantic and shifting to his personal life he said:

"I have been blessed with a wonderful family. My wife and I have four children and seven grandchildren. The other day, on the occasion of my wife's birthday, as a present, I had breakfast with her. . ."

Nathan listened to those words and felt a powerful sensation of nausea deep in his soul. Ever since he had met Rebecca, he had wanted to spend as much time with her as possible. He always had made a point of having breakfast with her; only on those occasions when he worked overnight at the hospital he did not and then, he felt he had betrayed her. He could not imagine the world he had seen without her by his side. There was no image, no landscape and no music that Jacob would not wish to share with her. There was no enjoyment of beauty without being reassured that Rebecca was by his side enjoying it herself. And here, the Congress of Neurological Surgeons was honoring and savoring this man's psycho-babbling about his life of dedication to the profession and abuse and neglect of his wife and family. Amazing as it might seem it was possible to study and practice neurosurgery having clinical rounds at 7 in the morning. In fact, most of the fifth generation neurosurgeons were doing exactly that.

36

Jacob Nathan's neurosurgery practice thrived. He was now one of the most respected neurosurgeons in New York. He finally had opted for a private practice. This had not been his original intention, but after the Birmingham fiasco and the Florida Jew roasting, the Nathans had decided it was time to go back to New York.

They had started in a small office space about two blocks from Raimondi-Dupertin Hospital. At first, Rebecca served as receptionist and secretary, and even assisted Jacob during the occasional dressing changes that were carried out in the office. Her previous experience working for Doctor Rosenberg, the neurologist, came in very handy during these initial years. The patients liked her enormously and never felt neglected or abandoned, not even during those instances when Nathan had to cancel clinic appointments because of a surgical emergency. Rebecca had a way with patients –she too had been exposed to the effects of cruelty of the invading Nazi hoards and having survived had learned to cope with suffering– that reassured and calmed them, even if they needed to be re-scheduled. Soon, by word of mouth, from patient to friend, the practice began to grow to the extent that they needed a second secretary for the office, one that could keep up with dictations, while Rebecca dedicated herself to scheduling and billing.

But Jacob never felt comfortable practicing where he had been a student. He suspected that others still looked at him as an apprentice. He could not help feeling that his old teachers, with whom he now shared the use of the wards and the surgical suites, were still somehow his superiors. There was great wisdom in the saying that one cannot be a prophet in one's own land. Those that knew you as a child or a student confused familiarity with respect or achievement with mere presence and Jacob knew this. At first, the pleasure of being back in the New York area and of having his practice flourish had eased these concerns. Still, as he became more successful, it became clear to him that he needed to change the location of his practice. He discussed this with Rebecca. She understood, but it wasn't easy to pack and leave a successful practice for an unknown destination. Nonetheless, as his discontent with the Raimondi-Dupertin situation grew, the attraction of leaving became greater and clearer.

Living in the Bronx was not the same as living in New York City. They seldom went to Manhattan to take advantage of all the cultural riches that this amazing island offered. They missed strolling on Fifth Avenue, taking hikes in Central Park and walking through miles of museum corridors with their incredible displays of art. Most of all, they missed the opera. So, three years after they had started in the Bronx, they moved both home and office to the Upper East Side of Manhattan.

At first, the office on Fifth Avenue and 90th

St., was like a deserted cave. They began to think that it all had been a huge mistake. But by sharing the on-call schedule with other neurosurgeons, Jacob began to pick up a few patients that came to him by way of the emergency room and an occasional referral from a busy colleague that wanted to take a day off. Soon, Rebecca's office charm and Nathan's surgical skill began to pay off just as it had been the case in the Bronx. The practice grew as his surgical successes began to be recognized by other doctors and Jacob never again experienced that feeling of still being seen as a student or not being respected by his colleagues. Now Jacob and Rebecca were able to afford subscription seats at the Metropolitan Opera. Their past had become distant on this island of many accents and diverse cultures.

Living in Manhattan brought a new dimension to the Nathans' way of living. They lived within walking distance of the Metropolitan Museum of Art. Sundays, when he was not on call, were reserved for a walk in Central Park and a short visit to the Met. Often, they were joined by Erzon, whose success now permitted him to live a life he never dreamed of. It was precisely during one of these Sunday outings that Erzon voiced the idea of retrieving the paintings he had buried in the concentration camp. They were standing in front of El Greco's "View of Toledo" and Jacob was saying:

"Do you realize that in spite of the expressionistic imagery and the fact that it was painted four centuries ago, Toledo looks now exactly as it does in this painting?"

Erzon did not respond, rather, Jacob felt that his friend was acting as if he were standing over hot coals.

"What's bothering you?"

Jacob noticed the extreme pallor on his friend's cheeks. In a tremulous voice Erzon began to voice his thoughts.

"Jacob, you know I have never talked about the sketches and paintings I did in the camp".

"I know. And I never, ever brought up the topic either."

"Well, it is I who is breaking the silence now." His eyes were looking at the wind that seemed to be battering the walled city of Toledo. "For the last few weeks, I have been thinking that it is time to retrieve those paintings." Nathan's muscles stiffened –he too was looking at the wind. "At night, as I begin to doze off, suddenly find myself fully awake and covered in sweat. The only thought that comes to my head is almost crazy. I think that my paintings are buried alive and that they are suffocating and that they must be rescued."

Finally, Jacob dared to look at his friend, "Let's sit on that bench and talk about it".

The two of them walked like two old men, supporting each other, to the solid wood bench and sat, still facing El Greco's masterpiece. It seemed that the night was even darker and the winds were blowing even stronger over medieval Toledo.

Still holding hands: "All I know is that I

must go back and find them. As much as in the past I closed my life to them, now it seems impossible to live without them".

"Erzon, I understand. You have finally achieved artistic success. People look at you with respect. They see you for what you are, and yet, you realize that they, your public, are missing half of the story."

"Yes! Yes, Jacob. It is that…and also, I am beginning to feel as if I am only half a person and part of me is buried back at the camp."

"Well, if you feel this strongly, then, you should go back."

"But Jacob, I cannot do it alone. You have to come with me. I need you."

Silence fell over the two friends. Now Jacob's thoughts were rushing in, as if his skull were too small for all of them to happen at the same time, making him feel dizzy. He had come a long way, since those years when Europe had covered itself with a mantle of darkness and loathing and murder and had finished with his family, leaving him like a living carcass. He had managed to pick up the pieces and continue with his studies, after a long and dark night where he had been a teenager before going to bed and had woken up a grown man after a protracted nightmare. What his friend was asking of him, was to go back into that long and awful night that he tried so hard to keep suppressed but never could.

"Do you know what you are asking of me?" The palms of his hands were drenched in sweat.

"Yes, my friend. I know, I know. But no

matter how horrible it may be to go back you too need to confront your past."

Deep down Nathan knew that part of him was, somehow, buried with his friend's paintings. "I don't know, Erzon. . . I have to ask Rebecca. . . I have an active surgical practice that also needs attention."

"Jacob, if there is a will, there is a way."

That night, when the two of them were resting in bed, after turning the lights off, Jacob asked Rebecca's advice.

"What should I do? Erzon is right but I am also afraid I'll go crazy if I go back."

Rebecca turned towards him, even though in the darkness of the room, she could only see his silhouette. "Jacob, my dear Jacob, I am afraid that the time has come for you to begin opening the door to the past. The two of you should go back and look for the hidden paintings. I think that when you find them, you will find also angels' wings."

It was a strange thing that Rebecca had said, about finding also angels' wings, but he was too busy covering up his pain, so he let it pass. The next morning, he discussed with Rebecca the logistics of how to take a couple of weeks off from his practice. First, he needed to get another neurosurgeon to cover his practice; then, he had to inform his patients of the impending trip, and lastly, he needed to give those patients that were scheduled to have surgery the option of canceling or being operated by another surgeon. When it was clear that he could accomplish these, he phoned Erzon and they chose the date for the trip.

A trip that he never thought to make, for he never thought he would survive his oppressors.

The two friends met at Kennedy International two hours before their scheduled departure. They felt as if insects were crawling under their skin and laughed when they discovered their common feelings. Their travel would take them by plane to England and then to Germany. From Germany they would take the train into Poland and after an overnight stay in Krakow, another short train ride to their final destination.

During the flight to Heathrow, they realized that the Polish government would not let them dig around looking for something inside the campgrounds. To get such a permit, they knew, would require intervention at government level, probably a formal request from the American and even Israeli governments. This would take months if not years. Now that they had made their minds to do it, they did not have the patience or the fortitude to wait. So, the decision was made to go the illegal way. They figured that what the Poles had done to them was far worse than what they were planning to do by simply digging in the middle of the night in search of the paintings.

On arrival to London, Jacob and Erzon took a taxi to The Central House Hotel, a small hotel located close to the business district. They had been told it was in walking distance to Buckingham Palace and the Tate Gallery. Although they were happy that their room had a bathroom with shower and toilet facilities, its peeling paint and dilapidated furniture were in great need of renovation. They decided to remain for a couple of days in London –a neutral territory– to adapt to the six-hour shift in their biological clocks. The last thing they needed was to be irritable and sleep deprived while entering the camp. So, the two friends spend two days visiting the wonderful art collection at the Tate and eating in inexpensive Indian restaurants that peppered the neighborhood. In their mind, they were trying to cope with the next leg of the trip, Germany.

From London to Berlin took less than two hours. It had taken them years to prepare mentally for this short hop, and now they were walking in the new Berlin, meandering and losing themselves among the congested pedestrian traffic, waiting to be stopped at any minute by a policeman or a soldier –"*Halt, verfluchte Juden* – Stop, damned Jews!*" Mindful that perhaps they could even recognize a guard from the camp – what would they do? It was so difficult to see all these people minding their own business and not wonder what they had done during the war. Had they spit on the Jews being herded to the train station? Had one of them saved a family by hiding them in the cellar of his home? Were they still Nazis or was it all forgotten? Jacob and Erzon knew these were questions that would never be answered. It had been difficult, especially at the beginning, when America was so involved in the reconstruction of Germany, to accept that Nazism was dead. Of course, they knew that not every German had been a Jew hater and that many wore Nazi hats to keep their families on the good side of the SS troupers, but still, it was very hard for the two of them to walk on the sidewalks of Berlin and to listen to a language that once was theirs and then became their enemies'. But as hard as this was, they also knew that the next leg of the trip, entering Poland, would be even more painful.

Berlin was just a stop on their way to the concentration camp and the paintings. They did not attempt to visit the old quarters of their childhood. Their families had lost all during the war. This was not to be the trip where they would confront the façades of their ancestral homes. To them, Germany was just a stop on the subway line to the camp in Poland.   Trains to Krakow did not leave from the central Berlin *Hauptbahnhof*, but rather from *Bahnhof Lichtenberg* on the eastern district. Approaching the train station with its loudspeakers announcing with precise German diction the arrivals and departures and the sound of screeching wheels and the voices of the passengers speaking in German, made them feel as if a frozen rod had been nailed through their spines.   They bought tickets and walked slowly towards the gate. They were not in a hurry to step onto a Polish train for this last leg of their trip.

They waited until the last moment before boarding the train.   Fortunately, the conductor spoke to them in German and not in Polish and indicated with his finger and a slight bow of his head the direction of their seats. This was not a cattle-car, far from it. It was a regular 2nd class passenger compartment and yet, as the train began rolling out of the station and the rhythmic crack, crack of the wheels and the bobbing of the car reached a constant beat, Jacob and Erzon interlaced their fingers in a grip that lasted for several minutes. The absence of fecal stench and the fact that there was no generalized grief in the rest of the passengers brought them back to reality. Little by little, looking at the landscape that glided fast on the other side of their window, they relaxed and fell into a deep sleep.

"Krakow! Krakow *Glowny!*" They woke up just in time to see the decaying city neighborhoods and the failing attempts to bring them back to life as the train, now traveling considerably slower, approached the center of town. There was no doubt that the post-war communist government had imposed some punishment on the Polish people –a kind of poetic justice, for what they had inflicted on the Jews, although not for that reason. The miraculous recovery of war-damaged West Germany had not been shared by Poland. The evidence of ruins and poverty were everywhere one looked. The average attire of people on the street was closer to that of a homeless person in the Bowery in New York.

This time, Erzon and Jacob had suitcases and American dollars that made the local people behave somewhat subserviently towards them. From *Krakow Glowny Station* they took a taxi to the Maximillian Hotel where they spent the night, not bothering to do any sightseeing. Early next morning, after a simple breakfast, they boarded the train to their final destination. The very sound of the Polish language was offensive to their ears. Intellectually they knew that the language itself could not be blamed for the actions of the people that spoke it, but the psychological laws of association are inescapable, and they could not help the feeling of repugnance that drove them almost to a constant state of nausea. Years before, when they first made this trip in those specially built "cattle-cars", they recalled seeing, through cracks in the wood-planks, the locals gesturing that they were doomed by sliding their extended fingers across their throats, and it had not escaped them that they were laughing and spitting in disgust as the wagons loaded with Jews approached their final destination: the camps from where the stench of burning flesh never stopped.

37

The two friends felt they were sharing a nightmare, but it was far worse for they knew they were not asleep. The train had stopped at the new station, just a few blocks from where it had stopped for them once before –rewriting history. They exited the train station and turned right on Powstancow Street and after going through the round-a-bout continued on Stanislawy Street from where both camps could be approached. Instinctively they checked if they were wearing the obligatory Star of David and quickly realized it was not required of Jews any longer. They could not believe that they were actually buying tickets to get into the camp. Here, the Carmelite nuns were planting crosses in memory of the Christians that had been slaughtered by the extermination machine. Sure, there was a need to remember those dead, but by excluding a proportional number of stars of David, an act that might have been motivated by piousness became offensive – the crosses should have been planted in the middle of a field of stars. But the two friends had not come to argue with the locals about the politics of memory, they had come with a single purpose in mind. They showed the tickets to the person at the gate, a man in his fifties, wearing a gray-green uniform and stinking to cigarette that automatically ripped them at the upper corner with his nicotine-stained fingers looking indifferently at the two friends as if they were transparent. A few feet away they could read on the metal bars of the entrance gates "*Arbeit Macht Frei*", Work Sets You Free. They were in.

This was the original camp. The Germans had commandeered existing Polish Army barracks that suited their purpose and saved them a good deal of money and time. Most buildings were stone sturdy, and they had remained basically unchanged. At the same time, the camp was too clean, it lacked the built-in factor that cemented all events during the war years, it lacked the smell of death, of fear, of hopelessness. Jacob and Erzon had not been part of this camp, but on one occasion they had been brought to clean up a building, Block 11. When they entered, they found eight bodies, the thinnest people they had yet seen. Later they learned that they had been killed by withholding food and water from them, after being tortured for some days. Their job was to carry the cadavers and deposit them against a stone wall next to the building; from there, another group of prisoners took the remains outside the camp.

But Erzon and Jacob were not tourists, they had come with a purpose. They exited the camp and began walking in the direction of their previous home, a sister camp so vast that at one point it had housed ninety thousand prisoners. A camp so deadly, that almost anyone that entered found death within its barbed wire confines. At its peak, several thousand prisoners were murdered each day. Death came either by gas, or disease, or by bullet. Bodies were disposed of in large pits dug just at the outskirts of the camp or incinerated in specially designed ovens.

They walked on the road next to the rail tracks and then turned to the west until they faced the massive brick building, with its central tower and ample arched gate –opened wide like the mouth of a hungry giant– through which trains brought hundreds of thousands of horrified prisoners to their final home. The parallax effect of the rusted tracks pulled them with a force that neither of them could resist even though they were petrified to proceed. It was as if it was calling them to approach:

> *"Come,*
> *come back to me,*
> *who failed to kill you*
> *so many years ago,*
> *let me show you*
> *how fertile is my ground today".*

The two friends walked under the great arch and entered the area where the trains used to stop and the prisoners used to disembark. This time, there was no train, no transport cars, there was no music, no barking dogs, no shouts of desperation, no Anna bleeding on the floor with her head pierced by a bayonet, only silence broken occasionally by a tourist guide.

How can it be put into words what two innocent inmates feel upon returning to a place worse than hell? Hell was a place where bad people were supposed to go after their death. This was no hell, here innocent people had been brought to suffer, to agonize and be murdered by individuals that should have gone to hell. If churches sanctify their martyrs because they suffered, this should be the holiest place on Earth; it should be walked upon without shoes. Jacob and Erzon stood there, just a few feet inside the entrance gate, their arms interlaced at the elbow, their bodies convulsing like puppets following the jerky rhythm of rapid bursts of breathing, their pupils dilated, their sight fogged by the tears welling and then running down their faces – marionettes jerked by their own sobs. They stood there for several minutes, holding to each other like two scared children, until they had emptied themselves of years of suppressed and repressed pain. They cried for all those years they had not cried. Finally, Erzon broke the spell.

"Jacob, we must mingle with the public, we cannot let our emotions sabotage our mission."

Yes, we do have a mission", he said drying his face with the sleeves of his jacket. "Let's move."

The camp was and was not the same than the one they almost died in. Some of the buildings were there, but everything had changed, as if time had twisted with one jerk the edge of reality. The large reception building where they were forced to take off all of their clothing and furtively had written their names on the walls, was still there, but it was silent and closed momentarily for repairs. The grounds where they were assembled day after day, after day, standing for hours on end, listening to the shouting of the guards and witnessing beatings and hangings, still was there but it was empty, void of people, of blood, of misery –just inhabited by the ghosts of all those who had died then and were still living today– now covered by the greenest grass one could imagine. Many of the barracks where they were corralled and forced to live under incredible filthy conditions remained standing and those missing still left an imprint over the tended ground, their presence announced by brick chimneys standing like a forest of fingers pointing to the sky. At the distance, they identified the building that once served as a "hospital", and not too far from it the shower building were tens of thousands of their fellow prisoners had been gassed to dead. The tall chimneys that bellowed continuously incinerated Jews were now ruins, not one reaching full height, some unrecognizable – twisted rubble of stone and rebar eagerly destroyed to erase what could never be forgotten.

The two friends walked like ghosts amidst the alleys between the barracks, at times expecting to hear a guard shouting at them, commanding them to stop. They passed several blocks of barracks or their remnants still scarring the ground. Jacob recognized Shimen's barrack, where he treated his first patient. Close to it was his own barrack, number 14, where once Abrum had cautioned him about the forced marches. Jacob knew he could not enter –coming this far was as far as he was willing or able to come. Erzon signaled his friend to follow him. Erzon's barrack was just a few yards away. They slowed down and began scouting the area, making sure no one was watching them. Erzon recognized his old dwelling. Two cement block steps led to the entrance door. On the left, as one faced the building, at the very corner between the steps and the concrete base of the barrack, he had buried his art treasure. The structure appeared intact. Now it was a matter of waiting until the camp closed for the night before they could dig for the paintings. Of course, they had no idea if they were going to find anything at all.

Erzon was still familiar with his barrack. The front door was locked, probably for security reasons. He was hoping that the barrack had not undergone major repairs. He remembered that the wooden planks next to the latrines where loose. He had used them as his escape route when he had to leave the barrack in the midst of darkness. Close to closing time, the two friends crawled by the side of the building, Erzon leading the way. After a few yards, Erzon began tapping the boards. One of them gave way. Now they had to do the unimaginable, they had to get into the barrack and wait for darkness before attempting their dig.

All was quiet inside. After liberation, the allied forces had forced the locals to clean the camp. Now, years later, all had been sanitized. But memories cannot be sanitized and perhaps because of their imagination or because their noses were gathering a few remaining molecules of the misery that once reigned here, Jacob and Erzon were assaulted by the stench of the barrack, just like in those horrible nights. All of a sudden, all their memories became alive. Squatting on the dirt floor, they heard the sounds of agony and they saw, just as clear as one can see a tree on a sunny day, Death walking in between the stacks of wooden bunks where once humans slept.

Jacob began to rock back and forth chanting those two nonsense words: "Ungehpuk
Ungehpak, Ungehpuk
Ungehpak, Ungehpuk
Ungehpak, Ungehpuk
Ungehpak, Ungehpuk
Ungehpak. . ." over and over as he had done so many times decades before when time was taking too long to pass by or hurt was too intense to withstand. He was rocking, like a lullaby, like a mother would rock a baby to hush the violent cry away. Erzon scooted close to his friend and placed an arm around him, like friends do in moments like this.

After a while, all began to quiet down and the barrack returned to its usual state of apparent solitude, inhabited by the thousand souls that once lived there. The sun had gone down and darkness prevailed.

Jacob whispered without looking up, "Do you think it's time to dig?"

"Yes, let's get to what we came here for."

The two, already exhausted by the wait, crawled out of the barrack and approached the concrete steps. They had brought two short garden spades from home, which they proceeded to unwrap and under the light provided by a decreasing quarter Moon they began to dig the hardened earth. Ten minutes later, Erzon felt the softness of cloth under the tip of his spade and dropping it began to scrape the dirt with his hands; Jacob joined his friend. Two minutes later they had exposed all around the bundle and with great care, Erzon freed it from its earthen confine. At that moment, they felt the presence of God. It was as if He had kept them alive to bear witness. They both felt as if an angel was hovering over their heads, and Jacob whispered, "Before the trip my wife said to me: '*I think that when you find them, you will find also angels' wings.*'"

It had seemed so big years ago, the package, and now it seemed so small. How could it be that all his painted memories were confined to that simple bundle? Yet, Erzon knew that half of himself had been buried along with his small paintings and that now, for the first time in years, he could attempt to feel whole once more. There was no time to waste. Unwrapping the package now was dangerous and it could damage its contents; Jacob had brought a pillowcase from the hotel and they placed the parcel inside. Now, more cautious than when the camp was teaming with Nazi guards, they began moving to the main exit gate. Lighting of the camp was not what it used to be but the incipient moon's rays allowed them to follow the rail tracks to the very entrance of the camp. The gate was locked. They retraced their steps and decided that the best way to exit the camp was by crawling under the barbed wire on either side of the gigantic building that extended on the sides of the central arched tower. This time there were no reflectors and no guards with dogs, and the fence was not electrified. They found a stretch of fence where the ground was eroded with more space to crawl under and made their escape through there.

When they arrived at their hotel, the night watchman almost did not let them in, but they showed their passports and produced a ten-dollar bill which seemed to do the trick. Once in their room, they extracted the package from the pillowcase and placed it on the floor under the one light that hung from the ceiling. They were fearful and excited.

"I think we should wash before unwrapping them."

"Yeah, that's a good idea."

Those were the only words said that night. When they woke up the next morning, the room was lit by sunlight and the noise of the traffic outside was almost unbearable. They realized that they had washed and fallen asleep without ever having opened their precious cargo. Exhausted or fearing a meltdown their brains had shut off. But now, after some sleep, they had collected themselves and were more ready to face their task. They approached the package in the middle of the room and as if following a signal, sat simultaneously in front of it. Erzon's hands were trembling as he proceeded to peel off the old dirty rags, exposing a layer of rubberized paper that cracked into a hundred pieces when he pulled at it. The paintings were stacked neatly. Only the top one had been damaged by a small water smudge. They counted forty-three paintings. At this point, Erzon placed them on the small table on one side of the room. They still had not mustered the courage needed to look at them. Jacob and his friend stood, each floating on a sea of memories and thoughts, like shipwrecked survivors in a storm waiting eagerly for the calm.

"I think it is time to look at them, Erzon."

"I know. All these years, when I looked in a mirror, I saw half a person, now, I will be able to see myself whole. I can't believe that this has happened… is happening."

They approached the stack and Erzon lifted delicately the first painting. The gallery text would read:

"Josaleh'
Burned wood and blood on wrapping paper
15 x 12 cm
1943."

One by one, they went over each painting. Each one bringing more pain than anyone could imagine. Finally, Erzon got to the last one:

"Cart with Bodies'
Earth and ashes on blanket
15 x 15 cm
1944", the gallery ticket next to it would read.

It was time to go back home, to New York, to their new friends and old habits, to their renewed world, to the work that was awaiting them.

38

Upon their arrival in New York, Jacob was confronted with a stack full of clinical consultations waiting for him in the office. Rebecca also had managed to reserve operating room time. She knew that several of the consultations would result in surgical procedures and although she did not know which ones would, thanks to her good standing with the surgery secretary in charge of reserving and assigning operating times, she had reserved one surgery slot every afternoon for the entire week. Jacob was astonished and pleased, and in no time had written real names to the reserved surgical blocks. He needed to work as much as possible to give his mind time to digest and absorb all that he had experienced in Europe.

As traumatic as the trip had been, it had helped Jacob begin to realize certain important concepts. At first it had all been dark, but little by little, like clouds dispersing after a stormy night, repressed thoughts and painful memories began to shape more clearly in Jacob's mind. And a thought began to take root: that after all he had experienced and overcome, he had survived his enemies and yet, he was still their prisoner. So was the cruelty of the Holocaust, that as long as the survivors lived holding on to their memories, they were in fact still prisoners. Only dying would bring final liberation. He was beginning to understand that just as a fire is not completely dead until there is no further smoke, so the Holocaust was not completely over but until there was no more pain. The experts and historians were wrong, it had not ended in 1945, it was still going on, he was being tormented and others were feeling pain and their children too and their children's children. It was a flame that could not die.

His days began with clinical rounds at seven in the morning and ended when, exhausted, he retired at ten in the evening after a quick dinner and a shower. What he had gone through during those few days in Europe was beyond anything he could put into words. He had told Rebecca some of it, but even speaking about it brought too much pain. Rebecca did not push. She knew that Jacob needed time to absorb and digest all the raw emotions generated by his trip. She was there ready to support him if needed. She knew that this workload was necessary and did not protest her husband's absence from home.

In the meantime, Erzon found renewed energy for his new project. On the morning after his arrival, he had called Robert to his studio and had shown him his old work for a new exhibit. Robert was so touched by it that for a few minutes he could not speak. He always had known that there was a part of Erzon that had always been closed to him, even to Erzon himself. But now, upon seeing these forty-three little sketches and paintings, for the first time he was able to penetrate that elusive part of his friend's soul.

"Erzon, these works are not only of great historic value but they also are small art jewels. You must exhibit them."

"I never thought they would see the light of day again."

"They are precious. They must be shown in a museum or a serious gallery. Tomorrow I will start looking for a venue."

"Thanks Robert. You know how important they are to me and I would not entrust them to anyone but you."

"Well, first things first. We have to photograph them. So, I'll contact John Pasternak and send him your way as soon as possible."

Robert's work paid off. The Jewish Museum on Fifth Avenue liked the work. The curator, Miriam Hohlköpfig, who had been searching for a good idea for an exhibit for quite some time, saw the value of the work immediately. She would see to it that the Museum publish a catalogue and she would write the introduction. Because of those quirks of life, the Museum had cancelled an exhibition on Nineteenth Century African Jewry and had an empty slot for that winter, in just a few months. A contract was negotiated. Needless to say, Robert was instrumental in representing Erzon. Because of him, Erzon got a large commission and a twenty-five percent cut on all proceeds from the catalogue sales. Robert also got the Museum to use its connections to secure a half hour PBS segment about the exhibit. In exchange for all these concessions, Erzon had to produce one new painting, inspired by the old works.

The weeks that followed demanded great emotional stamina from Erzon. He, like Jacob, was also confronting the demons of his past. Discovering his old, buried sketches had been liberating, but the liberated memories were a mixed bag of good and bad experiences. In order to paint the new work, Erzon was forced to confront every day his old work: Each image conjuring almost infinite pain and agony. It was not just the image of Josaleh that he saw, but he heard his soft, raspy voice with the sentences ending on an up lilt, as if questioning. He also saw Josaleh on that morning when they placed him on the cart, still alive, moving his jaw like a fish out of water. And he heard the squeaky wheels when the cart, pushed and pulled by two inmates, took him away forever, leaving the imprint of the wheels behind.

Each image became alive. Each image burned his flesh. At night, in his apartment, he was confronted with the living ghosts of those scenes he had visited during the day. Erzon spent his nights tossing and turning and sweating and crying. And then, one night, suddenly, it came to him. He rushed to his studio and began to sketch the preliminary lines of his new work. It would be a large roll perhaps as long as thirty feet. It would begin on the right with Hebrew and English words quoting the Scriptures "*Veatem Edai Veem Adonai* - Am Your God And You Are My Witnesses". Little by little, as the images moved to the left of the roll (as if one was reading Hebrew), the two sentences would be replaced by progressive graffiti, until at the very end on the left side of the role, only a dripping blood-colored word would remain "*Jude*".

When he finished painting his roll, Erzon was not aware that he had not left the studio and that he had not eaten in two weeks. When Robert found him, on that Tuesday morning, he first thought his friend was dead. He ran to Erzon who was lying on the floor.

"Erzon, Erzon", he shook him up in desperation, as if he could shake death out of a body. He was surprised when Erzon opened his eyes.

"Hi, Robert. Did you see it?" –referring to the painting. But of course he had not seen it, his mind concerned only for his friend's life.

"Seen what?"

"The painting!"

It was then that Robert looked at the wall behind him where Erzon had stretched his roll. He took an involuntary gasp and was not aware his mouth hung open. Still holding Erzon in his arms, he turned to confront the work head on. He looked at it in silence for several seconds, and then, in a voice as tender as an angel's said to his friend that now was fully awake and was supporting part of his weight on Robert's forearm:

"This is the most magnificent work of art I have ever seen. This is your masterpiece. You know you can die now and you still will be known forever."

He took his eyes away from the painting and looked at his friend and saw that he was smiling at him. Then, Robert came back to the reality of the moment and realized that Erzon needed to be taken to an emergency room. He placed him carefully on the floor, slipped a small pillow under his head, and ran to the phone to dial 9-1-1.

During the weeks preceding the opening of the exhibition, Erzon regained his strength. He was excited and happy. Painting had helped him control his demons. He visited Jacob and Rebecca on Friday nights and little by little the two friends opened up in front of Rebecca and recounted to her their experience in Germany and Poland during their recent visit. Jacob again was able to reach a compromise between his past memories and his current life and all began to normalize. They all were eagerly waiting and looking forward to the exhibit. Jacob was so proud to see the announcements in the New York Times:

"Erzon's Buried Treasure:

At the Jewish Museum from October 5 to January 11

Opening reception with the Artist at 8 p.m., October 5.

Tickets on sale at the door and by Ticketron"

He felt utterly happy for his friend that after so much bitterness was finally going to drink from the cup the sweet nectar that is the vindication and goal of all living great artists.

39

Jacob had finished operating on Ms. Paula Kenneth. She had suffered from a ruptured disc that compressed a nerve root to her right arm, giving her great pain. The surgery was curative. As was always his habit, he had just finished speaking with the family and was dictating the operative note when he heard the hospital page. He finished the paragraph and dialed the operator.

"Operator, this is Doctor Nathan."

"Doctor Nathan, one moment please, you have an outside call." After a few seconds of electronic gibberish, a human voice.

"Jacob? This is Robert."

"Oh, hi Robert, what can I do for you."

Silence and then: "Jacob, Erzon is dead."

Erzon, the man that had confronted and defeated Death on so many occasions during the horrible years of the war, the man that dared go back and face his accusers –or rather their ghosts– on the old torture turf had succumbed to a fourteen-year-old ghetto punk. According to witnesses, the boy recently minted by one of the many ghettos found in the South Bronx, had accosted Erzon on the corner of Madison and Eighty-Six.

"Mothaafucka, geehme yoa money", he had threatened with a knife. Erzon had handed him his wallet.

"Whoa. Seven dolla? And he had stabbed him seven times in the abdomen and chest. Erzon had not had time to be scared.

By the time the ambulance came. Erzon was dead. He had managed to write with his own blood something on the sidewalk. At first no one knew what it meant. But a Hassid passing by clarified the mystery, it says: "*Atem Edai*" (You are Witness). Three days later, a picture of the sidewalk with the Hebrew writing –Erzon's last drawing on this Earth– hung next to the twenty-six-foot-long painting on the Museum's wall. The line of people that formed to see the exhibit curled outside around two corners and never seemed to decrease, just advancing in silence, surrounded by the city noise that enveloped the good and the bad New York offered with equanimity.

Rebecca and Jacob never went to see their friend's paintings hanging on the Jewish Museum's walls. Jacob had seen them once in the camp before they were buried and then again fOllowing that horrible night when they had returned for them. Now, once more, Jacob felt betrayed by God.

40

Erzon's death created a wave of news articles against urban violence. People were disgusted with such an untimely and tragic death. Jacob knew that all this hype was as transitory as a shooting star in the darkened heavens. The world had tolerated the Holocaust, the Armenian genocide, the Cambodian killing fields, the Central African tribal massacres, the Argentinian *desaparecidos*, certainly the death of one artist was practically irrelevant, if not for the momentary soul cleansing that it afforded the sophisticated modern urban animal. But for Jacob, his friend's assassination had sealed shut forever any hope of ever reaching peace with God or man on this Earth. Besides Rebecca, the only thing he had left in this world was his work.

The Nathans' success in New York could not have happened without their failure in Birmingham, his first professional job. Even though Berlin was a distant memory, upon finishing his neurosurgical training, Jacob still wanted to teach and do research, to be an academic neurosurgeon. During his senior year in the training program, he had been voted as the most likely person to become chairman of a neurosurgery department within five years. So, it was with great pride that he accepted the position of Assistant Professor of Neurosurgery at Ivory University in Birmingham.

From talking with trainees from other neurosurgery programs, Jacob had become aware of how frequently sociopaths were in charge of academic neurosurgery departments. When he found out about the opening at Ivory, he asked his professors about Doctor Standall, the chairman at Ivory. All those who knew Doctor Standall, mostly from national meetings, had vouched for him: "He is a gentleman" was the consensus. Clearing this first obstacle, Jacob accepted an invitation to learn more about the program. Standall himself, came to pick him up at the airport. This gesture pleased and reassured Jacob.

There was no doubt, John Standall ran a tight ship and a very successful neurosurgery teaching program. There were ample laboratory facilities for research, and the equipment in the operating rooms was top notch. During his visit Jacob made sure to sound out several students and a couple of faculty members about the personal attributes of the chairman. All spoke very positively of him. At the end of the two-day visit, Standall took Jacob to the airport. Jacob would never forget the paternal and protective way in which Standall looked at him as he walked to the gate. He told Rebecca that his dream was coming true. A week later, Jacob received a letter formally offering him the position. The nightmare in Birmingham was soon to begin.

As part of his responsibilities and duties at Ivory, Doctor Nathan was to establish a research laboratory. He was given about 1200 square feet of space on the third floor of the research building.

During the first year, the department also provided enough funds to get him started while he obtained funding from the National Institutes of Health. As part of the program, the residents were required to rotate for four-months in a laboratory, so that Jacob did not have to spend money on assistants. In addition, Jacob was given an office in the clinical building, two doors away from the chairman's. He was assigned a secretary that served both as office manager and typist and took care of scheduling his patients. He was given operating room time on Monday mornings and Thursdays in the afternoon. Life was good.

During the first months at Ivory, Standall continued to show interest in Jacob's welfare. He visited the lab on several occasions and seemed to show a real interest in his research project. During Wednesday Conference, all seemed to have welcomed Nathan with open arms. Jacob had been a bit apprehensive when he had found out that Helen, one of the third-year residents, was Standall's wife, but during these first months, Jacob did not notice any preferential treatment toward her.

The colleague with whom he had the most contact was an Associate Professor who had come into the program four years earlier. His name was John Maxon. With a relatively empty surgical schedule during the first weeks, Jacob asked Maxon if it was all right to observe his surgeries. There was no doubt about it, Maxon was a superb surgeon. The way he handled aneurysms and arterio-venous malformations was excellent and Jacob did not mind learning from him. He and John hit it off well. John had gotten divorced just a few months before Jacob's first visit to Ivory. A cloak of secrecy surrounded the circumstances of that divorce, but all indications pointed at a rather abnormal relationship leading to an attempt at severe bodily harm.

Jacob's laboratory began to take shape little by little. The initial group of rats that had been injected with "compound DSB 24" was ready to be sacrificed. Jacob was curious to find out if this treatment had produced the Pituitary tumors that he was expecting. Four weeks after the original injections were given Jacob sacrificed the dozen experimental rats and their paired control group. He had perfused them with formalin and had placed their heads, duly marked, in small jars.

"Hey, John, I am about to start my autopsies on these guys. Do you want to come and watch?"

It was a Wednesday evening. Neither he nor Maxon were on call, making it about the best time to work and not be interrupted. Rebecca did not mind Jacob's absence; she knew how important this first experiment was for his academic success.

"Don't start without me. I'll be there in twenty minutes".

Jacob had put on a plastic apron and latex gloves. He definitely did not like to get formalin all over. He hated the odor that reminded him of his days at the morgue studying anatomy on his assigned cadaver. With small Lecksell rongeurs, he removed the skull vault of one of the control rats; he did not want to practice the opening technique on one of the DSBs. Maintaining the rodent's head fixed between his thumb and index finger, he expertly lifted the exposed brain, sectioning the olfactory bulbs, exposing the base of the skull. There, seated on the Sella Turcica, was the glistening white of a normal gland.

"OK, let's get one of the DSBs", he said to John full of excitement.

Jacob removed the skull and the brain with confidence. As he exposed the Sella, a large hemorrhagic tumor originating in the Pituitary gland could be seen.

"Oowhaooo!". John was impressed.

They proceeded to expose the remaining glands. Eleven out of twelve contained tumors; none of the controls had them. It was a perfect experiment. Now, having a reliable way to induce tumors in the Pituitary, Jacob could begin investigating what were the factors that would make them grow worse, or inhibit their development. He had the perfect grant proposal to write.

A week later, Doctor Standall visited the laboratory and got all the results firsthand from Jacob, who made no effort to hide his excitement. In the meantime, his clinical practice began to grow. Nathan's first case was an unforgettable one. He had overheard Joan, his secretary, in a telephone conversation.

Joan had said, "Good morning Mrs. McFadden."

…"Oh, he is very good"…

…"No, he just joined the clinic"…

…"No, he was not born here"…

..."Germany"...

..."He is as good as any American"...

..."If you insist, I can transfer you to another "...

..."You'll be pleased"...

..."Next Tuesday at Nine".

"Joan, what was that all about?" Jacob inquired.

"Oh, some folks from South Georgia that never have seen a foreigner and were concerned that their daughter be seen by the best".

Claire McFadden was the name of his first private patient at Ivory. Her parents brought her on Tuesday. As soon as they entered the office, Jacob observed that the girl had a big head, but even worse, it appeared as if she had a second head growing off the side, behind her right ear. She did not appear in great distress. Her parents were both short, and somewhat obese. They had dressed up for the occasion. Claire was 14 years old and lived in an institution for "chronic children", where she was visited by her parents about once or twice a year. Suddenly, after all those years, they had finally been overcome by guilt and had decided to do something about Claire's situation.

When she was one year old, Claire had contracted meningitis. A few weeks after she was successfully treated with antibiotics, she had become sleepy and had stopped eating. Her parents took her to the local doctor and he in turn transferred her to Municipal Hospital where a diagnosis of hydrocephalus secondary to complications arising from her meningitis was made and had placed a ventricular shunt to divert all the cerebrospinal fluid from her head into her belly where it got reabsorbed back into the blood stream. As Claire grew older, they realized that she was not developing like their other children and eventually placed her in the "home".

Jacob ordered a CT scan of Claire's head and asked Joan to re-schedule them for the following day or at their convenience. The CT scan demonstrated that Claire's shunt had stopped working many years ago, but instead of killing her, the cerebrospinal fluid, under pressure, had escaped around the surface of the tubing and into the space between her scalp and the skull. There, somehow, it got reabsorbed into the blood. But throughout all those years, the excess pressure and irritation from the fluid had made the bone of her skull react by producing more bone; in fact, she had what looked like a sea-sponge growing from the skull behind her right ear. The whole thing was almost of the size of her head. It was truly grotesque. Jacob explained all the facts to the parents and the girl, who did not appear to be mentally retarded, and they all agreed that she needed surgery to repair the damage.

Decades after that surgery, Jacob still could not forget the peculiar odor that came from the bony mass after he exposed it. It is practically impossible to describe an odor except by approximating it to other familiar odors, but Jacob could not think of any. It did not smell rotten, or sour; it wasn't a sweet odor, the closest thing Jacob could come up with is that it smelled dusty, even though wet. In any event, in conjunction with the appearance of foamy bone, this became one of the most memorable surgical cases of his life.

With Claire anesthetized, Jacob positioned the child on her side, mass side up. The growth was about the size of a grapefruit, covered sparsely with tufts of hair. The incision needed to account for extensive resection of the excess skin. When he cut deep into the skin, he saw the white, spongy bone and then he was hit by that peculiar dusty odor. He drilled the exuberant bone away, and then he proceeded to introduce a new shunt system to divert the cerebrospinal fluid. After the final sutures were in place, Claire's head was that of a normal looking person. On a clinic visit one month after the surgery, her parents took many photographs of their daughter standing next to her foreign- born savior.

A few months later Standall asked Jacob to visit him in his lab. When Jacob arrived, Standall handed him a grant proposal that he had written. He wanted his opinion; it was clear that he was not permitted to take the proposal out of the lab. Jacob sat down and began reading. It was about developing Pituitary tumors in rats. Jacob was quite disturbed by it. The proposal was along the same lines of his own. But how could he tell this to his boss? Or even worse, had his boss copied Nathan's proposal?

"Well…" said Standall, "What'd you think?"

Jacob had to be careful. He was potentially walking on razorblades.

"I think it is good, but I would expand on the histology section. It seems somewhat weak to me and I think they could question you on it."

Standall appeared to take Jacob's criticism without any problem.

Both Jacob and Standall had submitted their grant proposals to the National Institutes of Health. Four months later, Jacob's was approved and Standall's was not, precisely on the grounds that it had a weak histology section, as Jacob had suggested. One week later Jacob learned that Joan was no longer his full-time secretary.

Jacob continued developing his laboratory and his clinical practice. On one occasion, during Wednesday Conference, Standall questioned Nathan's handling of a particular case. He suggested that the patient could have been served better if he had had a posterior lumbar inter-body fusion instead of the old fashion lateral fusion. At the end of the conference Jacob had asked Standall about the new procedure.

"So you think a posterior lumbar interbody fusion (PLIF) would have been better?"

"Oh yeah." Standall had replied. "It is a beautiful surgery, very complex and difficult. I have been going to Ohio two days a week for a couple of months to learn the procedure. You should learn it too".

Jacob was aware that his boss knew he had neither time nor money to be going off to Ohio, where the surgeon that developed that particular surgical technique worked. Jacob thought that Standall had mentioned it more to rub in the fact that he was the only one doing the

PLIFs at Ivory. On the other hand, Jacob thought that indeed, this could be a very good way to expand his surgical armamentarium to deal with many spinal problems. So, he called the chairman of the Anatomy Department and asked permission to work on a cadaver. He went to the library and studied the surgical technique that had been published in one of the recent issues of the *Journal of Neurosurgery*, made a Xerox copy of the paper and went to work in the Anatomy Lab. He remembered how much he hated the smell of formaldehyde and cadavers, but there was not much he could do about it. He had brought with him some surgical instruments that the paper recommended for the technique and began to expose the lower back of this unknown person that now was occupying the metal table in front of him. He retracted the muscles on either side of the spine, exposing the bony arches of the lumbar vertebrae number four and five and with the small chisel and hammer, sculpted away a window in between that permitted him to expose the spinal tube that contained all the lumbar nerves. He retracted it delicately to one side and again, working with the chisel he carved a square space between the two vertebral bones, taking part of the disc space as well. Then, from the hip of the cadaver, he cut out a small square of bone that he then tapped solidly into the inter-vertebral space he had just made. The surgery was finished. He thought the procedure was not as difficult as Standall had made it out to be. He practiced it again at another spinal level and felt he was ready to perform it on a real patient.

Soon enough, Jacob had the opportunity to perform his newly acquired surgical technique on one of his patients. The surgery went just fine. After that, it became routine for Jacob; no major problem. What Jacob did not know was that Standall deeply resented the fact that he was now performing PLIFs. Standall was a good surgeon, but he was not a superb surgeon and learning new techniques did not come easily to him. This business with the PLIF had been perceived as another personal blow after Jacob's research grant proposal was approved while Standall's was not.

Next, Standall complained to Nathan, that it was time to give more surgical experience to the residents, that he had not been hired to learn new surgical techniques but to teach old ones to the students. As of that moment Standall took away Jacob's access to the operating theater on Thursdays. In addition, Jacob was expected to share his Mondays' operating time with the residents, starting with Helen Standall. That evening Nathan called Maxon and the two of them went to a quiet bar near the hospital.

Jacob confided to John all the events that had transpired since the time Standall visited his laboratory culminating in the restrictions of secretarial help, operating time and the imposition of Standall's wife as his surgical student with further restriction on his personal surgery time. It was then that, for the first time, Maxon spoke of Doctor Richard Adsen. He had occupied the position that Jacob filled. He had lasted three years in the program, but after a series of humiliations, he had quit or been fired. Nathan learned also, that before Adsen there was a Robbins. He had lasted two years before being fired. And before Robbins there was a Richards. Maxon did not know of other particular cases, although he knew there had been others. Jacob was astounded by this information and saddened that his friend had never told him about the history of the position he now occupied. It appeared that Professor Standall used junior neurosurgeons as cannon fodder –just another kind of slave.

Jacob returned home and told Rebecca what he had learned that evening. It was a major let down. He had wanted to be a teacher of medicine since he was a teenager in Berlin. Now, once more, he had confirmed the accuracy of his observations while a student of neurosurgery: The chances of finding a departmental head that did not abuse of his power and was not a sociopath, were very small. He knew that he had to resign before he was fired. He would not allow Standall the pleasure of firing him! He also knew that his chances of finding another academic program that would take him without a letter of recommendation from Standall were zero. The only person that could have saved his academic life with a solid letter of recommendation and some personal calls was his old professor, Karlsman, and he was dead. How he missed his old professor. He had not just killed himself; he had killed his student's chances in the academic world. Now, the only option open was private practice. It was then, almost by chance, that he heard from a medical recruiter about the opening at the Graham Clinic in Florida. And Jacob saw that it offered him a kind of intermediate position between academic practice and solo practice. It had been God sent, he thought.

41

Jacob needed Rebecca constantly. She was to him the very ladder that would permit him to climb out of his personal hell towards the light. He saw in her all the beauty that so long ago had left his world; the very essence of goodness that he had thought did not exist any longer. The softness of her skin counteracted the memories of the sandpaper hardness and splinters of his barrack's bed. The perfume of her skin, especially around her mouth would serve as an eternal balsam against the putrid odors that surrounded him from the moment he had lost his freedom during all those nights and days he spent buried in his dark Paris apartment after the war had ended. Before he had met Rebecca, he had smelled the dead. His pillow, the air in the room, the food he ate when he could not stand the hunger any longer, the back of his hand when he checked it to see if it was rotten too, all had smelled of death. And then, she had appeared in his life.

After their chance meeting at the *Parc de Montsouris*, Jacob had wanted her with the same intensity he had craved solid food in the camps. He needed to be by her side in order to peel away the barbed wire he had worn all those years. At first, they continued meeting by the little lake in the park. They would promenade along the twisting path that led from one side of the park to the other and back. The trees were no longer green and most of the leaves were graying, but nothing had been as full of life as every inch of grass and trees and birds on that particular autumn in Paris.

Each afternoon, after lunch, they met by the bench. Then, they decided to meet in the mornings so that they could spend more time together. Jacob could not afford to pay for lunches at the local bistros. Rebecca, realizing Jacob's predicament, began bringing a small basket with bread and cheese and watery wine. Jacob adored her. He loved her from the first instant his eyes had seen her and every moment thereafter. She could sense the intense feelings that emanated from him and the dark pit that held so many secrets within his heart. She began to see in his intelligent eyes the very essence of his soul and she loved that soul.

The weeks passed and their love for one another began to soften the edges of the wounds they both carried. She knew of her parents' death and just as she remembered the two of them standing by the train station in Berlin when they sent her away to Paris, she also remembered what she had not seen but now imagined: those last moments before they died. The convoy train stopping at Buchenwald, unloading their cargo of human flesh –trash to the German eyes. She could sense, see, her mother holding on to her father's arm as she so often did when walking along the elegant promenades of Berlin on Sunday afternoons. She could hear the German soldiers' shouts and see the terror in her mother's eyes as they were separated. She could feel the tears in their eyes as each one in their own time realized they were going to die away from each other's reach.

Jacob was reluctant to take Rebecca to his apartment. He had known better living conditions than what he had now. There was nothing he could do to improve the empty, dark cavern that constituted his living quarters. Rebecca, suspecting that Jacob needed a helping hand with the décor of his room insisted on visiting him at home. Finally, one day, surprised by a sudden downpour while walking in the park, they had run for cover the few short blocks to his apartment. They climbed the stairs still chilled by the penetrating, cold rain. Her eyes darkened when she saw the prison cell that Jacob inhabited: dark, wasted, empty. They sat side by side on his bed and she leaned against his shoulder, her heart constricted by the desolation that surrounded this man she loved so much.   It was then that he had, for the first time, let her see some of his inner landscape; a sensitive and dark landscape that she would explore for the rest of her life. For an instant, he was immobile and his eyes were covered in tears.   In an almost inaudible voice he had said:

"I took bread away from dying men".

He began sobbing. How could he convey to anyone the eternal agony he experienced every waking moment, assaulted by the memories of such a simple gesture, a quick move of the hand as he passed by the crouching prisoners, too weak to lift their bread ration to their mouths. But if he had not done so, others would have. He knew he was a monster; he had murdered those people who had names and families and friends and he had taken their food away. How could he describe the pain of constant hunger gnawing at his entrails day and night, never quenched by the watery soup and the single piece of bread? How could anyone feel pity for him when he had stolen food from the dead? This was the very essence of the Nazi's wisdom, the ultimate crime, to make their victims feel like criminals, to convert a whole person into a fugitive within himself, thus, not capable of running away. Only death could free their souls, life, the very thing they had fought so hard to keep, was their jailer.

Rebecca remained still against his body until he calmed down. What could she reply to him that would make sense, that would sooth his open wounds? Nothing, she knew. Silence. And then:

"Jacob, we have to do something with your room. It is not possible to live here and not be depressed". She said playfully.

Jacob sat on the low bed, thinking of the color of his world. Night and day had the same dull opacity. Like when it is dusk and things lose their color for lack of light and yet one can tell that they are what they are, a rose is red, a jasmine is white, and the grass must be green as it used to be when he was just like any other child. But all the colors had been covered by ashes, stained by human residue.

"Look at the color of these drapes! They hardly let any light come through. No wonder you are sad most of the time" —as if she did not suspect the horrible ghosts that persecuted him.

"Jacob, would you let me change your room a little bit? Perhaps add a little color here and there?"

"Yes, Rebecca, you may change my room, just don't expect that I will change along with it".

But Jacob had been wrong. The new drapes, the small flowerpot with the decorative Van Gogh sunflowers, the small, bright blue carpet by his bed, they all added life to his room and a little crack of hope into his life. Rebecca could see a smile on his face where before there had been but the frown of dark desperation.

Rebecca had said: "How can you learn about Paris if you don't ride the *Métro*?" Jacob still resisted getting into the *Métro* and would recoil to the sound of a passing train. For him, the sound of wheels grating against the cold metal of railroad tracks brought horrible memories of his daily life in the camps. Once a week and at times almost every day, at eight-thirty in the morning, the train would stop a few hundred feet from his barrack and the story would be relived one more time: People with eyes temporarily blinded by the sudden light, erupting from the wagons, confused by the barking of the dogs and the shouting of the guards, eyes wide open in vain searching for dear ones, lines moving slowly, desperately and inexorably into certain death, realizing at one point that there would be no further opportunity to hold hands or embrace husbands, wives, children, parents or friends and say good-bye —and the acrid odor of the smoke billowing from the dark brick chimneys on the other side of the camp.

The war had ended. Jacob knew this. He also knew, logically, that the trains did not bring about death and desolation, so little by little he began to object less and less to Rebecca's idea of taking a ride on the *Métro*. Finally, on a Tuesday at eleven in the morning, the two had walked to the *Métro* station *Cité Universitaire* and climbed aboard. Rebecca did not tell Jacob he was hurting her as he held on tightly to her hand. They got off at *Luxembourg* and walked the few steps up to freedom and *Boulevard Saint Michel*. He had made it! It would take a few more rides for him to be more comfortable about it, but he had taken the first major step. They walked one block toward the large esplanade and then they strolled in the direction of the *Palais du Luxembourg*. The garden and the fountain had survived the occupation. Their beauty moved Jacob and made him feel even closer to Rebecca.

"I want to live the rest of my life with you", he said, "when I open my eyes in the mornings, your face should be my rising Sun". They embraced and kissed and felt as if God's finger was delicately touching them. They continued their walk, passing by the magnificent façade of the *L'Odéon*, and sat in a small sidewalk café on *Rue Racine*. It was the first time he had felt, if only briefly, like any other Frenchman.

The newly gained mobility permitted Rebecca to show Jacob the beauty of the city. Jacob was enchanted by the boulevards, the parks, the magnificence of the palaces and museums, the quiet beauty of the River Seine and the awesome skeletal height of the *Tour Eiffel* –all spared by the destructive power of the German war machine. Jacob liked especially the *Arc de Triomphe* and they often would sit on a small wooden bench by the corner of *Avenue Kléber* and watch the crazy traffic going round and round.

One day, Rebecca took Jacob to see *Notre Dame* – the church that had been built over the old church that had been built over an ancient Roman temple to Jupiter, establishing Christianity as the one main religion in the very core of France. Upon crossing the church's threshold, they fell into a gigantic space of cold and darkness, and then, as they followed the central corridor, the magnificence of the stained-glass windows with their solemn color prisms –still the original stained-glass installed centuries before– covered them in a protective blanket of subdued light and warmth; the old gothic church had done its miracle once more. When they exited *Notre Dame*, they crossed the Seine towards the left bank and turned left on *Rue St. Jacques* and then right onto a narrow street. The old church of *St. Séverin* seemed almost like a toy in comparison to *Notre Dame*. Attracted by the sound of music, they walked in. They sat on one of the benches towards the back and listened to the most beautiful concert they ever heard –the sound of the cello bouncing against peeling plaster and stone walls acquired a mellowness that made it almost as if angels were chanting the glory of love. Jacob could not take his eyes away from those gnarled fingers that seemed to sculpt the sounds away from the old instrument. Memories of his childhood rushed into his brain, memories boiling his entrails. He saw children's eyes –dark pupils– like a kaleidoscope of feelings covering a land that once had been shared. There were no sounds, no talk, a memory void of sentences and phrases, like a leafless winter tree, all silently marching on a rainy Sunday morning, naked feet splashing –chop, chop, chop– like drops of melting glory, like tears from dark angels hitting against the crystals of Jacob's window of memories, and Jacob felt his mouth curled in a smile as the past took one more step back, away.

"I want to listen to music with you at my side", he had whispered in her ear, and she turned and whispered: "Yes".

With marriage on the horizon, Jacob began to metamorphose. Winter in Paris can be gray and depressing, but for him, a clouded sky was nothing but the promise of more sun, and the dampness in the air was just but a soothing balm. The promises the future offered diminished his fear of trains, allowing them to explore more of the "City of Lights".   One day, they proposed to visit the *Tour Eiffel* and then have a picnic under a tree in the *Parc du Champ de Mars*.   Instead of getting off at *Ecole Militaire*, they exited at *Duroc*. They realized their error and began walking towards *Ave. de Saxe*. On their right they could see numerous buildings and then they saw the sign: *Hôpital Necker*. As if inspired by the same thought, Jacob and Rebecca came to the same idea: Jacob always had wanted to become a doctor. Perhaps, it was time he started working and what better place than at a hospital. Since his arrival to Paris, Jacob had had no desire to work. He had died at the camp and only his carcass had survived. At least he had thought so. But now, with a wedding in the near future, it was time to rejoin society. They sure could use the extra income.

They entered the main building and asked directions to the administration. A toothless nurse in a nun's habit took them across the street to a two-story brick building and wished them luck. And as luck would have it, there was an opening for a male, nurse assistant. Jacob began working on Monday of the following week. With his first paycheck also came an unexpected gift: he felt worthy. He was no longer a post-war parasite. He felt comfort in knowing that the money he received from the American Jewish Joint Distribution Committee could now go to someone else. He had been born again.

Now that the two of them were working, they could only visit with each other during evenings and weekends. Paris at night was as mesmerizing as during the day, just a different landscape. The town looked as if it were on a perpetual Christmas celebration. The weekends were reserved for long walks and visiting new neighborhoods. They discovered the palace of the *Louvre* and walked endlessly on the *Champs Elysées*. They ventured way passed the *Arc de Triomphe*, promenading on *Avenue Foch* and never ceased to be amazed by the luxury of the townhouses along its endless gardens. Then, they discovered the *Bois de Boulogne* and the infinite peace and solace that it offered –a preamble to New York's Central Park. They took boat rides on the lake and picnicked under a Willow tree by the water's edge. They lay next to each other on the grass and watched the clouds pass by. The winter was not as cold and spring brought with it a beauty that neither of them had expected as the graying grass became alive and the trees brought forth phosphorescent life in the form of verdant leaves.

They married in August of 1947, just weeks before *Rosh Hashanah*, the Jewish New Year. They married in the synagogue on *Rue des Tournelles* across the street from Rebecca's apartment. The temple had lost most of its furniture during the German occupation and now it was but a shadow of its glorious past. The rabbi had set a *Chuppah*, the wedding altar, in front of the wooden armoire that housed the only *Torah*. The ceremony had been very simple at their request. He wore the dark brown suit and a white shirt buttoned up to the top. She dressed all in black. They both wore a white silk ribbon around their left arm. Uncle Max, her Parisian protector, accompanied the bride to the altar where Jacob waited for her, wondering if this was all a dream. In front of the altar, at their request, there were seven empty chairs. On each one there was a white rose. And as the rabbi uttered the Hebrew chants and she walked slowly around her Jacob seven times, seven ghosts caressing white roses cried for their loved ones.

"*Mazel Tov*", the rabbi said after Jacob had broken the glass under his foot. Jacob and Rebecca embraced and kissed, and then she had turned towards Max who looked into her eyes and saw that he had fulfilled his promise to the Ledermans. He was not needed any longer and was enveloped by a deep satisfaction having accomplished one of the Mishnaic dictums: that one who saves one human life saves humanity.

Jacob felt feverish with desire. Rebecca was as lovely as ever and his lust for her could not be contained any longer. They embraced and kissed, but this time they did not hold back. He felt her tongue probing his mouth as she pressed her abdomen against his, moving, dancing to a rhythmic melody that emanated from her own desires. She unbuttoned his shirt and caressed his chest. Jacob worked on the buttons on the back of her dress that slipped to the floor. His hands caressed her back and felt the smoothness of her skin. He took a step back to look at her. She was even more beautiful than he had imagined. He felt all the blood rushing to his pelvis. Rebecca removed her bra exposing her breasts. Jacob caressed them with his hands and then kissed and sucked the firm nipples. Rebecca wanted to be penetrated, to feel him inside of her. They scrambled to the bed. Instinctively, his hand moved towards her pelvis and began caressing her. He felt her moisture as she guided his organ into hers. She felt the pain of his penis braking through her hymen and then a wave of pleasure came upon them as they had never experienced before. Laying side by side, still breathing heavily, they felt that they finally were really together, that the war was now behind them.

Soon after the wedding, the Nathans completed their application for visas to the United States. The Assistant to the Consul, Mr. John Parker, promised he would do as much as possible to get them approved. But neither of them had family in the States and soon they became another statistic. Weeks became months and months turned into years. Then, in the spring of 1950, their visas were approved and within days, they found themselves floating in the bowels of the steamer *Americo Vespucci* on route to New York. Two third-class tickets got them the cheapest possible accommodations on the ship, two berths, one on top of the other, in a windowless room, with rights to a common table for their meals that offered them spaghetti and meat sauce day after day like a broken record forgotten by the ship's chef. They could see the sea from an upper deck on those days when they were not curled in bed sickened by the constant harassment of the ocean's waves.

New York had received them without a welcoming band. The city's constant movement and turmoil, its hyper-kinetic state came as a shock to the Nathans. Berlin was but a memory and Paris was a lovers' garden, and New York was like a cold shower simultaneously terminating their dreams and marking the beginning of a new life. With the help of the American Jewish Congress, they got an apartment on the Lower East Side on the fourth floor of what was obviously a Jewish tenement. It was even smaller than their Paris apartment and much noisier. Down below, humans moved like ants, propelled by the desire to succeed, driven by their own demons, all wanting to achieve more than their parents had, drunk by the hustle and bustle that emanated from New York, the city that never went to sleep. Rebecca began working as a seamstress in a shop about two blocks away, and Jacob washed dishes at a nearby delicatessen. Work was hard and pay was low. There were so many displaced people looking for jobs that employers could generate a hundred applicants in one hour, just by word of mouth.

The Nathans knew that this had to be temporary. Their lives had not been spared so that they would end up in sweatshops. Jacob began attending Friday services at the local synagogue perhaps because his boss had insinuated it, or perhaps because his father had done so during those days when Jews were as free as any other free man. As luck would have it, one of the parishioners was Leo Rabotnick, the "book worm". They called him so because he had a printing shop. As Jacob and Leo began their friendship, neither knew what God was anticipating for them. Leo and his wife Rivka took it upon themselves to teach the Nathans English –without the language, they would be nothing but third-class citizens in a country that offered anyone that wanted it the chance of becoming a success, the land of milk and money, the land where dreams could come true. The four of them made it a ritual to have dinner at a small Chinese restaurant on Mott Street where they mixed English, French, Yiddish and German in the most colorful ways.   But Leo could sense that Jacob was not happy with his job and one day asked him what he wanted to do with the rest of his life.   Jacob told him of his desire to be a doctor.   Leo was much more informed about the American system than his friend.   He told him that in America one had to go to college before entering medical school.   As it turned out, Leo was negotiating a contract with the University of Chicago to print their college catalogue.   Without consulting the Nathans, he phoned the Dean of the College and asked him if he could accept Jacob as a student, in return he would not charge the University for printing the catalogue.   The Dean had been so touched by this gesture that he offered Jacob a scholarship.   This is how Jacob and Rebecca found themselves in the Windy City by the summer of 1952.

42

Jacob was now putting his walking stick to good use. If he was not pushing himself up with it on an inclined slope, he was parting the branches that came to greet him from the surrounding trees. He owned that cane for many years. Once it had been just another fallen branch, it could have belonged to any one of these same trees, half eaten by woodworms, leafless, covered with dirt, but he had seen the beauty hidden in it. For years he had no use for it and it remained resting in a dark corner of a closet. But, after retiring, he had moved to New Mexico with Rebecca, and suddenly the old walking stick got a second life. Somehow, he always knew there was going to be a time for his stick.

"Verfluchter Schweinhund !
Verfluchter Schweinhund !
Verfluchter Schweinhund !
Verfluchter Schweinhund !
Verfluchter Schweinhund !"

Each shouted "damned dirty dog" was followed by a horrible blow with the cane. The guard had rolled up the sleeves of his shirt. His muscular forearms were tattooed with swastikas. Nathan's arms had been tied behind his back and his feet were tied to a chain and hooked to a crossing beam resting on two large wooden posts about eight feet above the ground. The wooden stick with which he was being beaten was covered with blood and pieces of skin –his and others. Jacob had lost all sense of time. At first, he had been overwhelmed with utter horror. Each blow to his body produced so much pain that he wished for death. Then, almost imperceptibly, the pain began to ease and the rhythm of the blows began to lull him into a hypnotic state. He saw himself dressed in a white doctor's coat, wearing a white hat, walking down a long hospital corridor. Then he saw his parents applauding as he, covered in a black robe, received his diploma from the director of the medical school. Then, when he opened his eyes again, he felt horrible pain, as if his head was connected to his legs by a column of fire. All he could feel was the swooshing of the wooden cane followed by a flat resonant sound as his chest was struck and then, a profound pain as his battered flesh became a mass of contused muscle. Then darkness came to sooth him once more. The cane, the wood, the cane covered in Jewish flesh. His flesh.

43

God had begun to smile on the Nathans. The University had given Jacob a small stipend and a small apartment, a ten-minute walk to the quadrangle. Chicago was very hot in the summer and very cold in the winter, but to them, weather was not a concern. Jacob applied himself to study and Rebecca got a job as a secretary to a professor of French literature. At first, Jacob encountered great difficulty understanding academic English, it was a distant cousin of Leo Rabotnick's Lower East Side argot. Sentences appeared to have no end and some professors appeared to speak without making use of punctuation. But after a period of adjustment to the nuances of this "new language" Jacob's performance jumped to the top of his class. The years passed by like puffs of clouds on a windy day. At the beginning of his fourth year, he applied to Medical School. He was not surprised to be admitted on the first draft and to be given a full scholarship. He was again dreaming his Berlin dream.

Medical school was not easy. Jacob found that although the day had twenty-four hours, it seemed as if that was not enough to prepare the material for his classes. He was assigned a cadaver for anatomical dissection. This did not come as a surprise to Jacob, but after all the death and suffering he had seen, he did not expect to be so touched by this silent, formalin impregnated, human being. What bothered him the most was the lack of a name, so he baptized him "Erzon" in remembrance of his artist friend during the time in the camp and who he thought had died during the struggle of liberation. He spent many nights in the company of his new friend, Erzon, in turn learning all the secrets hidden in his cold, lifeless body.

Physiology opened to him a world he had never fathomed. Acquiring information was tedious and difficult, but it was never a chore. After finishing the basic sciences, Jacob moved into the clinical aspects of medicine. His teachers were surprised by what appeared as his almost innate ability to relate on a deeper plane to the sick. Pathology and medicine came and went and then, Jacob was confronted with surgery and he knew instantly that he wanted to become a surgeon. Then, a rotation in Neurology made him realize the complexity of the human brain and awakened in him a curiosity he never had before. Jacob realized he wanted to combine the two disciplines he liked the most. He consulted with Rebecca, for this had to be a decision made by the two of them. In addition to a year of internship and a year of surgery, he would have to train for five more years. Rebecca saw the enthusiasm in Jacob's eyes and recognized the spark of life and could not help but to live his dream as well.

44

The vegetation was quite dense in some places and Jacob had to watch carefully for openings between the branches so that he could pass without damaging the trees. During the hundreds of walks he took in his later years, he never damaged a tree. Sometimes he felt uneasy for hours after having stepped, inadvertently, on a sapling. He wondered how that young tree might have looked a hundred years later, and the sight of a flattened Piñon-child crushed by his boot horrified him. He always walked carefully, for he knew that even though this was high desert and the ground appeared to be mostly sand, it was really full of life. There had been occasions when he had seen thousands of large, black ants marching from one hole in the ground to another, carrying on their little backs small pieces of dried Piñon bark. Once, he was surprised to see out of the corner of his eye, something moving on the ground in a stealth fashion. When he looked again, he saw nothing and then it moved again. It was the first time he had seen a horned lizard. It stood, motionless, with its flat belly and its large head, covered with spines that gave its body the appearance of the rough sandy soil that surrounded it. Jacob realized he was never alone when he walked these hills. A gentle breeze brought two small birds to rest on a nearby branch and again he was assaulted by an old memory:

"But, he will be all right, won't he?" Jacob could hear those words and see the woman, with her baggy eyes, uttering them as if she were standing right next to the two little birds. But he knew she was decades away.

He had tried to be kind to her. Jacob had sensed how utterly dependent Mrs. Bartoli was on her husband. She had brought him to the hospital that morning, holding on to his arm, walking along the long corridor with its gaping doors –wounds– that led to the many private rooms along the neurosurgical floor. She had spoken for her husband when Jacob wanted a clinical history. Anthony Bartoli had taken good care of his family. He had always provided for all of them and now at age fifty-five, after forty years of smoking two packs of cigarettes a day, death had caught up with him. Anthony was lying on the bed, with his head high on two pillows and his shoes still on. He did not appear too ill. Only the barrel-shape chest and his rapid, shallow breathing and flaring nostrils insinuated his chronic emphysema. He made no attempt at answering the questions Doctor Nathan was posing to them, only she did.

And at the end, when it was time to explain to her what was going on with her husband, Jacob had taken some time to bring reality to Mrs. Bartoli in a way that would cause the least pain. He had gotten a copy of the X-rays and held them against the light coming through the window, as two little birds rested on the outside by the ledge, saying:

"You see Mrs. Bartoli, do you see this little ball here –pointing at a tumor in the cerebellum – well, that little ball alone could kill a person."

"But he is going to be all right, right?" she had urged, her voice coated in anxiety.

Jacob knew he had to be more assertive. "Well, do you see this other little ball here?" He looked at her, pointing at the right cerebral hemisphere on Mr. Bartoli's CT scan. "Well, this one alone could kill a person, but your husband has this one and this other one".

"But he will be O.K., will he? She had asked.

Jacob felt anger and irritation. Mr. Bartoli was paying the biological dues for his smoking sins. Each one of his five brain metastasis was an affirmation of the genetic laws that determine who could and who could not escape the consequences of smoking cigarettes decade after decade, even if his wife could not accept it.

"Mrs. Bartoli" Jacob had said in a soft, tender voice. "Your husband not only has these two tumors, but he also has another three on the left hemisphere of his brain, and I am not even counting the big one in his lung."

"Yes, yes, I know doctor, but will he be fine?"

Defeated, Jacob had replied, "We will do our best, Mrs. Bartoli. Our best". And he had walked out of the room never to forget her baggy eyes, dark, sunken, moist, sad, begging, wanting to be blind to reality.

How often he had walked that gray-walled corridor with blue green, soft carpet –that universal path to the daily rounds of pain– eagerly wanting to heal, to see a family holding hands, walking towards a home full of waiting smiles. But Death also walked that same corridor. Jacob felt betrayed and defeated when he approached the room of a condemned patient. He, the healer, had to remain calm while walking under the weight of a thousand years of sorrow. His eyes had to look into those eyes that held a thousand years of tears and in an almost casual, unaffected manner he would hear his voice saying:

"I don't have very good news to tell you. You have something in your brain that needs to be taken out... I cannot predict the final outcome; it may be years, or months, or even now".

And then, he would watch himself walking back into that long corridor with its gray walls and the carpet softened by the rivers of tears and sorrows that poured from under those doors, and he would feel his skin wrinkle.

How many times had he remembered that strange interaction? How many times he had heard those terrible words full of hope, how many times he had felt the pain in those eyes? And now, decades away, the whispering wind had brought those words back to him. The two little birds fluttered their wings and flew away, bringing him back to the moment.

He saw an opening between the branches of a large Juniper and a Piñon tree and determined he could go through. He followed the path indicated by the vegetation and passed by the only spot from where he could see to the west the distant Opera House on a ridge, perhaps four miles away. From where he was standing it looked like a spaceship with its wings suspended by giant cables descending from the clouds. The Opera became alive only during the summer months and attracted audiences from all over the world. The building was solid even though it resembled a giant tent with its sides opened to the air and its proscenium exposing the horizon and the distant Jemez Mountains and the starry New Mexico sky as backdrop for the performances. An early tailgate dinner had become a tradition, combining champagne, food, magnificent sunsets and blowing dust into an indelible experience.

45

Rebecca and Jacob held subscription tickets to the best seats in the Metropolitan Opera House. This was certainly quite a contrast from their experience during those first years in Paris. Then, poverty was queen and on the very few occasions they had gone to the opera, they could afford only the very cheapest of tickets, standing room. Then, like now, they marveled at the splendor of Beethoven's music. The darkness of the theater was soothing and the music, caressing. At first, one voice could be heard, and in a few bars a second voice joined in, and then a third one, and then a fourth. The vocal lines undulating in a hypnotic rhythm as the characters stood still, stiffened in their own thoughts, prisoners of their own destiny. And all along, that glorious music interlacing, like four ribbons of silk in the wind. Of all the operas he had ever heard, nothing touched him as much as the music of Beethoven's *Fidelio* quartet. He grabbed Rebecca's hand and squeezed it sweetly as she looked at him for an instant and watched, without disturbing him the tears brimming in his eyes. Jacob thought that if God had composed music, He would have written *Fidelio*.

Jacob's neurosurgical practice had brought success and money. For years he and Rebecca had sacrificed in order to accomplish something and now they could enjoy the fruits of their efforts. But Rebecca knew that Jacob did not react to beauty in the same way others did. For that matter, not even as she did. For him, beauty never came alone; it always carried the fears of a past devoid of it. But if Jacob was a prisoner of his eternal battles with humanity's cruelty, he was also capable of great enjoyment, a natural result of the contrasts that good and evil played in his heart.

Seated comfortably with Rebecca by his side amidst the splendor of the opera house and the magnificence of the music that engulfed him like warm caressing waters, Jacob was transported to the day when he and Rebecca first made a date to go to L'*Operà*. It had been during the winter of 1946. Paris was bursting with vitality as the post-war brought to the City of Lights a renewed energy.

46

Jacob had met Rebecca almost by accident and yet with the certainty that their meeting was as destined as the path of the stars in heaven. It had been so long since Jacob had wandered outside his apartment to enjoy a sunny day that his skin had turned a yellowish-white color. He had been victim to another wave of guilt and depression and, save for the brief periods when he ventured out to get food or to check with the relief organization, he confined himself to his boarding house room. He kept the shutters drawn shut, often contemplating the color print framed in a thin ribbon of wood, hanging from the wall opposite the window of his dilapidated one-bedroom apartment. That color print of a painting by an unknown artist depicted a landscape of sand dunes in the Saharan desert under a light blue sky –the same colors that would captivate him decades later in New Mexico. Jacob would sit for hours on end, in silence, contemplating the little picture of sky and sand. Time would pass as if the life bursting at the seams outside his window did not matter, as if he had been forgotten by the Angel of Death during a last pass at the concentration camp and now, he needed to wait for another, this time, successful pass.

But then, one day –a Thursday– he had left his room and ventured out. He even walked down *Rue de Rungis* and for the first time in months dared cross the wide *Rue de L'Amiral*

Mouchez and had walked into the *Parc de Montsouris* that years of war and turmoil had not damaged. It was still resplendent with its trees and grass and little lake. Perhaps it had been the Sun that on that autumn day was offering the last of its warmth before winter took hold of Paris. Perhaps it had been destiny. He had been walking for almost an hour when he decided to sit on a bench by the tip of the lake on the northeast corner of the park. The pigeons that had flown away when he approached now began to land close to him expecting to be fed, but Jacob had nothing to offer. He had lost track of time and then was awakened by the crystalline voice of the most beautiful woman he had ever seen:

"*Pardon, il est un tres jolie lac, n'est ce pas*? She said in fluent French with a slight accent. Her skin was light olive and her elongated face and green eyes covered him with a blanket of desire that would never abandon him for the rest of his life.

"*Oui, il est tres jolie*", Jacob replied with a heavy German accent, afraid to disperse the spell.

She sat at the other end of the bench and they both watched the gentle waters covered with lotus and the pigeons trying to peck at food where there was none. Soon they realized that they both spoke German and then forever their lives became intertwined. How could all change in so little time? Just as he had seen his life swallowed into the darkest hole by the single command of "*Juden Raus*", his life now bloomed as he first saw her smiling. Suddenly, the 13th *arrondissement* ceased to be gray and instead it became lively. The apartment was not a jail any longer. They took short walks and discovered the magnificence of the *Place d'Italie* and the gigantic solemnity of the *Hôpital Salpetrière* and the boisterous life that continuously moved like flowing waters from a cascade along the many boulevards.   All of this just around his one-bedroom apartment!

That winter, Jacob and Rebecca went to the opera. He had taken her to dinner at an eatery on the corner of *Rue Tronchet*, just behind the *Eglise de la Madelaine*. It was the most expensive place he had ever eaten in since the war had started, and the food had tasted heavenly in her company. Then, they had walked on the *Boulevard de la Madeleine* to the *Place de l'Opèrà*.

He had bought tickets in advance and showed them to the usher with a pride that had been absent from his countenance for many years. It did not matter that his suit was wrinkled and a size too big or that the tickets were for the very back of the theater, in the standing room section; all it mattered was that he had taken her to the opera. They had marveled at the beauty of the interior of the house with its pastel and gold atmosphere and when the lights dimmed and the orchestra began pouring its hunting sound, it seemed that all the horrors of the war were being covered by a gentle ointment, a magic potion. Beethoven's only opera was taking life and soon they both became slaves to the hypnotic power of the rhythmic music that with the might of the genius of its composer covered all spectators with its magical tapestry of deep thoughts and love and soaring freedom.

Rebecca was the perfect woman for Jacob: as he was impulsive and assertive, she was reserved and moderate; as he was dark and moody, she was light spirited and stable. His stubborn determination was balanced by her flexible approach to life. But life had not been easy for Rebecca. She had arrived in the "City of Lights" in 1939. The move had not been pleasant or comfortable, but given the alternatives, it turned out to be the best decision her family ever made.

47

Things were getting more and more difficult for the German Jewish community. Rebecca's grandfather, Albert Lederman, had been a decorated war hero of the German army during the Great War for having rescued two wounded comrades that had been left behind on a stretch of no man's land on the Western Front. His son, Friederich, had gotten the best education a young man could get, and had obtained his degree in Medicine at the University of Munich. He had a successful practice that permitted him to marry Eva, Rebecca's mother, and build a house close to the *Englischer Garten* on *Königinstrasse*, close to the university in Berlin. Eva and Rebecca loved their daily promenades on the magnificent winding paths of the garden. But during the 1930's, the beauty of the German culture and landscape began to be clouded with more and more edicts against people of Jewish descent. On a gloriously beautiful evening on May 10, 1933, Doctor Lederman witnessed the beginning of the destruction of German culture. Hundreds of students and even some professors, stormed into the University Library and into his own office, removing thousands of "impure" books and burned them in a gigantic pyre on the central quadrangle on *Leopoldstrasse*.

Two years later, German Jews were deprived of their citizenship as part of the "Nuremberg Laws". Now, the Lederman's were not being ostracized for practicing the Jewish religion, but for being of the Jewish race. Soon thereafter, Eva and her Rebecca had to shorten their daily outings into the *Englischer Garten* because Jews were forbidden to sit on park benches. The signs of *"Juden unerwünscht"* – Jews unwelcome– were everywhere.

Finally, when in July of 1938, Friederich was deprived of his right to see "German" patients and was limited to seeing only Jews, he thought it would be best to send their only daughter to a safe haven while things cooled down. The Ledermans had applied for a visa to the United States. Rebecca remembered the days of long lines outside the American Consulate offices. Being in line all day did not guaranty they would be seen. Often they returned home filled with anxiety, fearing that their visas having been approved had been cancelled and given to some other family while they waited outside the embassy in vain. The three of them would sit by the fireplace and dream of living in America. Friederich preferred New York. He had heard of the large medical schools; he would teach at one of them. Eva had heard beautiful things of a place called San Francisco, on the other side of America, far, far away from Germany. Rebecca had no opinion. She felt scared and excited at the same time. It had been weeks since she had gone to her regular school. Jewish children were being beaten by their Christian classmates. A place where she could play and not fear for her life sounded almost like a distant dream. In fact, that dream was shattered by the news from the

American embassy that their visas had been denied.

So it came to pass, that one rainy morning in the month of October of 1938, the Lederman's found themselves standing at the corner of *Luisenstrasse* and *Dachauer Strasse*, with the magnificent *Hauptbahnhof* –the rail station– looming in the drizzle at the distance. Rebecca was fourteen years old, and even though she did not know it at the time, she was saying goodbye to her parents for the last time. In just three weeks "*Kristallnacht*" was to take place on a cold November night. Government agents and German citizens, under instruction from Reinhard Heydrich, proceeded to attack Jews and Jewish property throughout Germany. At the end of the two-day rampage, many Jewish cemeteries were defaced, 270 synagogues were burned and many more damaged, more than 7,000 shops were destroyed, and 30,000 Jews were taken to concentration camps. Doctor Lederman spent most of the following week tending to the wounds of hundreds of Jews. A few weeks later, on Christmas morning of 1938, the Lederman's were taken to Buchenwald, a slave labor camp built amidst a beech forest near Weimar where its commander, Karl Otto Koch and his wife, *Die Hexe von Buchenwald* (the Witch of Buchenwald) spent their time adjudicating Jews to working in the ammunition factory, or serving as guinea pigs in medical experiments, or simply to dying in mass killings. They never left their German land.

48

After a daylong trip, Rebecca arrived at *Gare du Nord*, with a winter coat hanging from her arm and a single valise filled with clothing and a family photograph. The French connection that her parents had arranged for her was standing by the tracks holding a sign with her name: there was no music welcoming her to Paris. The drizzle that had framed her departure from Munich was now welcoming her to Paris. Paris –*La Ville Lumière*, the city of lights, the romantic heart of Europe, filled with magnificent museums and art galleries, with theaters, couples kissing under the shade of thousands of trees along its many boulevards and parks, physically transformed by Haussmann under the reign of Napoleon III– can be cold and windy and gray just before winter sets in.

Uncle Max was not really her uncle. He worked for the Displaced Persons Agency, German section. Max was built like a tank. He was short and muscular and wore a light brown raincoat and a dark blue beret. His face was square and indistinct except for a pencil thin mustache. The hardness of his body contrasted with the softness of his smile. He spoke German with a light accent but quite fluently. The Ledermans had sent five thousand dollars to cover resettlement expenses and room and board, as well as for a small living allowance that the Agency was to give Rebecca on a monthly basis. He explained to Rebecca that he was her contact with the Agency and that now he was going to take her to the home of the Giraud family. He reassured her that they would take good care of her during the few months before she could go back to Germany, after the nightmare ended.

The trip to the Girauds seemed to take an eternity. Rebecca was emotionally exhausted. Within a day's time she had been submitted to a very traumatic separation from her parents and an arrival to a strange city of which she knew practically nothing. It seemed that they changed *Métro* at least once and that finally they had exited by a large fountain and even larger plaza characterized by being the major intersection of several important streets. Max pointed at a tile sign on the wall at the exit from the *Métro* and reminded her that this was a name to remember if she was not to get lost in Paris: *Métro Daumesnil*. He took her valise and her hand and they walked on *Rue Claude* and made a left turn on *Rue Cannebière*. Just across from the church of *Saint Esprit*, through a set of double wooden doors painted in a light blue, lived the Giraud family. They climbed the stairs to the third floor and knocked at the door. After a moment, Madame Giraud opened the door and welcomed Rebecca with a brief embrace. Her husband was sitting on a large and comfortable chair next to the window that oversaw the side of the church. He stood and after shaking hands with Max, knelt on the floor in front of Rebecca. Eye to eye, he welcomed her to his home. Max translated: "Monsieur Giraud says that you are most welcome to his home… That you should consider it now also your home… That you and Giselle will now be his family". Giselle appeared on the entrance door to the apartment, out of breath as she had run from a neighbor's house. Giselle was about the same height as Rebecca, with brunette hair and light complexion. They probably were about the same age. She grabbed Rebecca by her hand and took her to her room closing the door behind them. This concluded Rebecca's welcoming to Paris.

During the weeks that followed, Rebecca was taught the rudiments of the French language. The Agency had given Madame Giraud a German/French dictionary and a book of French grammar. Mornings and afternoons the two of them sat by the kitchen table going over and over the lessons. Since no one spoke German in the Giraud household, Rebecca could only communicate in French with her adoptive family. At first, all she could pick up were a series of interminable sounds that had no breaks and no beginnings or endings, but by the end of her first month with the Girauds, Rebecca began to differentiate words that seemed to be embedded in the long sentences and would pop up once in a while. By the end of her second month, she was beginning to speak and could understand when they spoke to her slowly. It had been agreed that it would be best if Rebecca did not leave the apartment until she had a certain command of the language and for this reason alone, by the end of the fourth month, Rebecca was quite fluent in

French, having retained only a slight accent from her Teutonic past.

In January of 1939, Max came unannounced to visit her at the Girauds. Rebecca sensed immediately that something was wrong. Max sat next to her by the kitchen table where she was studying her French, held her hands and informed her of her parents' death. He did not tell her that on arriving in Buchenwald, her parents had managed to stay together and marched through the iron gates with their official welcoming sign: "*Jedem das Seine*" (Everyone Gets What They Deserves). He did not tell her that when all the deportees were gathered at the camp's *Appelplatz* and her parents had realized the degradation that they were about to suffer, without saying a word, they had embraced and then, running to the front of the group had shouted at the camp commandant: "You are a murderer! Hitler is a filthy murderer!" Within seconds, they had been shot. Dying, they kept looking at each other. It did not seem like the end, although they knew it was. They knew the day had brought the darkest tempest in their otherwise gentle lives. They missed the puffs of white clouds and gentle breezes bringing the scent of freshly baked bread. Their eyes touched each other knowing that there would be no more walks through curving paths, and that their hands would not hold each other during afternoon walks through the park as they watched the shadow of the Willow advancing silently over the gentle grass. As the sounds of the explosive shots reached them, Friederich remembered the day when he had first seen the smoothness of her face framed by all the shrilling noise of Berlin's rush-hour traffic and Eva remembered that he was wearing poetry on his head.

49

Giselle and Rebecca shared one bedroom. Giselle's bed was moved to one side of the room and a second bed was placed ninety degrees to it. The low table that previously occupied the center of the room was moved to fill the corner made by the two beds. They agreed to sleep head-to-head so that they could share a small lamp and chat late at night without having to raise their voices.

Giselle was a typical French girl. She was Catholic. Up to the time when her family was contacted by the Agency, she was of the impression that Jews were a kind of secretive, dangerous people. At school, at one point she had even heard that Jews had horns and tails, like the Devil, and that they sanded down their horns and covered the stumps with their hair. Most of her friends knew that the Jews had killed Christ and that because of this, they had been cursed. At home, she almost never heard her parents speak about the Jews. But one day, a man by the name of Max Rosenberg had shown up at their door and had asked if he could visit with them for a few minutes. From Max, Giselle learned that Germany was systematically taking away all civilian rights from their Jewish population. She learned that Jews were not permitted to sell their goods to Christian Germans and that they were being forced out of their professions and homes. She had seen her parents' reaction to Max's story. Max was asked to come back in a few days. Max had first approached Monsieur Giraud at his office. It was obvious that the Agency had already investigated the attitude of the Giraud family toward Jews. At that time, Max had suggested the possibility of housing a Jewish girl. During his visit to the Giraud's apartment, Max evaluated how safe it would be to house a Jewish girl in their household. It was a near perfect situation as the apartment was just across the street from a church. Only Giselle had to accept the new companion, without her cooperation Rebecca could not move in.

After Max's visit, Giselle's parents had spoken to her about the Jewish issue. It was important that she understood the predicament of the Jews of Germany –how for the past few years the Germans had been demonizing the Jews, blaming them for all the unemployment and poverty of the German workers, little by little making them look like vermin, too dirty to be part of the national health insurance, or to do business with Aryan Germans, or have the rights of citizenship and how they were being forced to dispose of their properties and flee to other countries throughout the world. They told her of a particular family that was going to send their daughter away, to keep her out of danger. For the first time Giselle was confronted with the reality of the Jews. How could they be devils and have so little power, not even capable of defending themselves? Her parents were not surprised to hear from their daughter all the misconceptions she had heard. Patiently they explained the truth to Giselle. More importantly, would she be willing to share her room and her life with another girl, her own age? How could she close the door to another human being? Had it not been Jesus himself who had said that we should love others?

The night of Max's first visit, Giselle had a dream. She dreamed that one day when she came back from school there was a hole where her house had stood just that morning. She ran back to the school, but her professors came running out, throwing stones and shouting "We hate girls like Giselle". Surprised, she had turned around and begun running away from them, but the harder she ran the slower she moved. Then, she saw a priest running at the front of all her teachers, he was foaming at the mouth. He was swinging a hammer and two horns and was shouting "I am going to nail them on your forehead!" And she awakened covered in sweat. At breakfast, she told her parents that she was ready for a sister.

On the day of Rebecca's arrival to the Giraud's, Giselle took Rebecca to her room closing the door behind them; then, taking Rebecca's face in her hands delicately searched for any signs of shaven horns. Rebecca remained still, thinking she was being greeted, albeit in a peculiar way. Then, Rebecca felt a kiss on her forehead and when she looked up, she saw Giselle's eyes brimming with tears and they embraced. During the first weeks, until late at night the two of them chatted, each tucked in her own bed, one in German and the other in French with the deep conviction that all that needed to be said was being said. They became best friends.

On the advice of the Agency, The Girauds did not place Rebecca in school, rather, Giselle shared her books and notes and homework assignments with Rebecca. It had been determined that it was safer if Rebecca was not placed in any institution that required formal applications, the less the paper trail the better. The two friends were free to roam the streets of Paris on their own and share all the beauty that was so easy to find at the turn of every corner. They especially liked to walk in the *Bois de Vincennes* and frequently took a small pouch with bread and cold cuts and had a feast by the shores of *Lac Daumesnil*. Sometimes they spent hours in one of the small rental boats by the lake, sharing their dreams, while reclining against each other, contemplating the rapidly changing Parisian cloud patterns.

Then, everything changed. In May 1940 the Germans punched through the beautiful landscape of the Ardennes region, considered by the French and British intelligence to be a terrain too wild and difficult to serve as a battle ground for the German forces, and by June, three weeks later, had occupied Paris and would not leave it until 1944. German uniforms were everywhere. Every time Rebecca saw a German soldier, she could not help but wonder if he had been the one that killed her parents –she feared and loathed them at the same time. The comings and goings of the two friends became much more restricted. They could not be spontaneous as they once had been. The Germans liked many of the sites the girls frequented. Giselle and Rebecca stopped visiting the *Champs Elysée's*, the *Arc de Triomphe*, and the *Louvre* and its magnificent gardens. They became much more cautious during their outings, often visiting Catholic churches and cemeteries, places it was assumed Jews would not frequent. Giselle gave Rebecca one of her golden crucifixes to wear and taught her how to make the sign of the cross every time they passed by a church. But once in a while, when the day was just irresistible, they would venture to the banks of *Daumesnil* lake.

50

Paris in early summer can be as beautiful as heaven itself. The parks, full of flowers surrounded by the bright green of early leaves sprouting, illuminated by a forgiving Sun, become the very gills of the city. Couples walking hand in hand like in no other city in the world; couples with their children sharing food over a blanket under the shade of trees, and youngsters soaking in the energy given away by a nature eager to share its colors and its warmth. It was in one of these parks that Rebecca was to secretly meet with Max. The appointment came in the form of a small folded note placed under the door of the Giraud's apartment. "For Rebecca: Meet me tomorrow, Thursday at noon by the tip of the lake at the *Parc Montsouris*. Max"

Rebecca's curiosity was piqued. This had been the first time that Max had been so secretive about having a meeting. Usually he visited the Girauds and discussed whatever was on his mind with her in the apartment. But now, for the first time he had requested a meeting elsewhere. Sensing that something was not right, Rebecca made a great effort to insure she was not followed. She took the *Métro* at *Daumesnil* and got off at *Bercy* and after checking that she was not followed, she took another train and got off at *Glacière*. She walked on *Rue de la Santé* and entered the grounds of *Hôpital Ste. Anne* –where years later, after liberation, doctors would develop a special radiation treatment for tumors of the Pituitary gland. Again, after making sure that no one was following, she exited and walked to the park on *Avenue Reille*. She walked casually along the lake until she saw Max. She could read from his face that something was wrong. Max went straight to the point:

"Rebecca, it seems the Germans are tightening the noose on anyone helping people like us. They are rounding up "the Jew lovers" for shipment to Germany or Poland". These words hit Rebecca's ears like molten lead.

"Are you sure?" Rebecca inquired, knowing that Max's sources of information had never failed before.

"Yes, I am sure. The day before yesterday I met with Monsieur Giraud at his office and informed him. I begged him to leave his home and take refuge with our Agency, but he was not sure he wanted to. I told him that the Germans were moving rapidly, that he did not have much time, at best forty-eight hours. He promised he would think about it."

Rebecca's face was contorted with anxiety. "But he never mentioned anything to us", she said.

"I was afraid of that and that is why I wrote you the note".

"Well, I must run home and ask them to leave immediately. There is no time to waste".

Max held her by her forearm: "No, Rebecca, you must not go now. It is too late and too dangerous. The Germans may be already there waiting for you. Come with me. Tomorrow we will go together".

Rebecca knew Max was right. She wanted desperately to be with her family but realized that there was nothing to do –her family had no telephone– but to follow Max's recommendation. So they walked in silence, hand in hand, she crying and he mumbling to himself until darkness swallowed them up.

The following morning, Max stood by Rebecca's improvised bed with a cup of hot chocolate. "Drink, we must go". The clock on the wall pointed at five. Outside it was still dark. They walked on the darker side of the street for a few blocks and then they entered a *Métro* station. Rebecca was not paying attention to the details of this trip; she was only anticipating her arrival at the Giraud's. They passed *Daumesnil* and got off at *Bel Air*. Then they backtracked towards the corner with *Rue Cannebière* from where they could see the entrance to the building where the Giraud's lived. There were no signs of abnormal activity, no men in trench coats were stationed anywhere nearby. The two of them entered the church of *Saint Sprit* and waited a few minutes protected by its cold cavernous darkness. Max again confirmed that all looked normal across the street before they dared enter through the double doors of the apartment complex. Still cautious,

Max climbed the stairs and after making sure the coast was clear, called Rebecca.

They entered the apartment with her key. The living room was in shambles, with the furniture scattered about, chairs upside down, lamps trashed on the floor. Rebecca entered Giselle's room. It looked as it had on the day of her arrival: one bed, a central table. Giselle's clothes were in the drawers and in the closet cabinet; there was no trace of any of her own belongings. It was as if the Girauds had tried to convince the Germans that there never was a Jewish girl living with them. But it had not worked.

All she felt was that she was living Giselle's dream, that the priest and the teachers were running with horns and hammers in their hands, shouting obscenities. The Girauds were running away in slow motion, but instead of escaping, they were running towards a room full of flames. Since then, almost unconsciously, Rebecca visited the lake in *Parc Montsouris* every Thursday —perhaps hoping that history would change. This is how she first came upon Jacob Nathan.

The Girauds, alerted by Max, had discussed their situation. It was evident that the Germans were suspecting them of hiding a Jew. The first thing they had done was to rearrange their apartment so that there was no trace of Rebecca. They hoped that if they were inspected, they could fool the Germans to believe that this was a one-child family. But the Germans had come with preconceived notions, their minds made up. Two armed soldiers and a Gestapo officer concluded that the apartment looked too neat. This made them even more suspicious, and just like two plus two is four, and the neighbors reporting of seeing two children playing, combined with a very clean and ordered one child bedroom, gave them enough confidence to accuse the Girauds of being Jew lovers and of harboring a Jewish girl. The family was taken to the Paris suburb of Drancy, where thousands of Jews and other undesirables were incarcerated waiting for transfer to other destinations, mostly Auschwitz-Birkenau.

After the deportation of the Giraud family in June, Rebecca moved from place to place as Max saw fit. It was not until the Germans left Paris in August of 1944 that Rebecca was finally able to settle in just one place. She was given a small apartment found vacant after the German retreat. It had originally belonged to the Leventhal family, but they had been shipped to Auschwitz. The apartment was located on *Rue de Tournelles*, a few feet from a synagogue. She could walk to the *Place des Vosges* with its lovely, covered sidewalks and miniature park. At one point, Jews had concentrated in this area, but now it was almost devoid of them, except for the few families that were returning from hiding as word got out that the Nazis had left. She got a job at the *Bibliothèque de L'Arsenal*, where she was asked to translate documents left by the Germans for archival purposes.   Rebecca was now 19 years old and self-sufficient.   She had turned into a beautiful woman, soft and kind and yet sculpted with an inner strength that allowed her to give without losing in the interchange.

51

How long had it been since he first entered the camp? The uniform he had been given on arrival was now as old and decrepit as a mummy's wrap. Living at number BIIb-14 had now become part of his daily dying. At night sometimes he would get wet by the urine dripping from Itzic, the tailor who lived on the bunk above his. But how could he complain to Itzic when Zeb the cook, one bunk below, occasionally got soaked by Jacob's own urine? It was the legacy of the barracks. Sometimes the stench was so overwhelming that he tried to hold his breath knowing that in just a few moments he would gasp for even more air.

The filth and odor that saturated the barrack was ever present, but it was most noticeable on entering the building, when Jacob could feel the warmth of the pus that covered the wounds of so many of them come to greet him at the door. On other occasions the stench of the watery diarrhea, that exploded out of the typhus' victims moments before they died, masked the odor coming from the infected wounds. At night, under the mantle of almost complete darkness and total exhaustion, Jacob had a chance to imagine he was lying on his own bed with the goose down pillow and the blanket he had known since he was eight years old. But darkness did not suffice to isolate him from the rottenness that surrounded him and of which he was a part.

Is there a good time to die? What will death be like? Death is just silence and quiet amidst the eternal movement of the surrounding world. It is crossing a river and never being able to cross back. It is like jumping from a tall building knowing that no matter how much one wants to go back up, one's descent is immutable; it has the finality of accurately pointing a rifle at a living thing and squeezing the trigger letting the bullet fly, and then wishing it back. Dying must be like knowing one is about to take that step from which, no matter how hard one wishes it, there is no return, accepting –willingly or not– that worms will partake of what once was oneself. Above all, dying is giving up all memories and dreams. But then the morning came to the camp and it was time to get up and leave the barracks for another day –those that didn't were dead.

One night, he saw light through a crack in the wall, he carefully left his bunk and looked through the crack, and he saw that the light was casting itself upon infinite darkness and evil. He saw SS guards playing soccer with the head of a person, it could have been a child's head, but he had no experience evaluating detached heads to be a better judge. He listened in horror to one of the soldiers named Johann argue with another one called Fritz about playing fair when one is playing for money, and demanding that they should get another ball – "Wier brauchen *einen neuen Ball*" he had said. Jacob fell to his knees and although he knew he was crying, his eye sockets were dry. There were no more tears inside his desiccated body. He now was skin, bones, and eternal agony. Pity had left him the night he ate a small piece of dry bread that had fallen from Shmuel Abramowitz's pocket. Passion had abandoned him when he was ordered to the cadaver cart team and had to wheel the women and children that had been poisoned upon their weekly arrivals to the camp. He sometimes would wonder why he still prayed or talked to God. He began to chant: "Ungehpuk

Ungehpak, Ungehpuk
Ungehpak
Ungehpuk
Ungehpak, Ungehpuk
Ungehpak
Ungehpuk
Ungehpak, Ungehpuk
Ungehpak
Ungehpuk
Ungehpak, Ungehpuk

Ungehpak. . ." over and over, rocking back and forth in an attempt to drown out of his brain any images and feelings and sensations. How many million times would he utter those stupid nonsense words trying to keep the world at bay? Perhaps God kept the tab.

52

He had begun masturbating when he was twelve years old. From his bedroom he had a clear view of Christa's window across the street. She was perhaps fifteen years old and they had never spoken. She was much older and moved in a world as alien to Jacob's as if they inhabited separate planets. He was the son of a relatively poor Jewish family. His father mended broken books for a living. She was the daughter of a local Christian politician. Her side of the street was lined with manorial homes. On most Sunday mornings, Christa dressed up to go to church. On sunny days, she would open her window and he could see her naked. It was during one of those mornings, watching her, when he felt an erection and the need to caress himself and had his first orgasm imagining her next to him –not a dream.

When Hitler came to power, Christa's father jumped on the National Socialist movement bandwagon and became a little wheel in the Nazi machine that eventually would all but wipe out Jacob's family. But during that summer of 1933, Jacob was consumed with passion and desire for Christa. He had caressed her soft, round breasts and had felt her thighs opening to the pressure of his body against hers dozens of times. He imagined her soft white skin, every inch of it, and had caressed it with his thirsty hands. He dreamed of being kissed with passion and of kissing her back. Now in the camp, far from that passionate summer, he had no passion left in him, he had no desire, his penis hung like wrinkled skin, an atrophied useless appendage. He had lost all sexual desire. Now he was tortured by the memory of his mother's chicken soup as he gulped down a bowl of lukewarm watery barley soup –his only desire in life.

THE LAST WITNESS

53

Jacob walked carefully between the two Piñons and found a narrow trail that gently curved toward the hills and he followed it. He felt sure he could hear the sound of rushing water and he was confused and cautious for he knew there was no river or waterfall in this part of the countryside. Was he losing his mind? He was aware of his advanced age; certainly he could be experiencing the first signs of some degenerative brain disease. But why now? He was so familiar with all these mountain paths. Surely his brain would show the first signs of Alzheimer when confronted with a less familiar situation! How could his brain betray him and his memories? He had searched for most of his life for a reasonable explanation of what had happened to him and all the others and he was so close now. He knew these were his last years on Earth and was thankful for the opportunities that had opened to him after the war. He never forgot what he had seen done to others nor did he forget any part of his experience. No, refusing to be a victim of some degenerative dementia, he would not rest until the very end. Jacob, who always had a clear mind, needed a clear mind now. He sat down on a large granite boulder by an ancient Piñon, extracted the flask from his back pocket, and took several swallows of water. A small red cardinal was singing not fifteen feet away. The shade of the tree was comforting and he rested for a while.

"Is there a purpose to my living? Is there an end? Is there a question or is this a game some superior being is playing with me? Is there a reason for dying or a reason for not? Am I to be a witness to all the experiences that my senses have registered, even after I am dead, or will I die raving mad? And if I survive, will I remember and will anyone believe?" How many times these thoughts had crossed Jacob's mind? They seemed to come back to him at every turn in his life.

54

The rainy season had come to the camp replacing hot and dry days with unbearable humidity. During the weeks that followed his arrival to number 14 Jacob had been assigned to several labor contingents, and he developed a friendship with Leibish Baruch. Except for Erzon, the two friends were the only ones left from the original group, all the others had died and been replaced by new faces that in turn had shriveled and died. Almost half had succumbed to natural causes, mostly typhoid and pneumonia. A good number had died from gangrene. A cut not bigger than a nick was commonly followed by a major infection, and given their weakened bodies, these infections often became rampant and purulent. There was no hygiene and no serious attempt at medical treatment; an ill person was not worth the effort. The remaining half had died at the hands of the guards, and even though the turnover was so high at number 14, Jacob and Leibish had survived.

During the rainy season they were assigned to the graveyard. Every morning at six they joined others from other barracks and marched to the graveyard with their heads sunk between their shoulders and their bodies clinging to a desire for survival that they themselves did not want and could not understand. On approaching these hallowed grounds, they could hear the dead from deep under the earth burping a thousand burps of prayers foul like rotten meat as their intestines ruptured their gaseous contents into the murk. As they walked over filled in grave trenches, their feet sunk into softened mud with the stench of death. Of all the problems of the camp, this one posed the greatest challenge to German intelligence: How to avoid the telling smell of death. They had experimenting incinerating all the bodies, but this had proven to be too costly and slow. They tried burying bodies in deep trenches dug by tractors; the cadavers were piled in them and covered with lime. But the moisture of the entrails sooner rather than later would form gases that bloated the cadavers and eventually exploded releasing their horrible contents into the ground, converting it into mud. The wind carried this horrible message of death along with human ashes from the ovens into nearby towns where on Sundays they joined the incense from the churches and ascended to the heavens above. Jacob and his friend would never forget how their feet sank into the decomposing carcasses that floated in this miasma of hell.

55

Had he ever told any of his colleagues what it feels to walk mid-calf deep in cadaver mud? Would anyone have believed him, or for that matter, could any person even imagine it? There were occasions when Jacob had recognized a friend or an acquaintance floating in this quagmire of death, but for the sake of his sanity, Jacob preferred to think that here, all faces looked alike because they wore the uniform of total waste: Scalps thin as diaphanous membranes allowing the skull bone sutures to show through, bald eye-brows and wide opened eyes too big to fit any of their faces, long narrow fallen noses, lipless mouths, sunken cheeks and large, huge swollen ears. In them he recognized his friends, his parents, even himself. And as horrible as the visual experience was, how could he ever convey the stench, that terrible overpowering sweet, putrid, humid odor that contrasted so harshly with the sacred source from which it emanated? In his impeccably white doctor's coat, surrounded by other doctors and nurses in white coats, how could he see them as his equals, how could he touch someone and not feel their vital flesh as alien from his own?

The little red cardinal kept singing and the song appeared to ascend into the clouds that were forming as Jacob neared the foot of the mountain from which all the hills seemed to come from. Jacob noticed a mystical quality to the bird's song; he could swear that some of the tones came straight from the *Kohl Nidrei*, the chant of atonement that Jews had recited for centuries during the High Holiday of *Yom Kippur*. He felt a knot in his stomach and a strange sense of being in a magical world. For the first time now, he remembered all the stories he had read about New Mexico and its magical qualities. Was it not called "The Land of Enchantment"? How did it come about that he had never experienced this before? A smile crossed his face as the thought occurred to him that perhaps Mategooh, the old Indian woman with magical powers that Martha Gallaway consulted, had been right all along. Were these lands inhabited by ghosts? He picked up his walking stick and continued up the path that was clearly visible between the trees, and as he walked, he could hear rushing water louder and louder.

56

Victor Danilov joined the army when he was 18 years old. The war was happening far away, it was, as the song said it clearly, *"over there"*, far away. He had finished the lyceum and intended to become a lawyer. But his dreams had to wait; he had become a victim of the intense propaganda machine that was rolling over the Soviet Union. In fact, Germany's invasion of Russia's western borders had a lot to do with his becoming a soldier. During the months preceding the invasion, General of the Army Georgy Zhukov had undertaken a strong advertising campaign to encourage bright Soviet men to join the army. Viktor had done just that, planning to enter Law school after the war.

In August of 1939, the Germans and the Russians signed a non-aggression pact. As part of this agreement Poland was divided and shared by the two, and Russia was able to conquer by mostly diplomatic means Estonia, Latvia and Lithuania. Victor Danilov was part of a contingent of Soviet troops send to occupy Vilnius. It was in this capital city that he met Miriam Silberwasser. It had not been a meeting of equals, he was an occupier and she was Jewish. Her family, that before had been suspected of being communist sympathizers, now was suspected of being fascists spies. During the few weeks that it took to send the Silberwassers to Siberia, Viktor and Miriam became lovers. Miriam's plans to enter university never came to fruition. She saw in Victor a gentle man that had become a soldier and he saw in her a beautiful young woman of intelligent eyes, sweet disposition and great inner strength. Viktor was not prepared to fall in love with a Jewess. Although he had never met one, he had been taught about their evil, easy and avaricious nature; Miriam changed all that. Then, on the summer of 1941, the Germans began their offensive against the Soviets, surprising them in the Baltic States. Viktor was part of the retreating army that after pulling back behind the Dnieper River was commissioned to dismantle heavy industry installations to be taken farther inland. By miracle, he survived the brutal German advance, and eventually, was transferred to a battalion that was to retake Poland. He never saw Miriam again. What remained of the Silberwasser family became part of the German spoils of war, they were killed, even though to this day it is not known as to what the mechanism of their murder was. No tombstones can be found with their names.

Mikhail Kruvchenko enlisted on his eighteenth birthday. He wanted to leave home, to go to exotic places, to see things others had never seen. His father died when he was five and his mother had remarried a few years later. Mikhail never learned to love his stepfather. He had no idea what he wanted to become when he grew up, he only knew he wanted to experience something new, so he joined the army. His platoon had been sent to Siberia, along with many others, in preparation for a Japanese invasion. But when Russian intelligence determined that Japan was not interested in conquering them, but rather expanding into the pacific, they transferred most of the Siberian contingent to the front that eventually confronted the Germans at the doorsteps of Moscow. He survived the brutal battles and the frigid winter to eventually be commissioned to recapture Poland.

57

The winter had been terrible. The feeling of cold crept into his body during the first wintry night in autumn and never parted from him. There were no blankets and no heat in the barracks. Body heat was their only defense. During the times they were left inside the barracks, the survivors huddled together hoping to keep warm by the heat of their souls. But their souls had been left dry and their emaciated bodies were as cold as the blowing snow. Many had died during those months. Then, one day in what was probably mid-winter, Leibish called to Jacob in the silent language they had developed. The train had not come. It was the first time ever that the weekly train had not come. The two friends were now so thin, so dry of their flesh that walking had become almost impossible. Standing from a seated position was unbearably painful. They often helped each other crawl over the ground. Yes indeed, the train had not vomited its contents of human flesh on that week.

The survivors of barrack number 14 had no idea that the Allied invasion was taking a great toll on their captors. In the barracks, they had never heard the names of Eisenhower, Montgomery, Patton, Zhukov, or Danilov and Kruvchenko, or any of the many soldiers that were advancing towards them. But the prisoners noticed that during the last three days the killing rate at the camp had increased. Forced marches were organized daily and if this were not enough, shootings and hangings had tripled as well. The camp commanders were trying to fulfill their last order to exterminate all the Jews still alive in the concentration camps. Thousands of prisoners had been taken away from the camp in forced marches back into German territory. Most of them never made it to the Fatherland. Leibish and Jacob and the remaining forty inhabitants of their barracks expected to die on that day. Somehow, they were suffused with a feeling not so much of peace but of the promise of no more suffering. That morning, as they heard the commotion, the two friends touched their hands together and whispered: "*Shema Israel Adonai Eloheinu Adonai Echad*" (Hear Oh Israel The Lord Our God Is One) –the last words often uttered by a dying Jew. They had remained motionless with their eyes half closed and dry, surrounded by flies and maggots and memories that no man can ever describe.

"Hey Mikhail, these two are still alive," said one man in an excited but soft and reverent voice.

"I am Sergeant Viktor Danilov. You are free! Can you hear me?"

The two friends first thought they had died, but then, little by little began to realize that they had been spared. Their sight darkened by dried mucus that was gluing their lids almost shut, they tried to turn their heads towards the new sound. They were temporarily blinded by the light that was shining, without apology, through the open barrack's door. The back lit figures that moved in front of them were more like shadows than a positive image. These were soldiers, soldiers that spoke a language other than German, and they were crouching next to them. It had been four days since they had gotten their usual rations. The sense of weakness was no longer a sensation, it had become an integral part of them. One of the soldiers got some chocolate from his pouch and offered it to them. Jacob let the morsel melt in his mouth savoring that velvet feeling of warmth and sweetness and joy that he had long forgotten. Another soldier gave them water to drink. They were all squatting around the two of them. At that moment, these soldiers knew that this was to be the most profound experience of their life. They felt total decay assaulting them through each of their senses. They were floating in darkness partially relieved by two prisoners on the verge of death that had survived –flotsam of horror– to serve as witnesses to a God who had forgotten the meaning of pity.

Viktor Danilov never married his Lithuanian high-school friend. He suffered a nervous collapse and remained hospitalized for many years at St. Petersburg's Psychiatric Hospital #3 by the Fontanka Canal. His nurses reported that he never bothered to watch the beautiful blue cupolas of the Holy Trinity Church, just a bird's fly away. He eventually died from complications of a urinary tract infection. Mikhail Kruvchenko returned to the Ukraine soon after the war was over. He attempted suicide on one occasion, right in the middle of the loading docks of Sevastopol, but his faithful army semi-automatic pistol misfired. He evaded hospitalization and left his home and has not been heard from since.

58

The ground was not as soft as the sandy soil by the dry arroyo; it now had become firm and rocky. The vegetation was changing as well with Aspens clumping together in magnificent bunches reaching up high, as if praying to the heavens. The lighter color of their leaves contrasted with the dark solemnity of the twisted Piñons, and the light blowing wind made the leaves of the Aspens flutter like the wings of a thousand angels projected against the pastel blue of the sky. Jacob knew that Aspens required much more water than Junipers and Piñons. A feeling of uneasiness began to fall upon him, for he never had seen water in these parts.

Uneasiness was a condition experienced often by the old man. After that first night at the camp, when his nostrils had closed to the horrible odor that permeated every inch of his surroundings, when his ears became accustomed to the quiet rapid breathing of those with high fever that were rushing to meet death before the morning, he had heard for the first time the piercing, unforgettable cries of unspeakable pain brought by the wind in waves of varying intensity. It was impossible to determine whether the cries came from men or women. Agony has no gender. Then, Jacob had begun rocking and chanting:

"Ungehpuk
Ungehpak- Ungehpuk
Ungehpak- Ungehpuk

Ungehpak". . . attempting to drown out all the agony that surrounded him with this sequence of nonsensical words accompanied by an almost catatonic rocking of his body. And his chant mixed with shrieks of pain in a cacophonic poem where the tempo was dictated by how quickly the camp guards wanted to finish with their victims. Those horrible screams became his nightly lullaby and afflicted him with the ever-present fear that the next one howling would be he. And so, to the ever present feeling of hunger, cold, illness, desolation, and hopelessness, he had added the burden of constant apprehension, always waiting for the worst to come. And he felt it now, surrounded by Aspens, Junipers and Piñons and rocks and the clear piercing sunny air that always bathes the New Mexico mountains, and without realizing it he began to chant and rock back and forth:

"Ungehpuk
Ungehpak, Ungehpuk
Ungehpak. . ."

This was not a dream. The sound of rushing waters came from just over the ridge. Jacob helped himself with his stick and climbed the last few yards. He stood still, as still as he had during roll call in the camp. In front of him there was a river. It did not appear deep for he could see the rocky bottom. The waters' flow was interrupted by moss-covered rocks that added some sound and texture to this mysterious river. Jacob began to walk upstream along the bank. He lost all sense of time and place. He walked under branches, over rocks and boulders; he walked as if he knew where he was going. Perhaps five hundred yards farther up hill, a large granite boulder signaled the beginning of the river, and on it stood a man. Jacob Nathan was out of breath as he approached the boulder. In spite of the dryness of the mountain air, his garments were wet with perspiration. Something holy permeated the scene. Nathan walked closer to the boulder and he could see that the man was weeping. At times the sobs would stop, and Jacob could see his dark eyes, but when the weeping resumed a veritable river of tears would fall onto the boulder and from it to the ground and continue flowing down the ancient arroyo, down the hill, broken only by the moss covered rocks that stood in their path.

Jacob crouched and reached with his left arm to touch the waters. As he did, the tattoo on his forearm was exposed, reminding him of the eponym by which the Germans had known him. As he submerged his hand in the water, he was surprised to find it warm. Jacob knew all mountain waters are cold, or if they were warm, like thermal waters, then they had a sulfur smell, but the water Jacob held in his hand was pure and warm and perfumed like gardenias. He looked up at the man and understood that his tears gave birth to the river, and he knew that after all these years he had found God.

Although there was a breeze that swayed the vegetation surrounding the boulder, the long brown hair of the crying man was immobile, and such immobility acted as a frame to the simple figure of a medium size man dressed in white pants and shirt and naked feet. Jacob waited in silence until the man called him, as he knew he would.

"COME CLOSER TO ME JACOB NATHAN, SON OF MEIER, SON OF ISAAC, SON OF JACOB, SON OF SHMUEL", and the man added in the same soft, lingering voice "DO NOT FEAR ME".

Jacob walked tentatively and climbed the large boulder. He could see all the details of this man's skin, his wrinkles, the purity that surrounded him, the immense tragedy.

"I AM I AM".

"Yes, I know" Jacob replied.

"I WAS SILENT WHEN YOU CALLED ME".

"Yes, I know", Jacob replied.

"I KNEW THE MISERY, I HAVE ALWAYS KNOWN THE MISERY, I WILL ALWAYS KNOW THE MISERY".

"Yes", Nathan said.

"YOU ARE THE LAST ONE", God said.

"I HAVE WAITED AND I CAN NOT WAIT ANY LONGER".

"I ASK YOU TO FORGIVE ME", God said in a quiet voice. Then there was silence.

Jacob was breathing shallow and very rapidly and he was aware of his heart beating fast against his chest, and then he could hear his own voice trembling like the Aspen leaves in the wind as he replied:

"I am just a man; I cannot forgive you. The sin committed was too great to be forgiven by a man, only God can forgive such a sin".

And God cried sadly and bitterly, for he knew that the crimes he had allowed upon his people could not be forgiven, not now, not at the end of eternity. And his tears fell into the crevasses between the rocks and ran down the side of the hill into the ancient arroyo filling it with water that was crisp and tortuous like the feeling of hopelessness that some experience with the knowledge that there is no beginning, no now, no end.

Rebecca felt the sun warming her face and opened her eyes letting the beauty of nature filter through the bedroom window and into her soul. The distant mountain approached the bedroom with a series of ridges and meadows that both Jacob and she admired every day as they awakened. Rebecca turned to Jacob who was lying on his back, with his eyes still closed.

"Good morning Jacob. The sun is shining again. Our mountain is beautiful," she said sweetly.

But Jacob did not respond. The river had found the last witness on that sunny morning, and now Rebecca was alone and on becoming aware of her life companion's death, she began to rock in her bed chanting softly:

"Ungehpuk–*what is the purpose of living?*

Ungehpak, Ungehpuk–*after living as a couple for so many years I have lost the boundaries between him and me.*

Ungehpak, Ungehpuk–*but if so, have I not been living his life? And in doing so, am I not him, my Jacob?*

Ungehpak, Ungehpuk. . ."

Outside the sun was burning the last remaining clouds that still crawled between the canyons. Sometimes the mist of history does not settle until those living it become extinct and even then, it may skip one or two generations, just long enough so that people can forget and commit the same unthinkable atrocities. Perhaps, distracted, God got careless for a blink of an eye, again.

The End

ABOUT THE AUTHOR

Saul Balagura was born in Cali, Colombia, almost a decade after his parents emigrated from Romania. Throughout his life he moved in parallel universes of arts and sciences. He holds a M.D. from Universidad del Valle, a Ph.D. in Psychology from Princeton University and a Neurosurgery degree from Albert Einstein Medical Center in NY. He opened a studio, first in Tesuque, NM and now in Houston, TX, where he pursues the loves of his life, painting and writing. His expressionistic work is a direct result of the interaction of his clinical, scientific background with artistic influences from artists as varied as Willem de Kooning, Eduardo Guayasamin, el Greco, Pablo Neruda and Gabriel García Márquez. His artistic output has been exhibited in galleries and museums throughout the United States. His scientific work has been published in many prestigious journals. He writes novels, short stories, essays and poems.

THE LAST WITNESS